LOVERBOY

R.G. BELSKY

AVON BOOKS  NEW YORK

AVON BOOKS
A division of
The Hearst Corporation
1350 Avenue of the Americas
New York, New York 10019

Copyright © 1997 by R.G. Belsky
Visit our website at http://www.AvonBooks.com
Library of Congress Catalog Card Number: 96-27120
ISBN: 0-380-79068-8

First Avon Books Paperback Printing: February 1998
First Avon Books Hardcover Printing: February 1997

AVON TRADEMARK REG. U.S. PAT. OFF. AND IN OTHER COUNTRIES, MARCA REGIS-TRADA, HECHO EN U.S.A.

Printed in the U.S.A.

WCD   10   9   8   7   6   5   4   3   2   1

Prologue

June 1978

The killings started that summer as suddenly as they would again a long time later.

Jimmy Carter was in the White House then. Disco ruled the airwaves. White suits and gold chains were hot. So was the movie *Saturday Night Fever*. On TV, everyone loved the Fonz and *Laverne & Shirley* and *Charlie's Angels*.

On a steamy Saturday night in New York City, a boy and girl were making love inside a 1974 Chevy Nova parked on a ridge in upper Manhattan overlooking the Hudson River.

The boy was muscular, with dark hair and wearing a sleeveless T-shirt. The girl was blond, fresh-faced and dressed in a white blouse, jeans and platform heels.

Neither of them saw the person watching them until the very end.

"Hey, what the hell!" the boy suddenly yelled.

There was a figure standing alongside the car in the dark, near the open passenger window.

"Take a hike, will ya?" the boy said.

The shadowy figure didn't move.

"C'mon, we're busy . . ."

Still no response.

"Who are you anyway?"

Suddenly a hand came up and pointed in their direction. There was a glint of metal in it. Then the noise of gunshots reverberated in the quiet summer air.

Boom—boom—boom—boom—boom!

Five times the shooter fired.

Inside the Nova, there were screams and chaos. And then, finally, silence.

The girl in the car—who New York City newspaper readers would learn the next day was a twenty-three-year-old nursing student named Linda Malandro—lay dead in the passenger seat. Her boyfriend, whose name was Bobby Fowler, was still alive, but only barely. He told police later he didn't remember anything after the gunshots.

A few minutes after it happened, the shooter was in another car and driving away from the scene. The car got onto the Henry Hudson Parkway and headed south toward the skyscrapers of Manhattan.

The sound of the Bee Gees singing "Stayin' Alive" blasted from the radio.

The shooter laughed, pounded the steering wheel to the time of the music and sang along with the words.

From somewhere in the distance, police sirens began to wail.

Summertime.

New York City.

1978.

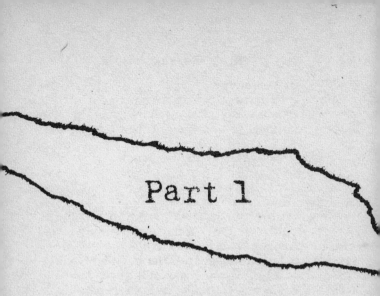

Part 1

START ME UP

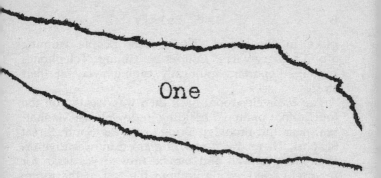

One

Everyone gets everything they want. I
wanted a mission. And, for my sins, they
gave me one.

—Captain Willard
Apocalypse Now

How do you call your loverboy?
I simply say . . . ''C'mere, loverboy.''

—Mickey and Sylvia
''Love Is Strange''

All I ever remember wanting to be is a newspaper
reporter.

When I was growing up, other girls dreamed about
being Billie Jean King or Lauren Hutton or Gloria
Steinem. Me, I wanted to be Lois Lane.

I always figured working for a newspaper was a
noble calling—like being a priest or a doctor or join-
ing the Peace Corps. I just never imagined myself
doing anything else.

Lucy Shannon, reporter.

God, I used to love it.

The first time I walked into the city room of the
New York Blade, I thought it was the most exciting

place in the world. There were people running around everywhere. Editors screaming. Telephones ringing. Reporters frantically typing away at their stories.

The *Blade* city room back then was located on the fourth floor of an old building in downtown Manhattan, near the Brooklyn Bridge and the South Street Seaport. There was a row of glassed-in executive offices along a wall and maybe fifty or so desks for reporters scattered throughout the rest of the room. The windows overlooked the East River on one side and a housing project on the other.

Once, when I was first there, someone in the housing project had a bit too much to drink and started taking target practice at one of the windows with a pellet gun, sending glass flying and all of us diving for cover. After that, the desks on that side of the room became known as the clay-pigeon area. And the waiting line for seats on the other side suddenly became longer than the one to see *Cats*.

In those days, the Associated Press machine spewed out reams of wire copy which would be punched onto sharp metal spikes the editors kept on their desks. One day two of the editors got into an argument and had a spike fight in the center of the office, using them like swords.

Another time, a frustrated reporter picked up a typewriter and threw it through a window.

I loved it all. Passionately. The kind of all-encompassing, no-questions-asked love you think will never die or grow old or turn bad. Just like the way I felt on my wedding day.

Of course, I was wrong about that too.

A lot has changed at the *Blade* since then.

A few years ago, we moved into a brand-new state-of-the-art building in midtown with carpeted floors, modular furniture and little partitions so that everyone has his own work area. The typewriters and

wire machines are gone. Reporters use computer ter-
minals to write their stories and store all the wire
copy.

I'm different too.

My love affair with the place ended a long time
ago. There's no excitement when I walk into the city
room these days. Me and the *Blade*, we're just like
an unhappy married couple living a lie. We don't
have much use for each other anymore, but we're
too tired to go to divorce court and put the damn
relationship out of its misery.

I sat down in front of one of the computer termi-
nals now, bleary-eyed and with morning coffee and
bagel in hand. The message light was blinking on
the screen.

I took a big gulp of the coffee, pressed a button
on the keyboard and read the message. It was from
Walter Barlow, the *Blade* city editor. He said I should
E-mail him back as soon as I got in.

"Do you remember when people used to actually
talk to each other?" I said to Janet Wood, a reporter
who sits at the desk next to mine.

She shrugged.

"Hey, Lucy, this is the nineties."

The '90s. Terrific.

"Whatever happened to the eighties?" I asked.

Walter Barlow was a big man—close to three hundred pounds, with a huge stomach that hung out
over his belt. He was pawing through a box of assorted glazed, jelly and cream-filled doughnuts when
I walked over to his desk.

"So many flavors, so little time," I said.

Barlow grunted. "Have you finished that feature I
assigned you on the flower show?" he asked.

"Sure."

That was a lie. But just a little one. I mean, I didn't

figure a lightning bolt was going to come down from the sky or anything.

Barlow had the daily assignment list in front of him.

The big story this morning was about a missing Brooklyn teenager named Theresa Anne Vinas; she'd gone into Manhattan a few nights ago and never been heard from since. There was also a piece about an early-summer heat wave—it was only June, but the temperature was already threatening to hit one hundred. A water-main break in Washington Heights. A political profile of the police commissioner, a man named Thomas Ferraro, who was being touted as the next mayor. And a press conference with a woman who won $27 million in the lottery by playing her dead husband's Social Security numbers.

"Let me do the missing Brooklyn girl," I said.

"Janet's already working on it."

"I could help her."

I looked down at the rest of the assignments. Most of them were pretty routine—press conferences, interviews. Then I saw something that wasn't routine. A feature about a Hollywood film company that was in town to shoot a movie about a mass murderer who had stalked New York during the late '70s and early '80s. The Loverboy killings.

"They're doing a movie about Loverboy?"

"Yeah. Your big story, right? The one that made you a star."

"That was a long time ago."

"I bet they're going to want to talk to you about it, Lucy. Hey, maybe you could be a technical adviser or something."

"I don't want to talk about Loverboy," I said.

Barlow shrugged and took a bite of one of the jelly doughnuts. "By the way, Vicki wants to see you," he said.

"Victoria Crawford? The editor?"

"I believe her title is editor in chief."

"She hasn't said a word to me in six months. I wonder what she wants."

Barlow looked up at me now. He seemed concerned. I guess I must have looked like I was in a state of shock or something. And not just over Victoria Crawford either.

"Lucy, are you okay?" he asked.

"I'm fine," I said.

That was a big lie.

But then I've been lying to men all my life.

I didn't see any reason to stop now.

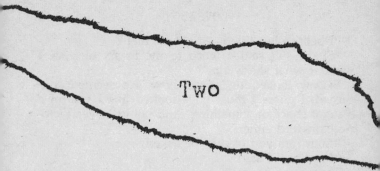

Two

Victoria Crawford had an impressive office in the executive suite. Plush maroon carpeting, a picture window overlooking the skyscrapers of Manhattan, framed journalism awards and memorable *Blade* front pages on the walls. On the desk in front of her was a baseball signed by the members of the New York Yankees. Next to it was a picture of Crawford on the cover of *New York* magazine.

She walked out from behind her desk and shook my hand.

"It's been a long time since we've talked, hasn't it, Lucy?"

"More than six months."

"Too long."

She gestured for me to sit down. Then she went back behind her desk. She was wearing a white silk blouse, a short pleated skirt and a pair of brown brushed-suede pumps that probably cost more than I make in a week. The only problem was, the short skirt made her look a tad bowlegged. I wondered if I should point this out to her. I decided against it.

Vicki Crawford and I had started out together as reporters at the *Blade*. Then, a few years ago, the paper was bought by a wealthy real estate tycoon named Ronald Mackell. Mackell spent a lot of time in the city room in the beginning, and he and Vicki became close. Very close. So close that he divorced his wife and married Vicki. Now she was editor of the paper.

It was bizarre for most of the staff to have to work for Vicki Crawford. But for me, it was downright torture. Things had come to a head at the *Blade* Christmas party when I got very drunk, not an unusual occurrence in those days, and told her she reminded me of the hookers in spandex pants and heels outside the Lincoln Tunnel.

"What are you talking about?" she'd said. "I'm worth seven hundred and fifty million."

"Yeah, and those women get twenty dollars for a blow job."

"So?"

"So it's like Winston Churchill once said about whores: 'We've already established what you are, now we're just haggling over the price.' "

But now Vicki Crawford leaned across her big desk and smiled at me.

"I think it's time we let bygones be bygones," she said. "Okay?"

"That works for me."

"Good."

Vicki relaxed a bit. She leaned back in her chair and picked up the baseball. She tossed it in the air casually as she talked, catching it in her left hand.

"Do you still talk to David?" she asked.

David was my ex-husband. One of them.

"Sure. My lawyer talks to his lawyer, and his lawyer talks to my lawyer. It's great. If we could have had the lawyers in bed with us when we were married, we'd probably still be together."

Vicki smiled.

"How many divorces is that?"

"Three."

"And how old are you?"

"Thirty-six."

She shook her head sadly.

"I don't do marriage well," I said.

"What about your . . . well, your problem?"

"You mean my drinking?"

"Yes."

"I haven't touched a drop since the beginning of the year. I drink bottled water in bars, diet soda at lunch, and I celebrated my birthday with a tall glass of carrot juice. I'm so healthy it's disgusting."

"I'm really glad to hear that."

She kept tossing the baseball in the air and catching it.

"Can I ask you a question?" I said.

"Sure."

"What's this all about?"

"I don't understand . . ."

"Well, I really don't think you called me in here just to check on the condition of my health or my marriage or to talk over old times together. You want something from me, Vicki. What is it?"

She looked at me blankly for a second, then nodded.

"Lucy, do you know who Leo Tischler is?"

"Sure. He owns Tischler's Department Store."

"That's right."

"Tischler is also one of the *Blade*'s biggest advertisers, if I remember correctly."

She nodded again. "Tischler's got a son, Barry, who works at the store. He's a vice president. Barry's wife is worried about him. You see, he . . ."

"Likes to sneak into the women's department at night and dress up in frilly lingerie?"

Vicki didn't laugh. "This is a very serious matter."

"Okay."

"A matter of some delicacy. Some sensitivity."

Her voice became very solemn.

"Emily Tischler can't find her husband," she said.

I shrugged. "Has she checked Lost and Found?"

Vicki Crawford dropped the baseball she was holding on the glass top of her desk. It made a loud crashing sound. She glared at me across the desk. She wasn't smiling anymore.

"You know, I really don't like you, Shannon."

I didn't say anything.

"I never did like you," she continued. "I thought you were shit when we were reporters together, and I think you're shit now. But you're in the union, so I can't do a damn thing about you."

I smiled at her.

"Have we gone past the part where we were letting bygones be bygones?"

"You want to know why you're here, I'll tell you. You're right—Leo Tischler is one of the paper's biggest advertisers. And he asked for you personally."

"Why me?"

"It seems you did a big feature on him a few years back, and he was very happy with it. Do you remember?"

"Oh, yeah." As I recalled, Leo Tischler had made a pass at me during that interview.

"I tried to put someone else on the story, but he insisted on you. I didn't know how to tell him you were now a broken-down alcoholic."

I let that one pass.

"Anyway, go up and talk to Emily Tischler, Barry Tischler's wife. She lives on the Upper East Side. After that, you can talk to old man Tischler too."

"Let me get this straight—the Tischler kid's disappeared?"

"That's right."

"Does anybody suspect foul play?"

"Not really. Barry Tischler has a reputation as a womanizer. In all likelihood, he's shacked up somewhere with some young thing."

"So do you really think it's a story?"

"If I really thought it was a story, I wouldn't be giving it to you."

"Oh."

"The wife wants to go public with this, so her father-in-law figures somebody should placate her and hold her hand a bit. You're elected. We'll decide afterward whether or not we're going to print anything. Understand?"

"Okey-dokey," I said.

I stood up.

"And, Shannon . . ."

"Yeah?"

"This is a million-dollar-a-year advertising account we're talking about here. Don't fuck it up."

I nodded and started for the door. Halfway there, I turned around and said:

"By the way, Vicki, here's a little fashion tip for you. It's not a good idea to wear short skirts when you're bowlegged."

I walked out and went back to the city room. Barlow came over. He was working on one of the cream-filled doughnuts now.

"How'd it go?" he asked.

"Not as badly as I expected," I said.

Three

Emily Tischler lived in an elegant new high-rise on the Upper East Side, near Gracie Mansion.

There was a huge circular driveway in front, with some red and white hyacinths planted in the center, where two limousines and a taxi sat parked under the blazing sun. The lobby had a running-water fountain, marble floors, a crystal chandelier hanging from the ceiling and sliding glass doors with the words "Summit House" written on them in big red letters.

A doorman stood stiffly at attention next to the water fountain. He was wearing a black uniform with white-piping trim and white braids hanging from the shoulder, a white cap with a black peak, highly polished black shoes and white gloves. I wasn't sure whether to say hello or salute.

I told him who I was and rode the penthouse elevator up to the top floor, where Emily Tischler answered the door.

She was petite, fair-haired and pretty, in a plain, nonthreatening sort of way. I figured her to be no more than twenty-three, with a clean, fresh look to her. No jewelry except for a simple pair of earrings. Almost no makeup. She was wearing a sleeveless white linen blouse, neatly pressed caramel slacks and brown leather penny loafers.

"Thank you for coming, Miss Shannon," she said. "Come in, please."

The apartment was all glass and chrome and metal. Modern and clean, but stark and devoid of any character. There was a yellow velvet couch in the center of the living room, along with two pieces of metal that I think were what modern furniture passes off as chairs. I opted for the couch.

"Do you want something to drink?" she asked.

"Sure," I said. "It's pretty hot outside."

She disappeared for a few minutes and came back carrying a bottle of beer and a tall glass on a silver tray.

"Is this okay?" she asked.

The bottle was icy cold, with beads of melting water dripping down the sides. She lifted it and the glass off the silver tray and held them out in front of me.

I summoned up all my willpower. "Uh—I'll just take some diet soda, if you have it."

She came back a minute later with a Diet Pepsi and handed it to me. Then she sat down in one of the metal monstrosities.

"My husband left home two nights ago, and he hasn't been back since," she said.

"Uh-huh."

I took a sip of my soda.

"I'm heartsick with worry."

"Do you have any idea where he went?"

"Barry and I don't keep track of each other. Each of us is free to come and go as we please. This is an open marriage."

"Right."

I thought she had said that with a little too much intensity. I was going to say something about it, but I decided not to. I drank some more soda.

"Did he tell you anything at all the night he left?"

"Well, he said he was going to a bar near here. He

does that sometimes. But when I called the bar about two A.M., they said he'd already left."

"Has he ever done anything like this before?" I asked.

"You mean disappeared?"

"Well . . . not come home at night."

She bit down on her lower lip. "There have been a few times. I mean, we do have an open marriage."

"Right."

"But never for as long as this. And without leaving me any message."

"Your husband works for Tischler's Department Store?"

"He's a vice president of the company."

"And the store's owned by his father."

"Yes."

"I assume you've tried his office."

"They said they haven't seen him either. But that's not too unusual. You see, Barry's work schedule is very loose and . . ."

"Open?"

"That's right."

I looked down at my glass. It was empty. I could ask Emily Tischler for another soda. But I was afraid if she managed to get up from that chair she was sitting in, she might not get back down again. Besides, I didn't want to spend any more time in this apartment than I had to.

"Look, Mrs. Tischler," I said slowly, "what exactly is it you want me to do?"

"Why, find my husband, of course."

"What if he doesn't want to be found?"

"Meaning you think he could have run off somewhere?"

"There is that possibility. Have you gone to the police?"

"Yes."

"And?"

"They sort of said the same thing you just did."

"Suggested it was a domestic problem?"

She nodded. "I need to do something. So I thought of the newspapers. I figured if I got a story written about it, maybe it could spur some action."

Maybe it would. But what if it turned out that Barry Tischler was just shacked up with some babe? How would he feel about all that embarrassing publicity? More important, how would his father—who did a million dollars' worth of business a year with the *Blade*—feel about it?

Well, that really wasn't my problem. Vicki Crawford had told me to come here and be nice to the woman, so I'd be nice. I took out my notebook.

"Tell me a little about your husband," I said.

She talked for maybe twenty minutes, going over background about Barry Tischler. When she was finished, I asked if I could see some of his personal things—clothes and stuff.

"Why?"

"I don't know. Maybe it'll help me get a better idea of him. You know, atmosphere and all that."

She shrugged and led me down a long corridor to a bedroom with a window overlooking a park.

I spent a little time rummaging around in there. Emily got bored after a while and excused herself. After she was gone, I looked at a picture of Barry Tischler that was on top of a dresser. He was standing next to a sailboat, wearing a crew captain's T-shirt, white pants and little, round horn-rimmed glasses. Good-looking in a conservative, old-money sort of way.

The dresser itself was filled with the kind of stuff you'd expect to find. Expensive sweaters. Lots of khakis. Even a nice collection of Calvin Klein underwear. Then, underneath a pile of shirts in the bottom of a drawer, I hit paydirt. A small brown leather phone book was carefully hidden away in a corner.

I picked it up, paged through it quickly and found a lot of names and numbers. They were names like Kathy and Debbie and Ruth—all of them women. I checked the corner of the drawer one more time and came up with something else—a package of Trojan condoms.

Of course, he might keep the condoms to have sex with his wife, but somehow I doubted it. Kathy and Debbie and Ruth seemed a better possibility. All in all, it didn't look like ol' Barry was going to win a lot of points for marital fidelity.

I put the phone book and the condoms back where I'd found them, shut the drawer and looked around the room once more.

As far as I could tell, Barry Tischler wasn't hiding under the bed. He hadn't left behind a trail of birdseed or crumbs to mark his path. There were no messages written in invisible ink on the wall. I walked back to the living room, where Mrs. Tischler was waiting for me.

"Did you find anything that might help?"

I thought about the phone book and the condoms. "Maybe."

"Oh, Miss Shannon," she said, stifling a sob, "I'm so worried. I just hope Barry's all right."

"I'm sure everything's going to work out fine," I said.

But I didn't really.

Her marriage was in trouble.

And that trouble, before it was over, would touch a lot more people than just Emily and Barry Tischler.

Four

Leo Tischler, the head of Tischler's Department Store, was in his late fifties. He had silver hair, steel-blue eyes and a no-nonsense manner that made it clear he didn't like to waste time.

He also seemed to have come to the conclusion that maybe going public with this wasn't such a hot idea.

"I should have never let Emily talk to you," he said as I sat in his office overlooking Fifty-ninth Street. "It was a mistake."

"Your son has been gone for a couple of days. She's worried. Aren't you?"

"Hey, husbands leave sometimes. He's probably just out sowing a little wild oats."

"You mean another woman?"

"Look, Barry likes girls. He always has. Nothing wrong with that. I like 'em too."

He smiled across the desk at me.

"I don't know why he got married anyway. Why did he need it? I told him that. Of course, most of the time no one's the wiser, no one's hurt."

"Most of the time?"

He hesitated. "Are we off the record here?"

I shrugged. "Whatever."

"A few months ago"—Tischler sighed—"Barry disappeared like this. When we found him . . . well, he was holed up in a motel in New Jersey with some girl he'd picked up. I made up a cover story about a sudden business trip to tell Emily. Only . . ."

"Only what?"

"The girl in the motel turned out to be just seventeen. And then she got pregnant. He paid for her abortion, but something went wrong and . . . well, the girl died. It was a really messy business."

"A messy business," I said.

Jesus, Leo Tischler was really something. No wonder Barry had turned out the way he did.

"Anyway, Barry gave me his word he wouldn't do anything like that again."

"But now you think he could be doing a repeat performance."

Tischler nodded.

"What was the name of the motel?" I asked.

"The Route Four Motor Lodge. It's just across the George Washington Bridge."

I wrote that down.

"You think he might have gone back there?" Tischler asked.

"People sometimes follow the same patterns. I'll check it out."

He rubbed his hands together nervously.

"Look, I really don't want to see anything about this in the newspaper, after all. I've decided against it."

I wanted to tell him that wasn't up to him. But I was supposed to be nice.

"It's not my decision to make," I said.

"Who decides?"

"Vicki Crawford."

"Oh, yeah, that broad who's the editor now. Okay, I'll call Vicki and set her straight on how I want all this handled."

"That's a good idea." I smiled.

Nice.

I stood up to leave. He walked me to the door.

"Now, if you find out anything about Barry, you call me," he said. He wrote something down on a slip of paper and handed it to me. "That's my private number. Call me any time. Any time at all, even after this is over."

He winked.

Like father, like son.

"One more thing," he said. "That little incident about Barry and the abortion—that's our little secret, okay? I'm a respected businessman in this town. It might reflect badly on the Tischler family name."

"I suppose it might," I said.

You never know about a story.

Barry Tischler could have been at the Route 4 Motor Lodge. Screwing his brains out. Just lost track of the time and forgot about the wife and the job and all that stuff. Sorry.

But he wasn't there.

The motel manager said he had no one registered by that name. Of course, not everyone registers with his right name at a motel. I showed the manager a picture of Tischler I'd gotten from his wife. He recognized him. But he said he hadn't seen him for a few months.

My next stop was the Manhattan bar where Barry had last been seen.

It was called Partners, and it turned out to be your basic East Side singles place. A big long wooden bar. Lots of little tables with checkered tablecloths. A sign in the window which said: HAPPY HOUR, EVERY DAY 4–6.

The guy behind the bar was named Gary Savoy. He didn't seem very impressed when I showed him my press card.

"A reporter," he sniffed. "Another damn reporter. There's too many reporters around here."

I took out the picture of Barry Tischler and showed it to him.

"Recognize him?"

He studied the picture.

"What'd he do?"

"Nothing."

"That's why you're doing a story on him—because he did nothing?"

"His wife's looking for him. Do you know him or not?"

Savoy handed the picture back.

"Yeah, I've seen him around here."

"Doing what?"

"Making conversation with people."

"Women?"

"Hey, he likes to meet women. Women come here to meet guys. It works out nice."

"When's the last time you saw him?"

He thought for a second.

"A couple of nights ago. I remember his wife or somebody called here asking about him, but he'd left by then."

That would have been the phone call Emily Tischler said she made at 2 A.M.

"Did you happen to see who he left with?"

"C'mon, there's maybe two hundred people in here at night. I'm not a chaperon."

The place was already starting to fill up with the afternoon crowd. Girls in pleated skirts and silk blouses. Guys in summer sport jackets and jeans. Everybody looked hip and successful. I felt out of place.

"People really come to places like this looking for love, huh?" I asked Savoy.

"You got something against love?"

"It's highly overrated."

"Maybe you've just been with the wrong man."

"I've been with several of them," I said.

I gave him a card with my name and the *Blade*'s

telephone number. I told him to call me if he saw Barry Tischler again. He ripped the card into several little pieces and dropped them into an ashtray on the bar. Then he lit the pieces with a match and smiled as they burned.

The power of the press.

"We're not getting along too well, are we?" I said.

"Reporters, fucking reporters," he muttered. "Always busting my balls. Been busting my balls all week."

Five

" "Warren Beatty," Janet said. "In bed. After sex. And with a woman who's not his wife."

"How about Cher?" I countered. "From an infected needle while getting a tattoo."

Janet thought about that for a second.

"Okay, I've got a better one. Oprah Winfrey. She chokes on a ham sandwich. Just like Mama Cass did!"

"That's good," I said. "That's real good."

We were in the *Blade* city room the next morning. I guess we were getting kind of loud, even for a newspaper office. Barlow came over to us. He had a candy bar in his hand.

"Are you two playing the Someone Famous Died game again?"

"Absolutely," I told him.

He shook his head.

"You're crazy."

"What's crazy about playing a game where you fantasize about celebrities dying and which one would make the biggest front-page story?"

"It's sick, Lucy."

I nodded. "So what's your point?"

He sat down on the edge of my desk and took a bite out of the candy.

"The Breakfast of Champions, huh?" I said.

"What's your problem, Lucy?"

"I thought you were going on a diet," I said.

"I'm thinking about it."

"Does the term 'compulsive eater' mean anything to you?"

"Hey, you're a great one to lecture me about being compulsive.

"Okay, I'm compulsive—but I'm a recovering compulsive."

Barlow finished off the candy bar. "Any luck on Barry Tischler?" he asked.

I told him everything I'd done.

"I also made a few other checks," I said. "Barry Tischler has not been admitted to any local hospitals. He hasn't been arrested. He's not lying dead in the morgue. Pretty thorough, huh? Of course, I still don't have any idea where Tischler is. But then again, I'm not sure I really care."

"You don't."

"Excuse me?"

"Just drop it. There's no story."

I stared at him.

"His father called, right?" I said.

"As a matter of fact, he did."

"And Vicki wimped out."

"C'mon, you yourself said it sounded domestic— the guy just took a powder."

"I know."

"So?"

"So now I'm not so sure."

"You just want to be mad at Vicki."

"Well, there is that too."

After he left, I sat there wondering what had really happened to Barry Tischler. Maybe I should call his wife again. Maybe I should check some more hotels around town. The telephone rang. I picked it up.

"Is this Lucy Shannon?" a man's voice said.

"You got her."

"Miss Shannon, we're shooting a movie here in town. It's about the Loverboy murders. The serial killer who terrorized the city a number of years ago."

I squeezed the receiver tightly and took a deep breath. "Yeah, I know who he is," I said.

"Michael Anson would like to meet you."

"Who's that?"

"The director of the movie."

"Why?"

"We'd like you to be in it. You played such a big role in the real Loverboy case that we'd like you to play yourself in the film—a reporter covering the story. Of course, it would only be a cameo role, but the publicity could be beneficial for both of us."

I sighed.

"Tell Mr. Anson—"

"*Ms.* Anson," the guy said.

"Huh?"

"It's Ms. Anson. Michael Anson is a woman."

"Ah," I said, "cool name. Like Michael Learned of *The Waltons.*"

He cleared his throat. He seemed confused. I guess people generally get more excited when they're offered a part in a Hollywood movie.

"Ms. Anson would really like to meet you," he said. "We're doing some scenes right now at the Limelight—"

"Sorry, but I'm not interested."

"This is going to be a very big movie, Miss Shannon. It's a fascinating story."

"Not for me it isn't."

"Why not?"

"I lived through it, remember? And I still have the nightmares."

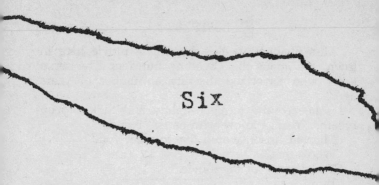

Six

That night I went to Headlines. Headlines is a bar on Sheridan Square in Greenwich Village. A lot of newspaper people hang out there.

There was a time, when I was drinking, that I used to regularly close the place down. I'd arrive after work at about eight or nine, have a couple drinks to unwind, and the next thing I knew, it would be 4 A.M. Sometimes things got out of hand, and on more than one occasion the manager had to tell the bartender to stop serving me and make sure I got home all right.

I didn't go to Headlines for the booze anymore. But I still went.

It was important to me. I didn't want drinking, or the lack of it, to change the way I lived my life. A good deal of that life was spent in bars—talking to sources, picking up tips or just schmoozing with politicians, cops or other newspaper people. If I couldn't drink anymore while I did it, well . . . that was the way it had to be.

I once met a woman at an AA meeting who worked as a cocktail waitress. She did this for two years while she stayed sober, hanging out with drunks every night and never touching a drop of the stuff. Then one time when she was on vacation in a remote mountain cabin in Vermont, she impulsively drove thirty miles to the nearest package store and proceeded to get royally blitzed.

Moral of the story: If you're going to drink, you will. If you're not, you won't. The circumstances don't really matter.

Janet Wood plopped down on the bar stool next to me.

"I think I'm in love," she announced.

"With who?"

She pointed to a guy standing at the end of the bar wearing a New York Jets T-shirt. He was dark-haired, handsome and muscular.

"What's his name?"

"I don't know yet. But I'm calling him Mr. Touchdown."

"Interesting approach."

"Speaking of approaches, how do you think I should try to meet him? My discreet move or the aggressive one?"

"What's the discreet?"

"I pretend to spill a drink on the front of my blouse and ask him to help wipe it off."

"I'm not even going to ask about the aggressive way."

The bartender brought us refills. A light beer for Janet and a Perrier for me.

"How did it go with the missing girl in Brooklyn today?" I asked her.

"I went out and talked to the mother. It's a sad story. Theresa Anne Vinas is a straight-A student, never been in any trouble, hardly ever even dated. And a real beauty too. Did you see the pictures of her?"

I nodded, remembering the smiling face framed by dark hair.

"Anyway, her friends decided to go to a singles bar in the city for a celebration because Theresa had gotten a big scholarship to Princeton. One thing led to another; the friends all drifted off with different guys and eventually wound up back in Brooklyn. All except Theresa. No one's heard from her since that night."

"What do you think happened to her?" I asked.

Janet shrugged. "Dead."

"Yeah. Me too."

We sat there in silence for a minute. To anyone else it might seem cold and heartless to talk about Theresa Anne Vinas so casually. But newspaper reporters, like cops, have to handle things that way. Otherwise every murder—every story—tears you apart.

A little later, Norm Malloy showed up with the first copies of the *Blade* off the press.

This was a nightly ritual. Malloy was a sixty-year-old desk assistant. He had never worked anywhere else but at the *Blade*, and insisted he would stay there until the day he died. Malloy lived alone and seemed to have no interests of any kind outside the newspaper.

"Better give your paycheck back today," he said as he handed a copy to me.

Malloy said that to everyone on the staff who didn't have a byline in the paper that night. When it was there, he called out the page number of the person's story in a loud, booming voice. It was irritating, but kind of nice too.

Janet's interview with Theresa Anne Vinas's mother was on page 1:

MISSING GIRL'S MOM
PRAYS FOR HER RETURN

by Janet Wood

On the mantel of Carmen Vinas's Brooklyn living room is a statue of St. Jude. St. Jude is the saint of lost causes.

Eighteen-year-old Theresa Anne Vinas is lost.
So her mother prays to St. Jude for a miracle.
"I get on my knees and beg the Lord to send
my Theresa Anne home to me," sobbed Mrs.
Vinas yesterday in her tiny apartment.
"I'll never ask Him for anything else again in
my life. I promise. I just want my Theresa. I
want my little girl back."
Meanwhile, Police Lt. William Masters said a
massive search had so far failed to turn up any
sign of the missing teenager.
Theresa Anne Vinas disappeared after going
to a Manhattan singles bar with a group of
friends. . . .

I idly skimmed through the rest of the story, sipping on my Perrier as I read.

Something was bothering me, but I wasn't sure
what it was.

I just had this nagging feeling I was missing
something.

I read the story from the beginning again, this time
more carefully. Then it hit me.

A singles bar!

The guy I had talked to at Partners, where Barry
Tischler was last seen, said he was in a bad mood
because he'd been hassled by reporters for the past
few days. Why were reporters hassling him? It didn't
seem important at the time. But now . . .

Theresa Anne Vinas had disappeared after going
to a Manhattan singles bar. Just like Barry Tischler.

Of course, it could just be a coincidence. There
were lots of singles bars in Manhattan.

I walked over to where Janet was now deep in
conversation with the hot guy in the football T-shirt.
They were staring intently into each other's eyes.

"Janet, I've got to talk to you."

"I'm busy," she said out of the side of her mouth.

She did not turn around.

"This is important."

"I'm very busy."

"It's very important."

Janet looked at the guy and smiled. "Can you excuse me for just one second? My friend here seems to have an emergency."

I pulled her off into a corner.

"This better be really good," Janet said.

"The singles bar Theresa Anne Vinas went to. What was its name?"

Janet stared at me. "That's what you called me over here for?"

"C'mon, Janet."

She thought for a second. "Uh, Partners, I think—"

"Jesus Christ!"

"What?"

"You know my guy, Barry Tischler, the missing department-store Romeo? I think he was at Partners the same night."

"You mean . . . ?"

"Yeah," I told her. "I figure when we find Barry Tischler, we'll find Theresa Anne Vinas."

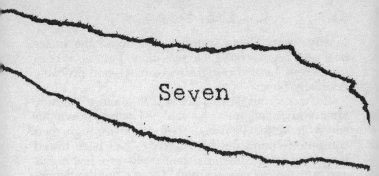

Seven

They found them both the next day.

It was late afternoon, and the temperature was holding at eighty, with bright sunshine glinting in through the window next to my desk, when the call came in to the office.

"Get over to the auto pound on West Fiftieth Street," the voice on the other end said.

It was Lieutenant William Masters, the cop who was heading up the search for Theresa Anne Vinas.

"Why?"

"You did us a favor last night by passing along the information about Tischler. Now I'm doing one for you."

"Okay, but—"

"You better get moving, Shannon, if you want this story first."

I got moving. When I got to the auto pound, Masters was standing next to a silver Mercedes sedan. The trunk was open, and a half-dozen cops were examining it. Masters said something to one of them, then saw me and walked over.

Masters was about fifty years old. He was wearing a pinstriped suit, crisp white shirt, silk tie and Italian loafers. Masters always looked good. Like he'd just stepped out of an ad in *GQ*.

I'd worked with him on a few stories before,

33

mostly when I was younger and doing the police beat on a regular basis. He was okay, I guess, as cops go. Decent, hardworking, street-smart—and probably relatively honest.

"I checked out Barry Tischler a little more carefully after you called me," he said. "Tracked down his car with Motor Vehicles. They ran it through their computer. Found out his Mercedes had been towed here from a pier down by the East River a few nights ago and never been claimed. There's two bodies inside the trunk."

"Theresa Anne Vinas and Barry Tischler?"

Masters nodded. He took a package of Tums out of his pocket and popped one in his mouth.

"They were both in various stages of undress."

So much for innocence.

One of the cops by the Mercedes came over and said something to Masters. The guy was a lot younger, closer to my age. If Masters looked like something from *GQ*, this guy was right out of *Rolling Stone*. He had shaggy brown hair—the longest I'd ever seen on a cop—and a mustache. He was wearing jeans, a khaki blazer and a T-shirt. He looked really rumpled, sort of a cross between Serpico and Columbo.

He smiled at me. I smiled back.

"What do you think happened?" I asked Masters.

"Not too hard to figure. The Vinas girl is innocent and naive, but she's pretty. So she goes to the singles bar with her friends and Tischler hits on her. I hear the guy had a thing for the ladies."

I remembered the phone book in his dresser drawer. "I don't think it will take exhaustive police work to prove that."

"Anyway, he probably offered to take her home and she got in his car. Only instead of going to Brooklyn, he convinced her to park with him and they started going at it. While they were in the mid-

dle of it, someone came up on them, opened the door
and shot them both."

I walked over to the car and looked inside.
"Where's all the blood?"

"Someone cleaned it up," he said. "That's why no
one noticed anything when they towed it away.
Wiped up all the blood and stuffed the bodies into
the trunk."

"Very thorough," I said. "And neat. Not to men-
tion weird."

"Yeah, ain't it?"

The ME's people were there now, taking the bodies
out of the trunk. They put them in green plastic bags
and then carried them over to the waiting morgue
truck.

I caught a glimpse of the faces before the bags
were zipped up. There wasn't much of Tischler's
face; it had been blown away by the force of the
blast. Must have been a powerful gun. Theresa Anne
Vinas still had an innocent look on her face, though.

"You got a motive?" I asked Masters.

"It sure looks like a jealous lover to me."

"You mean with Tischler?"

He nodded.

"Any ideas?"

"I'd say his wife is shaping up as a helluva
suspect."

I made a face. "Emily Tischler? No way. Wait'll
you meet her."

"Appearances can be deceiving. And she had
plenty of motive. He played around a lot—you said
so yourself. So she gets mad when he goes out again,
follows him to the bar and sees him leave with the
girl. She waits for the right moment and then—
bam!—no more Barry Tischler."

"Sure," I said. "Then she sticks her trusty cannon
back into her purse, drags the bodies into the trunk,
washes down the car and makes it back to her father-

in-law's store in time to catch the late Gucci hand-
bag sale."

The young cop next to Masters snickered loudly.

Masters gave him a dirty look. Then he turned
back to me.

"Well, it could have happened that way," he said.
But he didn't sound all that convinced himself.

"Yeah, and she could have pulled the Brinks robbery too, but she didn't."

"You don't like her for it, huh?"

"Nope."

"Maybe you're right," he said softly.

He walked back toward the car. The other cop
didn't move. He was still smiling at me.

"How ya doing?" I said.

He stuck out his hand.

"Detective Mitch Caruso." He nodded toward
Masters. "The lieutenant isn't very big on formal
introductions."

"Lucy Shannon. I'm a reporter with the *Blade*."

We shook. His grip was strong and firm. I thought
he held onto my hand just a little too long. But
maybe it was my imagination.

"You figured this out by yourself?" he said, gestur-
ing at the Mercedes.

"It was a lucky guess."

"Cool."

I pulled my hand away.

"Would you like to have dinner with me, Lucy?"

"Excuse me, Detective?"

"Mitch. Call me Mitch. Look, I don't like to waste
time. I mean, I could have led up to it with a lot of
small talk about people we both know in the department and stuff. But I figured I'd get right to the
point."

"Then you'll like my answer. It's short and to the
point too. No."

"C'mon, we'll get some Italian. I'm Italian, and

Italian cops know all the best Italian restaurants in the city. Think about it."

I pretended to ponder for a second.

"No," I said again.

"It'll be fun. We can exchange war stories. You tell me about all your big scoops and I'll tell you about the time I almost arrested John Gotti. Plus, if you're really good, I'll do my Jack Webb *Dragnet* impression for you."

"You do Jack Webb?"

He started talking in a clipped monotone.

"New York. This is the city. Everyone here has dreams. Some people want to be stars. Some want to get rich. And some people just want to steal other people's dreams. That's where I come in. I'm a cop . . ."

I laughed in spite of myself. It wasn't bad.

"Look, Detective—"

"Mitch. I know it's a toughie."

"Mitch, I just don't date cops."

"Is this some sort of religious or political statement?"

"I was recently married to one."

"It didn't work out?"

"None of my marriages did."

"How many are we talking about here?"

"Three."

He whistled softly. "Boy, you must be a barrel of fun to live with, huh?"

I smiled.

"How about you? I can't believe a charming guy like you hasn't lured some lucky bride to the altar yet."

Caruso shook his head.

"Unlike you, I'm waiting for the right person before I get married. I have this old-fashioned notion that marriage is forever. You know . . . love, honor, till death do us part . . . that sort of stuff."

"Yeah, I used to feel that way too. I thought my Prince Charming would come along one day and we'd live happily ever after."

"So what happened?"

"I was misinformed."

Eight

It had been a long time since I'd had a page 1 story.

I didn't realize how much I missed it. Before everything went wrong, I used to keep a scrapbook of all my newspaper clippings. I'm usually not good at stuff like that. I don't save letters from friends or pictures of my vacation or keep a diary. But I was very conscientious about that scrapbook. It was like a record of my life.

I took it down now from a shelf in the closet and began going through the pages.

There were a lot of clippings from when I first started with the paper. I was so young then—just in my twenties—but I found myself thrown into one of the biggest stories in New York City history. A serial killer was stalking the streets of New York, gunning down young women and couples—and sending taunting messages to the media. All the letters contained the killer's trademark phrase: "I love you to death."

I looked at some of the headlines: **"Loverboy Writes to Blade Reporter"**; **"Serial Killer Tells Shannon: I Want to Be Caught!"**; **"Crusading Young Woman Reporter One Step Ahead of Cops on Baffling Case."**

I remembered those days. How I had felt on top

of the world. Indestructible. Like nothing would ever go wrong. God, it seemed like such a long time ago.

Now they were making a movie about it.

Beautiful.

The pages in the scrapbook got emptier after that. Oh, I had some good stories along the way. I covered cops and the police commissioner's office for a long time. Got a city councilman indicted with a series on corruption in the city's urban-renewal program. Did a little rewrite, copyediting—even tried a brief stint as an assistant city editor until I decided that wasn't for me. But the truth is, my career was all pretty much downhill after that great start.

My apartment is on the sixth floor of a big building near Gramercy Park, just off Third Avenue. I stood by an open window, listening to the sounds of the city below. Horns honking. Car doors slamming. A radio turned up loud to a Top 40 station. A loud argument of some sort. I couldn't pick up all the details, but it seemed to be between two people named Ray and Maria and involved an alleged act of marital infidelity by Maria with someone named Hector.

Down on the street, I could see couples walking hand in hand, looking lovingly at each other. Everybody seemed to have somebody. Except me.

Of course, I had something they didn't have—a front-page story in tomorrow's paper.

I looked at my watch. The early edition of the *Blade*—with my exclusive about Barry Tischler and Theresa Anne Vinas having been found murdered—would be arriving at the newsstands pretty soon. I could go pick up a copy. I left my apartment, went outside and started up Third Avenue to Twenty-third Street, where there was a newsstand that stayed open all night.

Twenty-third Street and Third Avenue is not exactly what you'd call the garden spot of the city at night. I mean, you didn't find Donald Trump and Marla hanging out there.

The people around the newsstand tonight were a pretty typical bunch. A wino urinating against a wall. Someone asleep on the sidewalk who could have been a man or a woman—I wasn't sure which. And an old guy waving a cane at passersby and muttering something about Jesus and socialism.

The newsstand guy told me the papers generally showed up about eleven or so. I checked my watch. Ten-thirty. I decided to wait for the half hour.

Actually, it turned out to be forty-five minutes. During that time, several people asked me for money, one offered me drugs and a man made what I believe was a marriage proposal from a passing car.

Finally, at 11:15, a blue truck pulled up with the words *New York Blade* on the side. The driver threw out a bundle of papers. I slid one out of the pile, plopped down two quarters to pay for it and looked at page 1.

They'd played my story big, with a screaming headline across the top of the page:

MISSING TEEN, DEPARTMENT STORE HEIR FOUND SLAIN!

Below that, in fourteen-point type, was my byline:

Exclusive
by Lucy Shannon

I didn't think that mattered to me anymore, but it did. I still felt that little surge of adrenaline I'd had the first time I saw my name on a story. Nothing was ever going to take that away completely. I was hooked.

The people behind me in line were getting impatient.

"That's me," I announced, pointing to the byline.

Nobody said anything.

"First page one byline in a long, long time."

Still nothing.

I shrugged, folded up the paper and began trudging down Third Avenue.

I made it all the way home without anyone asking for my autograph.

Nine

"Murphy Brown," Janet said.

"Lois Lane," I told her.

"Lois Lane couldn't carry Murphy's hair spray."

"Lois doesn't use hair spray."

"That's because she's a goddamned cartoon character, Lucy."

Barlow walked over to our desks in the city room.

"What's the topic today?"

"Who's the better reporter?" Janet said. "Murphy Brown or Lois Lane."

"Murphy Brown doesn't even do real breaking-news stories," I pointed out. "It's all yuppie, TV-news-magazine kind of stuff."

"And Lois Lane never broke a scoop in her life. She just stood and watched while Superman did all the work."

Barlow looked down at my computer screen. It was blank.

"You got a follow-up on the murders?"

"I'm working on one."

"Doesn't seem like it."

"I'm trying to set up new interviews with Tischler's widow and the dead girl's mom."

"Gee, there's an original idea."

"Okay, it's a cliché. But it's an effective cliché. It'll make a nice sob story."

"See if you can find something better, huh?"

"Sure."

A cheer suddenly went up in the newsroom.

My face was on a color-TV screen hanging above the city desk. The story was about how my tip had broken the Theresa Anne Vinas case. I stood up and acknowledged the applause from the other reporters.

"Jesus, I've never seen anyone go from the outhouse to the penthouse so fast," Barlow muttered as he walked away.

"Speaking of outhouses," Janet said, "how's your love life these days?"

"What love life?"

"When's the last time you were out on a date anyway, Lucy?"

I thought about that for a second.

"Define 'date,' " I said finally.

"You been getting any offers?"

"Sure. One of the cops at the murder scene asked me out."

Janet made a face. "Yuck, another cop . . ."

"That was my reaction too."

Something plopped down on my desk. A white envelope. Norm Malloy was standing there.

"What's this?" I asked.

"Someone left it for you at the front door."

I picked up the envelope. There was a return address in the left-hand corner. It said: "Julie Blaumstein. 109 W. 81st Street, #3G."

"Who's Julie Blaumstein?" I asked.

Malloy shrugged. "I just deliver 'em. You're the hotshot reporter."

"Yeah," I said as I idly ripped the envelope open. "I'm the hotshot reporter."

It's funny how news works.

You knock yourself out trying to find a big exclusive. Make a million phone calls. Pound on doors all over town. And nothing comes of it.

Then, out of nowhere, someone drops the biggest story in the world right in your lap.

A lot of mail comes into a newspaper's city room. Most of it is just junk. Press releases, people trying to sell something, letters from crazy readers about men from Venus or neighbors they're convinced are enemy spies. Ninety-nine percent of it is worthless. But you never know.

Inside the envelope were two pieces of paper.

One was a clipping of my front-page article about the Theresa Anne Vinas-Barry Tischler murders. My byline was circled in red Magic Marker.

The second was another article from the *Blade*. It was a feature on the movie company that was in town to make a film about the Loverboy killings.

Written in the same red Magic Marker across this clipping were the words "I LOVE YOU TO DEATH."

Below that, it said: "I'm back."

Oh, Jesus!

This can't be happening.

Loverboy again.

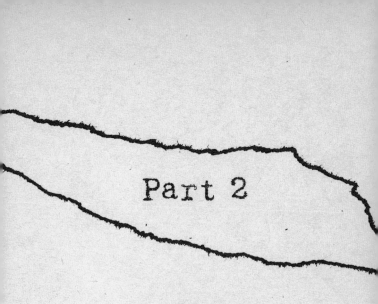

Part 2

LOVERBOY

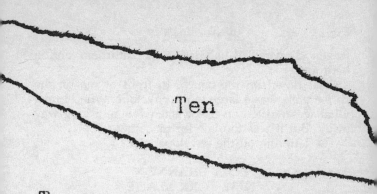

Ten

The address where Julie Blaumstein lived turned out to be a brownstone off Columbus Avenue.

I pushed open the front door and pressed the buzzer for 3G in the lobby. No answer. I tried a few other people in the building until someone finally buzzed me in.

I trudged up the steps to the third floor, found her apartment and knocked. Still nothing. I listened at the closed door for a minute to see if there was any sound coming from inside. There wasn't. So I took out a credit card, then jimmied it into the open space between the lock and the doorframe until the door popped open. A trick I learned once while interviewing a burglar for a feature on home break-ins. It was so easy I sometimes wondered why people even bothered with locks.

The inside of 3G had white walls, brown parquet floors and the feel of a new apartment where the tenant hasn't really settled in yet. There were only a few pieces of furniture—a couch, a coffee table, an easy chair and a stereo/CD set up by the window. On the wall was a print of the New York skyline that the peddlers down in Washington Square sold by the hundreds. The kitchen had a small stove and a refrigerator that was pretty empty except for a few

49

frozen dinners. A hall led to a bathroom and a bedroom.

I sat down on the couch. In front of me on the coffee table was a large white envelope. When I read what was written on it, I wished I were a long way away. But it was too late for that now.

The lettering on the envelope said:

LUCY SHANNON
NEW YORK BLADE

I sat there for a long time staring at that envelope. From outside, the sounds of the traffic on Columbus Avenue floated in through the open window. Finally I picked it up and tore it open.

Some things you just gotta know.

It was worse than I expected.

Dear Lucy,

Hello again, my lovely.

I've been away. I've been quiet. I've been good for so long.

PAUSE FOR JOKE

Q. How many Jewish-American princesses does it take to change a light bulb?

A. Three. Two to bring the diet soda and one to call her daddy to come over and do the work.

LAUGHTER

Do you remember those Death-Wish movies with Charles Bronson? If he saw anybody he didn't like, he just blew them away.

I used to fantasize about stuff like that.

I mean, you see some smug girl walking down Fifth Avenue in her miniskirt and heels and you try to talk to her. But she won't give you the time of day. So you just point at her and—presto!—no more girl. That'll teach her to ignore you.

If only life was that easy, right?
Well, I'll tell you a secret.
It really is.

Here's a riddle for you:

What has two arms, two legs, no face—and is red all over?
Think about that for a second.

ATTENTION WOMEN OF NEW YORK CITY:
I love you all. I really do.
I love you to death.
Now, due to circumstances beyond my control, I have begun killing again.
There's only one person who can stop this bloodbath.
It isn't me.

I've missed you, Lucy.
You and I, we shared something really special a long time ago. And you're going to be with me every step of the way this time too. I'm going to make you a hero again.
Just like old times.

Answer to riddle: If you don't know, go look in the bedroom.

Loverboy

The note was typewritten on white bond stationery. The letters were in pica type. The ribbon seemed to be worn, because some of the letters were not fully formed. I sat there staring at it for a long time. Maybe if I stared at it long enough, I'd find a clue. Maybe I'd find something I could use to help me track down the killer. Maybe I could avoid going into the bedroom.

Finally I stood up and walked down the hall. The door was closed. I turned the knob and pushed it open.

The bedroom was as sparsely furnished as the rest of the apartment. Platform bed. Wooden, four-drawer dresser along the wall. Venetian blinds on the windows. And that was it.

Except for the body on the bed.

She was young, in her early twenties, and might have been pretty once. I couldn't tell, though. A gunshot had blown away most of her face. She was wearing a black silk vest, Calvin Klein jeans and some kind of clunky black shoes. The vest had been torn open and the jeans were at her knees. Someone had written "SLUT" in bright red lipstick across her stomach.

I got out of there as fast as I could. I staggered back into the living room. The note was still on the coffee table, where I'd left it. I wanted to run out of that apartment, slam the door behind me and pretend I'd never been there.

But I didn't.

I walked over to Julie Blaumstein's telephone, picked up the receiver and did what I should have done in the first place.

I called the cops.

Eleven

Lieutenant Masters and Detective Caruso sat with me at the Midtown West Precinct and talked about Julie Blaumstein.

An army of police had descended on the apartment. They talked to other tenants, shopkeepers in the neighborhood, friends and relatives whose names they'd found in an address book. By the end of the day, they had put together a pretty good picture of her life. And how she had died.

Masters told me what they'd found out. He didn't look happy.

"Her name is Julie Rebecca Blaumstein. She's from Wisconsin, a little town called Silver Lake. That's not too far from Chicago. She came here about a year ago to try to be a writer. Took a tiny place on the Lower East Side, and struggled every day behind a keyboard.

"She didn't have much luck with that, but about six weeks ago, she landed a job churning out copy for a public relations firm on Madison Avenue. That gave her enough money to move into the spanking new digs off Columbus Avenue."

He took a deep breath.

"Okay, here's where it gets interesting. She had some money now, but she was still sorely lacking any companionship from the opposite sex."

"She wasn't getting laid," Caruso said.

Masters gave him a dirty look. "To put it crudely, yes."

He turned back to me. "Anyway, she signed up with a computer outfit called LifeMates. Know what that is?"

"Some kind of dating service?"

"Yeah. They're all the rage in these days of AIDS. You don't have to hang out in bars and get hit on by a lot of creepy guys. Instead you just sit at home and call up pictures and bios on your CD-ROM or whatever until you hit on someone you'd like to meet. It's really respectable too. They advertise in places like *New York* magazine."

"I've seen the ads," I said. " 'Harvard Ph.D., a hundred fifty thousand a year, summer house in Montauk—likes traveling, beautiful poetry, long walks on the beach, French-kissing and bondage.' "

"We found stuff for LifeMates in her apartment. She'd made a date for last night. The guy who offed her probably used the service to set it up."

"Does the company—"

"Have records of everyone—so we can find his name, address and what time he'll be home for us to pick him up for murder? No, it doesn't work that way. Everybody pays a fee to go on-line. But who you hook up with is your own business. Besides, most of those people use aliases and phony addresses."

"What about the gun?" I asked.

"We don't have the ballistics report yet, but it was a big one—maybe a forty-four."

"Does it look like the same gun that was used to kill Tischler and the Vinas girl?"

"Probably."

And the same kind of gun that Loverboy used to use.

I looked over at Caruso. "How do you think it went down?" I asked him.

He shrugged. "She invited the guy in for their date. He pulled out a gun. He shot her. End of story."

"It happened in the bedroom," I pointed out.

"Maybe they were having sex. Maybe they went out to dinner, had a great time and he got her in the sack. There was no evidence of that. But when the crime-lab report comes back . . ."

I shook my head. "I don't think so. I don't think they ever went out on the date. I think she went into the bedroom for something—maybe to check her makeup or change her earrings—and he followed her in with the gun. I just wonder what came first."

"Huh?"

"Did he shoot her and then pull off her clothes and write on her with the lipstick? Or did he do that stuff when she was still alive?"

"Does it matter?" Masters asked.

"Only for Julie Blaumstein. Can you imagine the terror she must have been feeling if she knew what was happening? But maybe her last thoughts were just about how great she hoped that night would be and how her life seemed to be turning around. Maybe she never even knew what hit her when the gunshot blew her face away. I hope it was that way for her."

I'd called in the facts of the story to the city desk a while ago. But I needed to get down to the office to write a first-person sidebar to go with it. Caruso offered to give me a ride.

I started to say no, but then changed my mind. I wasn't sure how long it would take me to catch a taxi. Besides, he might tell me something new about the case.

"Do you think this Loverboy is the same killer as before?" Caruso asked as we drove downtown.

"The guy who wrote that note is crazy," I said, not exactly answering his question.

"It must make you feel kinda creepy—the way he wrote to you like you were old friends or something."

"As a matter of fact, it does."

"But kind of exciting too, huh?"

I looked out the window and didn't say anything. This wasn't going as I'd expected. I was supposed to be asking the questions.

"So is he?" Caruso asked.

"Is he what?"

"The same guy?"

"No," I blurted out.

"How can you be sure?"

"There hasn't been a Loverboy murder in a long time."

"So?"

"That means the real Loverboy is dead."

"How do you know?"

"Because otherwise he never would have stopped killing."

"Maybe he was just lying low."

"Not Loverboy."

"So you think this is just a copycat? Someone who saw they were making a TV movie on the murders and decides it's such a good idea, he'll do it too?"

I nodded.

"I hope you're right," he said. "If not, it means that the worst mass killer in the history of New York City is still out there. And ready to start murdering people again."

We pulled up in front of the *Blade* Building.

"Let's talk again soon," he said.

"Officially?"

"Not necessarily."

"I don't think so."

I started to get out of the car.

"Look, I'm sorry if I came on too strong when we met. I just want to get to know you better, Lucy."

"Why? Do you think I'm that attractive? I'd figure a hip, happening cop like you could pick up all sorts of pretty young women."

"I think you're attractive, yes. But that's not the only reason. I think you're a fascinating person. But you've got all these barriers up. I'd like to strip them away sometime and see what the real Lucy Shannon is like. I'll bet she's pretty nice."

"Sorry," I said. "I don't do shrink sessions with horny cops."

Caruso shook his head.

"Are you ever *not* in your attack mode?" he asked.

I sighed. "I've got a lot on my mind."

He took out a card with his name on it and wrote something on the bottom. Then he handed it to me.

"That's my home phone number. Call me sometime. We'll just talk. Nothing more. Hey, maybe we can be friends."

"Doubtful," I told him. "Men friends generally don't work out for me."

"How come?"

"Sexual tension."

"You mean they want to go to bed with you."

"Or sometimes I want to go to bed with them."

I got out of the car without saying good-bye, entered the *Blade* Building and went upstairs to write my story.

But I kept his damn card.

After I finished the story, I waited around until the editions came off the press. Norm Malloy plopped one of the first copies down on my desk.

"Page one again," he announced in a loud voice. "You're on a roll, Shannon."

After that, Walter Barlow came over and told me I'd done a great job. Other reporters patted me on the back and shouted out compliments. Even Victoria Crawford had something nice to say.

I looked down at the headlines on the two stories, which took up virtually all of the front page.

COPS PROBE LOVERBOY
LINK IN NEW MURDERS

KILLER TALKS TO BLADE REPORTER

Exclusive
by Lucy Shannon

After all this time, I was a hero again.

I had a big story. My editors loved me. And a guy was even interested in me.

What was it the note in Julie Blaumstein's apartment had said?

Just like old times.

Twelve

I spent the next morning going through the clips on the Loverboy murders.

Most newspaper libraries are totally on computer now. If you want to read about an old case, you just press a button and it comes up on the screen. But the *Blade* still kept the actual clippings in boxes and drawers piled high on top of one another. The newsroom had joined the '90s, but the library was still somewhere around the 1940s. Like something out of a Humphrey Bogart movie. I loved it. I sometimes wished I could just disappear into the place.

I read through the stories about Loverboy. The first one was in the summer of 1978. The killer jumped out of some bushes and opened fire on a young couple named Bobby Fowler and Linda Malandro, who were necking in a scenic, secluded area in upper Manhattan, near the George Washington Bridge. She died, he survived.

After that, the killings continued. Slowly at first. Months would go by, sometimes years. It took a while for the cops to even realize they were connected. So the horror of a serial murderer roaming the streets of New York didn't fully emerge into the public's consciousness until much later. Near the end of the bloody spree.

During the summer of 1984 the killer—now calling

himself Loverboy—started writing letters to a reporter covering the story. Each of the letters contained the phrase "I love you to death." Maybe he
got the idea from Son of Sam. The serial killer as
media superstar. Son of Sam had sent his letters to
Jimmy Breslin. Loverboy picked one reporter to be
his friend too.

That reporter was me.

I was only twenty-four years old, and suddenly I
was thrown into the biggest story of my life. I became a superstar too. Linked forever with a madman.

There were thirteen killings in the six-year period.
Eight other people were wounded. All the victims
were young. The primary targets were always
women. And the killer used the same powerful .44-
caliber gun in each shooting.

The victims included a couple who'd just graduated from high school, a cocktail waitress, a college
sophomore, a nurse and all sorts of other assorted
New Yorkers. There was no predictable pattern to
Loverboy's madness. He struck at least once in
every borough.

Some of the wounded had been lucky—they were
able to get on with their lives. Others hadn't. One
girl was in a wheelchair, a paraplegic—paralyzed
from the waist down. A young man was legally
blind. I knew them all from when I'd first covered
the story, but a lot of time had passed since then. So
I wrote the names down in my notebook.

There were screaming headlines. Stories about a
city living in fear, its young people afraid to go out
at night and maybe become the next victim. "No One
Is Safe," the *New York Post* warned in one headline.

The circulation of every newspaper in town soared
by at least 20 percent during Loverboy's spree.

The police vowed they were zeroing in on prime
suspects. No one believed it. Neighborhood protec-

tion groups started sprouting up all over town. People went out and bought guns.

And then, just as suddenly as they had started, the killings stopped.

Everyone held his breath waiting for the next one, but it never came. Eventually the case drifted off the front page and out of people's minds. Loverboy was never caught.

The prevalent theory among law enforcement types was that he was dead.

"I think the guy offed himself," said Detective Jack Reagan in one yellowed clip I found.

It said Reagan had been one of the top investigators on the special task force hunting for Loverboy. The article was dated about six months after the last killing, when the special task force was being disbanded.

"The guy was a nut, we know that. So I think one day it all just got to him and he put the forty-four to his head and pulled the trigger. We'll never know for sure. But that's what I think happened."

Asked what made him feel that way, Reagan explained: "The killing stopped, that's why."

I smiled.

It didn't surprise me that Jack Reagan would have said that.

The most recent clip in the Loverboy file expressed a different view. It was from an interview with Michael Anson, the director in town making the movie about Loverboy's killing spree.

"I think he's still out there," Anson said. "Waiting. Waiting to start killing again."

Of course, it was in Anson's best interest to take that view. The idea that Loverboy was still loose helped drum up excitement in the movie.

There was another recent clip called "Where Are They Now?" It listed some of the main players in the story and told what had happened to them over the years. I was on the list. But I didn't need to read that.

I was interested in Tommy Ferraro. He'd been the head of the Loverboy task force.

Now he was Thomas J. Ferraro, and he was a big man around town. He was the police commissioner. And there was even a lot of talk about him running for mayor. There were pictures of his house in Pelham Manor, of his loving family and of him at fancy social events and dropping in at celebrity hot spots like Elaine's. He'd come a long way in twelve years.

Tommy Ferraro.

Jack Reagan.

And me.

Funny, how things had worked out for all of us.

But then no one ever said life was fair.

Thirteen

At 4 P.M. every day, Vicki Crawford had a news meeting in her office.

It had been a long time since I'd been invited to one of them. Most of the people on the desk went. Walter Barlow. A couple of assistant city editors. Brian Tully, the national editor. Karen Wolfe, the sports editor. And sometimes even a reporter who was working on a really big story.

This time they went around the room, talking about the rest of the stuff in the news before they got to today's big story.

My story.

"Here's the news item to make your day," Tully was saying. "A guy goes into the hospital in Chicago for hemorrhoid surgery. Only he's real nervous and has a lot of gas buildup. I mean, we're talking a lot of gas. Anyway, when the doctors start to cut him, he involuntarily lets it go on the operating table. An oxygen unit nearby catches fire, there's a big explosion and the whole operating team gets blown backward by the force of the blast . . ."

Everyone cracked up around the room.

"Anyway, the poor schmuck's lying there with half his rear end gone, the doctors and nurses had to get first-aid treatment, and now the hospital's looking at a huge malpractice suit."

"I guess the operation backfired, huh?" someone said.

"Is that why they call it the Windy City?" Karen Wolfe asked.

Even Vicki was laughing.

"All right," she said, "but do it short and straight. Very straight. And no bad puns in the headlines."

She turned to Wolfe.

"What's your lead sports story, Karen?"

"The Jets have offered their first draft choice five million dollars."

"Five friggin' million?"

"Yeah, but that's not even the story. The guy turned it down."

Vicki shook her head.

"Let's do a real breakdown of five million dollars. Put it in terms the average working stiff can understand. How many groceries it could buy, how many cars, how many shoes for the kids."

She turned to Barlow.

"What have you got on city side, Walter?"

"Well, there's a hearing on the budget, a bomb scare at La Guardia, an announcement from the Mayor's office that they're going to finish construction work on the FDR by the end of the year . . ."

"Didn't they say that last year?" Tully asked.

"They said it during the goddamned Lindsay administration," Vicki snapped. "C'mon, Walter—what have we got on Loverboy?"

"Okay, Loverboy's a big story, so—"

"No, Walter, it's not a big story. A big story is a cop being shot. Or some politician caught in bed with a hooker. This is a lot more than that. This is a gift from heaven. Do you understand what I'm saying?"

There were nods and murmurs around the room.

A newspaper war was going on in New York City. The players were the *Times*, the *Daily News*, the *Post* and the *Blade*. Of these four papers, most analysts predicted the city could support only two—possibly three at the most. So a desperate game of musical chairs was under way to see which would make it and which would be left by the wayside. The *Times* was pretty much invulnerable and above the fray. The *Daily News* and the *Post* had big money problems, but they also had a hard-core base of longtime readers to build on. The *Blade* had Ronald Mackell's millions.

Vicki wanted a big story. Not just for the *Blade*, but for herself. She wanted to make her mark in New York journalism to prove she wasn't just Ronald Mackell's little bimbo. I knew that. And I was covering the story that could give her what she wanted. Life works in strange ways sometimes.

"The only thing you can even compare this with is the Son of Sam killings back in 1977," she was saying. "Do you know what that did to newspaper sales? It sent them through the roof."

"People were terrified," Barlow said.

"I'm not so sure everyone's that scared this time," Tully pointed out.

"They will be by the time we're finished," someone suggested.

Everyone laughed.

"Hell, this is better than Son of Sam," Vicki said. "Son of Sam killed a lot of people, but he did it in one big spree. This guy kills a bunch of people, but over a six-year period. Then he lays low for more than a decade. Everyone figures he's dead. But suddenly he comes back and starts up again. Unbelievable."

"It's not the same guy," I said.

"What do you mean?"

"The first guy is probably dead. Or in a mental ward or something. This is a copycat."

"You got any proof of that?"

"No."

"So you don't know this for a fact?"

I didn't say anything.

Vicki thought about it for a second. "Screw it, let's assume we're dealing with the same guy. Loverboy is back. It's a better story that way."

"What if we're wrong?" Barlow asked.

"So what? Is the real Loverboy gonna sue? Is he going to claim we defamed him by saying he killed sixteen people when he really only snuffed out thirteen? C'mon, Walter, we can't lose either way on this one."

"I thought we dealt in facts," I said.

"You don't have any facts. Get me some."

"Well, I guess we just have to wait until the killer strikes again," Walter said. "Then we can—"

"Wrong!" Vicki's fist slammed down on the desktop in front of her. "That's exactly what we *won't* do."

"But—"

"For chrissakes, Walter, this guy might not hit again for days or even weeks. In the meantime, we have to put out a daily paper. We can't just sit around and wait for something to happen. We need to make news ourselves. I want to see something on this case every day that's going to keep the readers interested in it."

"What exactly did you have in mind?" I asked.

"It's your story," Vicki snapped. "You tell me."

I tried to think quickly. Everyone in the room was staring at me.

"Well, there's the movie they're making here about the Loverboy case. It's pretty bizarre that that's happening at the same time as these new killings. There's gotta be some kind of connection. The director called me—she wants me to be in the movie. I can do an interview with her."

"Good idea. Anything else?"

"I was thinking about the victims from the first

Loverboy spree. A few of them survived. Plus, there's the families of the dead ones. Why not go talk to them about all the terrible memories this brings back? Put a headline on it like, 'The Nightmare That Won't Die.' "

Vicki smiled broadly. "*Now* you're getting the hang of it. You know, you shouldn't give up on this reporting business, Shannon. You might figure out how to do it right someday."

When I got back to my desk after the meeting, Janet was waiting for me. She nodded toward Vicki's office, visible through the glass window.

"I have some dirt about our fearless leader," she said.

"Good news or bad news?"

"You'll like it."

I waited. Janet didn't say anything. She was milking this for all it was worth. It must be really good.

"I hear all is not well in paradise between our editor and her husband, our owner and publisher."

"There's trouble in the marriage?"

"Trouble with a capital D. As in divorce."

"She's getting one?"

"Him. I hear he's talking to his lawyers. My source says it's just a matter of time. There's another woman . . ."

"There usually is," I said.

I glanced over at Vicki in her office. She was on the phone and seemed totally in control. But if the marriage really was falling apart, Mackell wouldn't want his ex-wife to be editor of his newspaper. That meant the Vicki Crawford era would be over.

"I told you you'd like it," Janet said.

"I love it!"

Fourteen

The movie company was shooting at the Limelight, a nightclub at the corner of Sixth Avenue and Twentieth Street.

A fleet of trucks and vans sat parked on the street outside. People milled around carrying cameras, cables and lighting equipment. I walked up to a bearded man wearing a baseball cap and asked him where I could find Michael Anson. He pointed to one of the trailers near the front entrance.

A crowd of fans was being kept back by a rope, which had a sign on it that said: MOVIE SHOOT TODAY. NO PARKING. A policeman was standing next to the rope. I showed my press card to the cop, who let me through.

A woman opened the door of Michael Anson's trailer. She was over six feet tall and had muscular arms and a body like a female bodybuilder. She was wearing jeans, a sleeveless T-shirt and a necklace made out of some sort of animal teeth. She was also scowling at me. When I told her who I was, she motioned me inside. But she didn't stop scowling.

A half-dozen people were in the trailer, all of them engaged in animated conversation with a woman sitting at a table. There were lots of typewritten pages spread out in front of her. The woman at the center of all this looked up at me.

"You're Lucy Shannon?" she said.

"Right."

"I'm Michael Anson."

She shook my hand.

"Not bad," she said. "Not bad at all. You'll do."

"Thanks. I think."

Michael Anson was about thirty-five, with dark hair cut very short and a cute, pixielike kind of face. She was wearing a tailored black pantsuit with a cranberry silk blouse. Her makeup was perfect, despite the heat. She clapped her hands loudly and told everyone to take a fifteen-minute break. They all left. All except the big woman at the door.

"That's Micki," Michael said.

She was glaring at me.

"You mean, like Mickey Mouse?" I asked.

"No. Micki. With an *i*."

"How ya doing, Mick?" I said.

Micki just glared some more. She didn't really seem to be a people person.

"So you've decided to be in my movie, after all, Miss Shannon."

"Actually, I've come to ask you some questions about the case."

"Maybe we can help each other out."

"Meaning you'll talk to me if I take the part?"

"Why not?"

"I just always thought that if I got discovered by Hollywood, it would be more romantic. You know, like some producer sees me sitting at a soda fountain in a drugstore—like Lana Turner—and says, 'I'm gonna make her a star.' "

"They don't have soda fountains in drugstores anymore, Miss Shannon."

"Maybe that's why I've never made it into a movie."

Anson shook her head.

"Let's cut the crap, huh? These new killings have

raised the ante on the part. We're big news. I was going to have you do just a walk-on part, but now I'm thinking about a much bigger role. The real-life reporter who's still chasing the killer. What do you think?"

"It's catchy."

"Do yourself a favor. Grab a little of the glory. You could parlay this into something really big. You don't want to be a newspaper reporter covering fires all your life, do you?"

"There's worse things in the world than covering a fire," I said.

"Yeah. Covering two fires."

I hit her with the question that had been on my mind ever since I got the Loverboy note.

"It's quite a coincidence that these killings started up at the same time you began shooting this movie," I said. "What do you make of that?"

"I suppose the killer read about us—and that prompted him to do it."

"That would make you sort of responsible for murder."

Anson shrugged. "Oh, come on. I have no control over what other people do because of my movies. Any more than Martin Scorsese could control John Hinkley because he saw Jodie Foster in *Taxi Driver*. But hey, it's good publicity for the movie. It couldn't have worked out better."

"Which brings up another, much more disturbing possibility."

"What?" She laughed. "That I went out and killed some people all to get publicity for my movie?"

"You didn't have to do it yourself. You could have hired someone to do it." I looked over at the woman wearing the animal-teeth necklace. "Like Micki with an *i* by the door."

"Even you don't believe that, Shannon."

"Probably not."

"Actually, I could do the same thing with you. Your newspaper's circulation soared during the first wave of killings. So did your career. Maybe you thought that would happen again. So you . . ."

I held up my hand. "I get your point. Truce?"

Anson glanced toward Micki and smiled.

"Just out of curiosity," I said, "what's the Mickster's job around here?"

"She's my bodyguard."

"You need a bodyguard?"

"There've been threats against my life. People who say I'll die if I go ahead with this movie."

"From who—movie critics?"

"The threats are real. Just yesterday the police arrested some demonstrators outside who feel we're glorifying a mad killer."

"Well, Micki looks like she's capable of protecting you."

"That's why I keep her around me twenty-four hours a day."

I pondered that for a second. "That must be tough on your love life," I said.

"What do you mean?"

"Having Ms. Smiley-Face there standing guard next to the bed could really cut down on the ol' bedroom ardor with your lover."

Anson turned toward Micki now and laughed. Micki laughed too. I decided I'd said something funny. I just didn't know what it was.

"I don't get the joke," I said.

"Miss Shannon, Micki is my lover."

"Oh."

I stood up. It was time to leave.

"So will you be in the movie?"

"I'll think about it," I said.

Micki was still glaring at me when I left.

Micki and Michael.

Cute.

If they ever get married, they won't even have to change the monograms on their towels.

Jesus, how come I never saw that one coming?

Fifteen

One of the worst things about being a reporter is talking to victims and their families.

It's one thing to see a murder or accident victim's bloody body. That's something you can deal with. But it's a lot tougher actually meeting the families and seeing the grief they're going to have to live with for the rest of their lives.

Once, when I was just starting out, I had to ask a sobbing husband how he felt after his wife had chopped his baby son's head off and then begun reciting biblical quotations over it. Another time, I broke the news to a teenage girl that her father, mother, brother and sister had all been killed in a car accident. Both times I remember getting drunk afterward.

Now I was doing something different. I was going back to some crime victims years later to see what had become of them. What were they like now? How had they been changed by their ordeals?

The first person I met was Danny Girabaldi. He had been nineteen when he was shot; he was thirty-one now. He'd been with his date, an eighteen-year-old girl named Clare Cappadonna, in a parking lot outside a Bay Ridge dance club when the killer had struck. Clare had died instantly from a bullet to the head. Danny had suffered bullet wounds to the head, chest and back, and glass fragments in his eyes. He somehow had survived. But now he was legally blind.

"Yeah, I remember it," Girabaldi told me as we sat in his living room. "I go over it every day. I mean, what the hell else do I have to do?"

He wore a pair of dark glasses. In the pictures of him from before the shooting, he'd been a handsome teenager. Now he looked much older than his years. His parents sat on either side of him in front of a picture window looking out on a quiet Brooklyn neighborhood.

There seemed to be a sadness throughout the whole house.

"How are you getting along?" I asked.

"Oh, as well as can be expected. I don't get around much, but I'm not totally blind."

"Well, that's something."

"Yeah. I mean, I can pick up shapes and shadows and stuff. I can even see you sitting there, for instance. I can't tell what you're wearing or much about you or even if you're a man or a woman without hearing your voice. But I'm not totally blind."

He said this very firmly, as if it was an important distinction to make.

"Danny worked for a while a few months ago, you know," his father piped up. "Isn't that right?"

Danny nodded.

"I got him a job at the post office," he said. "I work there myself, been there for thirty-eight years. Anyway, we needed some help around Christmastime."

"How'd it go?" I asked.

"Not so well," Danny said.

"We probably pushed him a little," his mother said. "Asked him to do something he wasn't ready for yet."

"Maybe next year," his father said.

She nodded. Danny didn't say anything.

We went over the events of the night he'd been shot. The more we talked, the more subdued Danny seemed to get. This conversation was not doing him any good. I felt bad about that.

"There's been some more killings," I said. "I don't think it's the same person. I think it's probably just a copycat. But I'm trying to pick up anything—no matter how small—from what happened to you that might help me track him down."

"Why bother?" he asked. "It's too late for that now."

"It's never too late, Danny."

"It is for me."

Kathleen DiLeonardo was a different story altogether.

She'd been walking home after a night course at Queens College when the killer opened fire. She had been hit in the shoulder, but fortunately, the bullet had passed through without causing any major damage.

"I hardly think about it anymore," she told me.

She was married now and living in a split-level in Glen Cove, Long Island. She had three daughters and her husband was a stockbroker who worked for a big firm on Wall Street. They'd just put a down payment on a vacation house near Orient Point in Suffolk County, she said. Life had been good for Kathleen DiLeonardo since that night in Queens a long time ago.

"The only thing is, I still get this ache in my shoulder when it rains," she said. "Or sometimes when I reach up to get something with that arm. But I guess, all things considered, I was pretty lucky."

I thought about Danny Girabaldi and agreed that she was.

"Did you see the person who shot you at all?"

"Just for a second. A shadowy figure jumped out of some bushes. I mean, it was really dark. And it all happened so quickly . . ."

"What did he look like?"

She shrugged.

"Any possibility you might recognize him if you saw him again?"

She seemed uncomfortable with that thought. "Like I told you, it was a long time ago. I'm not sure anymore about any of it."

Jack Corrigan was bitter.

"My life ended when Katy died," Corrigan said. He nodded toward a picture next to him of a smiling teenager. "She was the apple of my eye. My wife died a year and a half later—from a broken heart, I'll always believe that. Me, I had to stop working soon after it happened because of my heart going bad. All the stress, the doctors said."

Corrigan lived in a dingy one-room efficiency in a hotel on West Forty-fifth Street in Manhattan.

"We had a little house in Jackson Heights," he said wistfully. "Had to give it up after I stopped working and the doctor bills ran up.

"Christ," he said, shaking his head, "I can still see Katy on that last night. She said she was going out dancing. I told her to be careful, because the papers were already writing about this nut with a gun who was killing young girls. She kissed me on the side of the cheek and said, 'I will, Daddykins.' She called me 'Daddykins' whenever she wanted something— like money to go out. So I gave her twenty dollars, in case she wanted to stop and get something to eat afterward."

Corrigan paused and looked down at the picture again.

"The twenty-dollar bill was still on her when they

found the body," he said bitterly. "He didn't even rob her. The creep just killed her for no reason at all."

I nodded. I really didn't know what to say.

"But you've kept going. That's important."

"I have to. I have my work to do."

"Your work?"

He handed me a pile of newspaper clippings. They were about committees being formed to fight for victims of crime. Petitions signed. Protests made to judges and prosecutors who were lenient with violent criminals.

"Do you know that Son of Sam tried to get money for the book-and-TV rights to his story? We stopped that. Got a law passed preventing a criminal from profiting from his crime. It's called the Son of Sam Law."

I nodded. "Yes, I'm aware of that."

"Do you know what will happen if the cops ever catch this guy you're looking for?"

"They'll send him to jail."

Corrigan shook his head violently from side to side.

"No, he'll get himself some fancy lawyer who'll say he's insane. And he probably is. So he'll be pampered in some hospital somewhere at taxpayer expense. And all the time they'll be writing books about him and TV-movies and he'll be trying to get his hands on that money. Do you know they're already trying to shoot a movie here about this case?"

"That's right."

"Well, it'll never get done. Not if I have anything to say about it."

"What do you mean?"

"I've been going down there every day, where they're shooting it, to try to talk some sense into that director. And I'll protest outside, every step of the way if I have to. It's not right for them to make money on my daughter's death. It's just not right."

I remembered what Michael Anson had said about threats against her life.

"This is a free country, Mr. Corrigan," I said. "If people want to pay money to see a movie—"

"It's blood money! Blood money off my dead daughter. And I won't stand for it."

At least one of the victims had turned to religion.

Bobby Fowler and his girlfriend, Linda Malandro, had been the first people shot by Loverboy. Sitting in a car overlooking the Hudson River, after leaving a disco one hot summer night in 1978. She'd died, but he survived.

Now he was the Reverend Robert Fowler. I found him at a little Baptist church on Queens Boulevard in Kew Gardens. He was helping to fill baskets with food for the elderly people in the area.

"I took the shooting as a sign from God," he said. "So I decided to devote myself to Him. As thanks for sparing me."

"Well, that sounds very constructive," I told him.

"It wasn't easy," Fowler said. He put some bread, eggs and milk into a basket and handed it to a volunteer. "I mean, I had some pretty rough times after Linda was shot.

"You know, we weren't just a couple of kids fooling around with each other. We'd lived together for a year, and had a daughter. But then we'd broken up. We were just getting back together when it happened. If we hadn't gone to that secluded spot that night, we probably would have gotten married. But . . ."

"What happened to your daughter?"

Fowler shrugged. "You see, I was really screwed up for a while. Started drinking. Did drugs. And since I wasn't married to Linda, I had no clear-cut right to her. She wound up with adoptive parents."

"Do you ever see her?"

He sighed. "Not really. It's too difficult. And anyway, she never remembered much about me."

"But you remember. . . ."

"She was all that Linda left behind," he said. "And I lost that too."

"Tell me about the shooting."

He went through it all. The lovers' lane. The shadowy figure by the car. The gunshots. Linda's body lying next to his as he struggled for consciousness.

"You know," Robert Fowler said, "the Lord saith we must not wish ill on our enemies. He asks us to turn the other cheek. Vengeance is mine, saith the Lord."

Fowler looked at me and said:

"But I hope they catch the bastard and he rots in jail."

On the way back to Manhattan, I thought about what I'd learned.

Mostly that Loverboy had affected his victims in different ways. Some, like the Girabaldi family and Jack Corrigan, had their lives ruined. For Kathleen DiLeonardo, the incident had been only a small aberration and her life had gone on normally. Bobby Fowler had experienced the depths of despair and now seemed to have picked up the pieces and made something constructive for himself.

Different lives, different outcomes.

I suddenly had an overpowering urge for a drink. A vodka on the rocks would taste great. Or maybe just an ice-cold beer. Hell, in the old days I used to be able to put away a six-pack of beer in no time at all. Not that I wanted to do that now. All I wanted was a single drink to quench my . . .

No, that wasn't right either. I wanted to get drunk. Disgustingly drunk. So drunk I didn't have to think about Danny Girabaldi or Katy Corrigan or Theresa Anne Vinas.

I pulled my car over to the side of the road. There was a tavern there. JOE'S PLACE, the sign said. Underneath that, it read: GOOD DRINKS, GOOD COMPANY. That sounded awfully nice to me. I could go inside, have a couple, and no one would ever know . . .

I looked down at my hands on the steering wheel. They were shaking.

My God, what was I doing?

Right after I had first stopped drinking, I went to AA meetings every day. I hadn't liked it much—the sobriety speeches and the crusading people and the little slogans—but it had helped me achieve a bit of discipline.

I'd gotten a sponsor while I was there, a woman I was supposed to call if I ever needed help. I'd never called her. But I'd kept the card with the number on it in my purse, just in case. I reached into my purse for it now—and found another card instead. Detective Mitch Caruso's.

I stared at his number for a long time. Then I looked at the tavern. Then back at the number.

Finally I put the card back in my purse, started the engine and got back on the road again.

By the time I reached the Midtown Tunnel, the worst of it was over.

Sixteen

I woke up with a start.

My heart was pounding. I was gasping for breath. I was having a terrible nightmare.

Normally I don't remember my dreams, but this time was different. As I got up and padded into the kitchen, it was still very fresh in my mind. I took a diet soda out of the refrigerator, pulled back the tab and gulped some liquid down. I looked at the time. Two-thirty A.M.

Damn!

All the talk about Loverboy had brought the memories back.

In my dream, the cops had finally caught Loverboy. Not only that, but the creep was tried, convicted and sentenced to death. I watched—horrified, but fascinated too—as they strapped him into the electric chair. The warden stood nearby, ready to turn on the current.

But there was one problem.

I couldn't see the killer's face. It was covered by a black hood. The kind of hood hangmen used to put on their victims in the days of the Old West.

But I had to know who it was.

So I stepped forward, stood in front of the frightened figure in the chair for a few seconds and then suddenly yanked the black hood away.

Now I was staring face-to-face with the evil
menace.

And that was when the real nightmare began.

The face of the person sitting in the electric chair—
the face of the killer—was my face.

Sitting there in the living room now, I thought it
still seemed too real. I drank some more soda and
clicked on the TV. Maybe I could Nick at Nite myself
back to sleep. Mary Tyler Moore was on. Lou Grant
was kidding her about what a lousy drinker she
was—how she hardly ever touched the stuff, but got
very funny after a few sips of a martini. Sometimes
I wished I were like Mary; she lived such a great life.
But then I remembered this was just fantasy. In real
life, Mary Tyler Moore was an alcoholic just like me.

And I thought about Jack Reagan, the cop from
the Loverboy task force who'd been quoted in one
of the old clips I found in the *Blade* library.

That brought back memories too.

Jack and I had had a lot of fun together. When we
were drinking—which was pretty much all of the
time—we had probably closed up every Irish pub in
the city at one time or another during the early-
morning hours. Shannon and Reagan. The cop and
the hotshot young reporter. What a pair they were.

Would things be very different if Jack were alive
now? Probably not.

I mean, what did I think would've happened—Jack
would've married me and we'd have lived happily
ever after? No way. Jesus, what a rotten combination.
A couple of drunks. We probably would have wound
up killing each other.

Except ol' Jack had killed himself first.

It was a little after 4 A.M. before I finally fell
asleep again.

I didn't dream any more that night.

Seventeen

"I'm glad you called," Mitch Caruso said.

"I found your card in my purse. That was a good move."

"You still had to make the call."

"I needed to hear the sound of a friendly voice."

"What happened to your 'I can't be friends with a man' rule? The credo you live your life by?"

"Sometimes I change the rules as I go along."

He smiled. We were sitting in a restaurant on Third Avenue. I still wasn't exactly sure what I was doing there. Why Mitch Caruso? I could have called Janet or someone else at the paper if I wanted someone to talk to. But he just seemed like the right person. Sometimes you have to go with your instincts.

Besides, maybe I could pump him for information about the case.

"Are you sure you don't want anything stronger?" Caruso asked.

"This is fine."

He had a beer. I was drinking coffee.

"Maybe a martini? Or some wine? You look like you need to loosen up a little bit."

"I don't need booze to loosen me up," I snapped.

I didn't want it to come out like that. But it had. Caruso looked startled.

"Sorry," I said.

"No problem."

I drank some of my coffee.

"Do you drink a lot?" I asked him.

"Sure. I like to go out and raise hell just like everyone else."

"No, I don't mean that. I mean really drink. Not just once in a while when you go out with people. But all day and all night. I'm talking about the kind of drinking where, from the minute you get up until you go to bed, you think about nothing else. The kind where there are mornings you don't remember what happened to you the night before. Your hands are trembling, your whole body aches and you feel like you want to die. Have you ever drunk like that?"

"No," he said slowly, "I guess not."

"Well, I have."

"You're an alcoholic?"

"That's right."

"For how long?"

I shrugged.

"Probably for a lot longer than I realized. Maybe I already was one when I was going to parties in high school. I don't know. Anyway, it kept getting worse as I got older. I tried not to let it affect my job, but it got harder and harder. Finally, it was impossible. The paper sent me to a clinic to dry out. It didn't take the first time. Or the second. I'm hoping the third time is the charm. I've been sober for six months."

He nodded. I could tell he wasn't sure what to say. There really wasn't anything. Terrific, Shannon. You sure are a fun date.

"Is the drinking what screwed up your marriages?" Caruso finally asked.

"It didn't help."

"Do you know why you drank so much?"

It was a question I'd asked myself plenty of times. I had a lot of theories. Some from stuff I'd read about the subject of alcoholism. Some I'd picked up from counselors and other drinkers at AA or during one of my stays in rehab. And some had come to me during bursts of inspiration while I was drunk.

But the only thing I really knew for sure about drinking was that I absolutely loved it.

I don't really have too many vices. I don't do drugs. I never smoked cigarettes. I like animals and little children, I don't rob banks and I've even been known to help a little old lady or two across the street in my time. Basically, I'm a pretty good person. Except for the drinking.

I took my first real drink when I was a junior in high school. It was a martini. I can still remember every detail about that moment, even after all these years. Where I was. Who I was with. The song that was playing on the radio. Most of all, the taste of the gin in my mouth and the warm glow it sent through my body and the way all my troubles seemed to slip away after just a few sips.

My real problems didn't start until after I came to New York City. I was drinking a lot in those days, but then something happened to make it worse. A lot worse. That was when I finally realized I had a problem. Of course, it took me twelve more years to finally come to grips with it.

"There's no answer for why I drink," I told Mitch Caruso.

"Okay. But if you had to pick one thing . . ."

"Well, I went through a very tough relationship."

"Which husband?"

"It wasn't even one of the men I married."

"Who?"

"He's dead now."

"And you were in love with this guy?"

I shook my head. "No. We were always a bad mix."

"Then why . . . ?"

"It's very complicated," I said.

I think he sensed I didn't want to talk about it.

The waiter brought our food. Mitch had chicken, and I had a pasta dish. While we ate, we talked about the case.

"The public has an incredible fascination with serial killers," he said. "Son of Sam here. Zodiac in San Francisco. The Hillside Slayer in Los Angeles. Until they're caught, nobody talks about anything else."

"Zodiac was never caught," I pointed out.

"Yeah, that's right."

"A few years ago, I read about another case like this one. Someone was sending letters again and claiming to be the serial killer. You know who it turned out to be? One of the cops in charge of investigating the case ten years earlier. He'd become so obsessed with it, he went right over the edge."

Caruso smiled. "Maybe that's what's happening here."

"Do you know who the cop was in charge of the original Loverboy investigation?" I asked.

"Thomas Ferraro."

"That's right—the police commissioner. The one who looks like he's headed for City Hall next."

"I don't think he's writing the letters."

"It would be an unorthodox way to run for mayor."

"Maybe someone else . . ."

"Ferraro's partner back then was a detective named Jack Reagan."

"You think . . . ?"

"Reagan's dead."

"How do you know that?"

"Believe me, I know everything there is to know about Jack Reagan."

Caruso nodded. Then it hit him.

"Is he the one who . . . ?"

"Yeah. Jack and I had a thing together."

"And then he died."

"I have that effect on men. They either divorce me or die. I'm like the Black Widow of dating."

Caruso's beeper went off. He excused himself to go to a pay phone.

I watched him walk away, wondering why I'd told him all that stuff about me.

I mean, I barely knew Mitch Caruso.

And yet I'd already opened up to him more than most men I've ever been with in my life—even some of my ex-husbands.

Was that because I just needed to release a lot of the things I'd kept bottled up inside me for so long?

Or was there something special about Mitch Caruso?

That's it, I decided. He *is* special. He's different than most of the men I meet. He listens to me. He seems genuinely interested in what I have to say. He's strong, he's smart, he's funny. . . .

Someone I might finally fall in love with.

I could love someone. I really could. I mean, it's not like I'm totally unfamiliar with the term "love." I love a sunny day. I love a great story. I love old Humphrey Bogart and W.C. Fields movies. I love to drink. So why can't I feel the same way about a man? Someone to share my life with. Someone like Mitch Caruso.

I shook my head. This was crazy.

All you're doing is having a simple dinner here, Shannon. Don't blow this out of proportion. Maybe you already scared him off with all your talk about drinking. The guy wants to have a good time. He doesn't want to listen to your sob stories.

Caruso came back to the table a few minutes later. He looked very serious.

"There's been another murder," he said.

"Where?"

"Queens. An airline stewardess. A neighbor found her after she got back from a flight."

"Is there a letter?" I asked.

"Yes."

I already knew what he was going to say next.

"It's addressed to you."

We rode out there together in his car.

"Why do the letters come to you?" Caruso asked as we made our way across Manhattan.

"I was never sure."

"It's definitely beginning to look like it's the same person as before."

"I still don't think so."

"What about the letters?"

"He's a copycat. He's copying Loverboy. Loverboy wrote notes to me about the murders. So does he."

Caruso thought about it.

"It doesn't make sense," he said. "There's got to be something more to it than that."

"Like what?"

"I wish I knew."

We drove down to Thirty-fourth Street and took the Midtown Tunnel to Queens.

"How did it all start?" Caruso asked.

The roads were still jammed with evening traffic. It was going to be a long ride. We had to talk about something.

So I told him about me and Loverboy. . . .

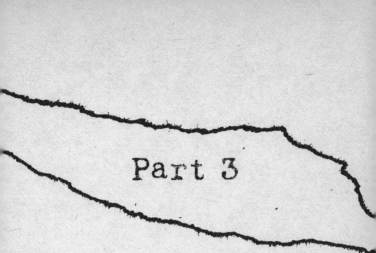

Part 3

MY BACK PAGES

Eighteen

I knew the story was going to be really big as soon as I heard about it.

It was a Saturday—generally the slowest day at a newspaper—and I was at the police shack on the four-to-midnight shift. Most of the other reporters there had already gone home for the night. But not me. I was on the phone, making the rounds of precincts and cop sources, trying to find something to put in the paper. In those days I thought a big story was the answer to everything. I was very young and naive.

"So this woman found stabbed to death in a playground in the South Bronx," I said to the cop on the other end, "she wasn't related to the Kennedys or anything, was she?"

I wrote down his answer in my notebook. Hooker. Drug addict. A rap sheet from here to Philadelphia.

"She was a real debutante, huh?" I said.

I dialed another number and went through the same routine.

"Okay, Sarge," I said, "this stiff in the abandoned building in Harlem with the numbers slips in his pocket. Was he a noted brain surgeon or what?"

You had to check them all out, even the ones in the crummiest neighborhoods, just in case a woman

killed in a brawl at a social club turned out to be
Demi Moore or somebody.

It was part of the routine.

"Damn, nobody good's dying today," I com-
plained to the duty cop who answered the phone at
the East Twenty-first Street precinct.

"I might have something," he said. "It's just happening now."

"What?"

"Report of a double homicide in Gramercy Park."

"Good address."

"There's two bodies on the street on the north side
of the park, across from the Gramercy Park Hotel. A
white female, early twenties, and a white male, a
little older."

"Uh-huh."

"There's something else too."

"What?"

"I hear there's an incredible amount of interest in
this one."

"Interest from who?"

"The brass."

I thought about that. It was unusual. Sure, Gramercy Park was a nice neighborhood and this probably was a high-profile homicide. But it takes a lot to
get the big shots downtown interested in anything
on a Saturday night. A warning bell went off in
my head.

Big story.

"What's going on?" I asked.

"I don't know," he said. "They're not telling me."

There were police barricades blocking the street
around Gramercy Park when I got there. A lot of
people from the neighborhood stood behind them,
trying to find out what was going on. I flashed my
press card at a cop and started to duck under one of
the barricades. The cop stopped me.

"Nobody goes past this line," he said.

"I'm a reporter."

"Doesn't matter. Those are my orders."

"Haven't you ever heard of freedom of the press?"

He had a bored expression on his face. "Take it up with the Supreme Court."

I didn't have time to argue, so I just nodded and backed off. Then I found a spot down the block, sneaked under the barricade there and made my way toward where two bodies lay on the street, covered by sheets.

There were two homicide detectives running things. One of them looked like a cop—he had a short haircut and wore a white shirt, suit and tie. His partner was a lot different. He was in his late thirties, with longish blond hair, blue eyes and a florid, heavy drinker's kind of face. I thought he looked really interesting.

They were talking to another man. I suddenly recognized who he was. A deputy police commissioner I'd met a few times named Wayne Cole. What was going on here anyway?

I moved closer and picked up snatches of their conversation.

"You think it's him?" Cole asked the cop with short hair.

"It sure looks like it. Same MO. Same kind of victims. Probably the same gun too, although we'll have to wait for the ballistics tests to be sure of that."

"But you're sure already, aren't you?"

"I've been after this guy for six years, Wayne. I know him. I can feel him. It's him, all right."

"So what happened?"

"The dead guy's named Joseph Borelli. He works on Wall Street. Has a wife and a new baby and a nice four-bedroom house up in Westchester somewhere. The girl's named Susan Lansdale."

"And she's not his wife?"

"Nope. She was an aspiring actress and a waitress

at a place near here called Gotham City. The two of them apparently met there earlier tonight."

"Where were they headed?"

"Maybe to her place. Maybe to a hotel room for a night of whoopee." He looked up at the Gramercy Park Hotel across the street and shrugged. "It doesn't really matter now."

"And you figure our boy followed them from the club?"

"That's the way he generally does it."

"Where's the witness?"

The cop pointed to a nervous-looking guy a few feet away. He was wearing a jogging outfit and carrying a Walkman.

"He heard the shots, came around the corner of the park and saw a shadowy figure running away. Then he heard an engine start and a car roar off down the street."

"But no real description of the gunman or the car?"

"That's right."

"Just like all the witnesses."

"We gotta get a break sometime."

I still wasn't sure exactly what they were talking about. I moved closer to try to hear them better. That was when I got caught.

"Hey. Who's she?" the short-haired cop yelled.

Cole made me right away. "She's a newspaper reporter."

"Jesus!"

He turned toward his partner. "Get her the hell out of here, Jack!"

The blond-haired detective nodded, grabbed me by the arm and began leading me back toward the crowd outside the barricade.

"Let go of my arm," I said.

"Just walk quietly with me," he whispered.

"What are you gonna do—shoot me?"

"Only if you resist."

He smiled. A great smile. We were back at the barricade now.

"My name's Jack Reagan," he said.

"I'm Lucy Shannon of the *Blade*."

We shook hands.

"Who's your partner?" I asked.

"Lieutenant Tommy Ferraro."

"I don't think Lieutenant Ferraro likes me very much."

"That's okay. He doesn't like me either."

He smiled again. I've always been a sucker for a great smile.

"How old are you, Lucy?" he asked.

"Twenty-four."

"Damn, they keep making reporters younger all the time."

I looked back over at Ferraro. He was still in conversation with Cole. They both looked very serious.

"What's going on here anyway?"

"I'm not supposed to tell you."

"I know it's something important."

"You're sure as hell right about that."

"Look, I've only worked at the *Blade* for a little while. I need to prove to them I can handle a really big story. This could be it. I'd protect you as a source. Believe me, they'd never know it came from you."

Reagan looked across the park at a bar a block or two away.

"See that place called Pete's Tavern?" he said.

"Yeah."

"Go wait for me there."

"How long will you be?"

"As long as it takes for me and Ferraro to wrap things up."

"How do I know you'll really show?"

Reagan shrugged. "What have you got to lose?"

He was right. I had nothing to lose. I called in the

facts I knew to the *Blade* office, but it wasn't much: a double homicide in a good neighborhood that the police seemed very interested in. Until I found out more, it was a pretty short story. So I waited.

Reagan showed up an hour and a half later. He slipped onto the bar stool beside me, ordered a beer and a shot of whiskey from the bartender and swallowed the whiskey down in one gulp. He ordered another one.

"So, Lucy"—he smiled—"what's a nice girl like you doing in a crummy business like newspapers?"

Nineteen

I had arrived in New York City for the first time on a bright December morning.

I was only twenty-two years old then and had driven all night to get there from Ohio, where I'd been working on a small weekly newspaper in Lorain County. At one point the Ohio Turnpike passed within sight of the newspaper's office. There was a sign that said: NEW YORK CITY—518 MILES. I used to look out the window at that sign and dream about going there.

I had a best friend named Carrie, who wanted to be an actress. She was working as a secretary for a firm in Cleveland that made automobile crankshafts, and performing at night with a little repertory company in Shaker Square. One day the two of us rode to the top floor of the Terminal Tower in Public Square, which is the tallest building in Cleveland. We could see the entire city from there—Lake Erie to the north, factories and smokestacks in the west, rolling suburban homes as far as the eye could see.

"Do you want to stay here?" Carrie asked.

"You mean the Terminal Tower?"

"No, Cleveland."

"Not particularly," I said.

"So let's go to New York."

"When?"

"Right now."

I told my parents first. They took the news very well. I think both of them had pretty much given up hope that I was going to settle down with a nice local boy and raise children and join the PTA. They probably came to that conclusion somewhere around the time a police car brought me home at 5 A.M., after a particularly wild night of partying. Or when the high school guidance counselor in my senior year wrote "Rebellious, overly opinionated and a real pain in the ass" on my report card. I still graduated with honors, though. I was always a maze of contradictions.

I grew up in Garfield Heights, which is a suburb of Cleveland. But it was really like living in a small town. Everybody knew everybody, and everyone knew everyone else's business. There're people I went to high school with who married other people from the same high school, and now they have kids of their own who go to that high school.

A lot of young people don't know what they want to do when they grow up. Not me. I wanted to get out of Garfield Heights. I wanted to go to some place big and exciting where people didn't look at me and judge me and where I didn't have to follow anybody else's rules on how to live my life.

"Maybe the problem is you, not this town or this school," the guidance counselor once told me. "Maybe running away to a big city won't help you run away from your problems."

But I didn't listen to her.

I knew where I was headed.

I was going to go to New York City to become a famous newspaper reporter.

And I did too, even though things didn't work out exactly the way I had hoped.

But I've never looked back. I've never for a second wondered what my life would have been like if I'd

stayed in Ohio and gotten a job there or settled down
and raised a family. Even now when I go back for a
visit—which is very rarely—I feel trapped and uncomfortable and out of place, just the way I did when
I was in high school. Suddenly I'm the girl who
didn't make the cheerleading squad all over again.
The one who didn't get invited to any of the cool
parties. The one who was afraid no one would ask
her to the prom. My throat gets tight and I have
trouble breathing and I desperately feel like a drink.
So I make up some excuse about an urgent assignment and hurry back to New York City.

I suppose my parents know I'm lying, but they
never talk to me about it.

Anyway, that's why I wasn't surprised when there
were no emotional farewells at my house when Carrie and I left fourteen years ago. My mother and
father seemed to have been preparing for my depar-
ture for a long time.

It was different at Carrie's house. Carrie's mother
cried. A long time ago, she had dreamed of being an
actress too. It hadn't worked out. She'd gotten pregnant by an actor who hit the road when he heard
the news, so she went to work on a factory assembly
line and raised Carrie as a single mother. Now her
daughter was going to make the dream come alive
again. It was a very touching moment.

They hugged each other for a long time. Then Carrie's mother gave her five hundred dollars, which
she'd saved from her job on the assembly line. She
told Carrie to keep it for an emergency so she would
always have a nest egg if things didn't work out.
Carrie promised she would. Carrie also said that
when she made her first appearance on Broadway,
she would fly her mother to New York City and
thank her publicly from the stage during the curtain
call. There were tears on their faces as we left.

A few hours later, we were driving across Pennsylvania in my 1975 Fiat. We spent some of the five hundred dollars on new clothes at a mall near Pittsburgh and the rest on beer. We played Go-Go's songs and drank beer the whole way, throwing our empty cans out the window and going eighty miles an hour along the Pennsylvania Turnpike. We both had that wonderful excitement and confidence about the future you still have when you're young and hopeful.

On our first night in New York, Carrie and I stayed at a motel near the Lincoln Tunnel where the rooms were very cheap. The clerk on duty leered at us when we checked in. Later, as we lay in bed, there was a noise outside the door that woke us both up. Visions of Norman Bates danced in our heads. We checked the lock, put on the safety chain and moved a large dresser in front of the door so that no one could open it from the outside. Nothing happened, and eventually we fell back to sleep.

The next morning I took a bus to the *New York Blade* offices. I told the receptionist I wanted to work for the newspaper. I had no appointment. I had no job application. Nobody would even talk to me. Finally one of the editors felt sorry for me and told me he knew someone who ran a small daily in New Jersey. He gave me the man's name and said to come back to the *Blade* when I had more experience.

The newspaper was in Wayne, New Jersey, about thirty miles from New York. It had a circulation of only ten thousand and an editorial staff of ten people, but I learned a lot. I covered City Council meetings and police stories, wrote headlines and laid out pages, and even learned how the presses worked. On my days off, I would go into the city and buy all the New York papers. Then I'd sit in a cafe and devour them, watching the people go by outside and dreaming about working there someday.

After nine months at the Wayne paper, I got a job with *The Bergen Record*. That was still in New Jersey—but it was much bigger and closer to the city. There was a school controversy going on, and I did a series of exclusive articles on a whistle-blowing teacher who revealed all sorts of shocking abuses in the educational system. It won an award and got me some attention and—best of all—caught the attention of the people at the *Blade*. They offered me a job. I'd finally made it to the Big Apple.

I was a cub reporter. I did anything the editors asked me to do. Obits. Boring press conferences. The police shack. I didn't care—I loved it all. I would have mopped floors if they'd wanted me to. I was just so glad to be a part of a New York City newspaper.

Carrie? Well, she lasted in New York for only a few months. Never made it as an actress on Broadway. Never even made it in Shaker Square. She moved back to Ohio, married some guy who went to high school with us, had a couple of kids, and now works part-time in the same factory as her mother. I haven't talked to her in years. Life goes on.

Anyway, that was me back then. Lucy Shannon. Ambitious young reporter. Budding alcoholic. And definitely a woman ready for love if the right guy ever came along.

Not a bad person, but not exactly Mother Teresa either.

Until Loverboy.

Twenty

' ' Do you remember a murder case about six years ago?'' Reagan asked me. ''This young couple were at a lovers' lane in upper Manhattan. A gunman opened fire on them.''

We were sitting at a corner table at Pete's, matching each other drink for drink.

All the small talk was gone. I'd told him about me. He'd gone through some of his police stories. Now we were getting down to it.

''Before my time,'' I said.

''The girl's name was Linda Malandro. She died. The guy was a kid named Bobby Fowler. He was pretty shot up, but he lived. They never caught the guy who did it.''

''Sounds like it was a big story.''

''Yeah, it was on page one for a while.''

He took a gulp of his drink.

''A year later, a woman was shot on a street in Queens for no apparent reason. The gunman just jumped out of the bushes and started firing. She died too.''

''You think it's the same guy?''

''There've been five more unsolved cases like that since 1978. Six people died, four were wounded. We have no leads. No suspects. No nothing. Except the ballistics reports. They all match. The same forty-four-caliber gun was used in all the shootings."

I stared at him. I couldn't believe what he was saying.

"Jesus Christ," I said. "There's a fucking serial killer out there. . . ."

He nodded.

"How come nobody knows about this?"

"Hell, we didn't even realize it ourselves for a long time. No reason to think there was any connection between any of the killings. I mean, they were in different boroughs and a few years apart. But then somebody at the crime lab stumbled across the fact that the bullets in two of the shootings seemed to match. They both came from a Bulldog forty-four revolver. That's a powerful gun, but a pretty rare one. So we started checking all the unsolved murders in our files. That's when we saw the pattern. Finally they set up this special task force to catch the guy. Ferraro's in charge. I'm assigned to it too. So far, we've found diddly-squat."

"And no one's ever told the public about any of this?"

"No."

"Why not?"

"The idea was it would be easier to catch the killer without the glare of publicity."

"People have a right to know if there's a murderer out there."

"You're probably right."

"Then why . . . ?"

"It wasn't my decision. It was the brass downtown at headquarters. I'm just a working cop."

I nodded. It finally dawned on me why we were here. He wasn't doing this for me. He was doing it for himself.

"You want this story published, don't you?"

"Yeah."

"Why?"

"I think maybe it'll help flush the killer out. Hell, we aren't getting anywhere the way we're doing it now. Anyway, I've got a feeling this guy wants publicity. I think he's frustrated he hasn't become a national celebrity like Son of Sam or Zodiac or one of those other nut jobs. So let's give him some—and see what happens."

"Won't you get in trouble doing this?" I asked.

"Not if you don't tell anyone where you got the information."

"I won't. I always protect my sources. It's a reporter's sacred duty to do that. It's guaranteed by the Constitution. I mean, I'd go to jail before I'd give you up to anyone."

I really believed in all that crap back then.

"That's what I'm counting on," Reagan said.

He stuck his hand out.

"So we got a deal?"

"Deal," I said.

We shook on it.

"I think we're gonna make a great team together, Lucy Shannon," Reagan said.

Then he smiled that killer smile again.

Looking back on it all now, I sometimes wonder what would have happened if Jack Reagan had been sixty and fat, with bad teeth. Would I still have jumped on the story the same way? Sure, I would have. But the rest of it would have been a lot different.

"So aren't you glad you decided to take me up on my invitation for a drink?" he asked.

"Absolutely."

Was he kidding? This was a huge story. And he'd dropped it right in my lap.

I finished off my drink. I'd switched from beer to vodka a while earlier, and I was starting to feel a buzz. Nothing I couldn't handle, though. I was still sober. Or at least not drunk enough for anyone to know, when I called in the story.

I was very good at hiding my drinking in those days. For a long time no one at the paper even realized I had a problem. I had a good act.

I called the *Blade* and told the night city editor everything Reagan had told me. It took a while. I could hear his astonishment at the other end of the line as I went through it all. He told the managing editor—who woke up the editor in chief at home to tell him.

Then they tore apart page 1—and made up a whole new one with my story for the late editions.

After I got off the phone, Reagan and I kept drinking. In fact, we wound up closing the place down. The bartender tried to stop serving us at about 1 A.M. But Reagan flashed his police shield and told him to keep them coming. It was after two by the time we finally stumbled out the front door into the warm summer air.

I suddenly remembered that the *Blade* had a printing plant in Queens, where I could get one of the first copies of my story off the presses.

"Let's go!" he said.

"Right now?"

"The night is young."

Reagan was driving a big, black Lincoln, and he had a bottle of tequila in the glove compartment. We passed it between us on the front seat as we made our way through the streets of Manhattan, along the Midtown Tunnel and then onto the Long Island Expressway.

The expressway was almost deserted at that hour. He floored the accelerator until we were hitting speeds of close to one hundred. Whenever a car did get in our way, Reagan turned on the police siren and flashing light as we roared past—probably frightening the hell out of the driver.

We didn't care. We were laughing and screaming at people out the windows and having a blast.

"This is a bitchin' car," I said.

"I love a Lincoln."

He started singing an old song from the '50s called "Hot Rod Lincoln" at the top of his lungs. It's about a drag-racing teenager and his car. I took a big swig of the tequila and joined along with him on the chorus.

It was a great night.

We got to the printing plant just as the first papers were coming off the press.

I showed my press card to one of the workers, who gave me a copy. I sat down on a crate in the parking lot—with the stars from a clear June night sky above me and the lights of the Manhattan skyline off in the distance and the roar of the presses behind me—and looked at page 1.

The headline said:

SERIAL KILLER TERRORIZES CITY

Exclusive
by Lucy Shannon

Reagan slipped onto the crate next to me and put his arm around me. He looked down at the paper.

"Are you happy?"

"Delirious. It's my first page-one story."

"Stick with me, kid." He smiled. "I'll make you a star."

Then he kissed me.

No one had ever kissed me like that back in Ohio. No one in New York either.

That night I made love with Jack Reagan for the first time.

Twenty-one

There was plenty of other news going on in New York during that summer of 1984.

Ronald Reagan was running for reelection against Walter Mondale. The Yankees and the Mets were both fighting for a pennant. And the city was going through a torrid heat wave.

But the news of the murders quickly became the only thing in town people were talking about.

The next day—on a Sunday afternoon—the Mayor and the police commissioner held a press conference to discuss it. The Mayor had to cut short his vacation to be there. The police commissioner helicoptered in from his weekend house in the Hamptons. Ferraro and Reagan were there too.

The Mayor vowed to spare no expense or manpower to catch the killer. He assured people that the city was safe. And he said he was assigning an army of cops to work with Ferraro and Reagan on the case.

"Do you have a prime suspect?" a reporter asked the police commissioner.

"No," he said.

"Any substantial leads?" someone else wanted to know.

"Not at this moment."

The story led every newspaper and news show in town.

*   *   *

When I got to work on Monday morning, I was a celebrity too. There were TV cameras waiting for me. Reporters from other papers. A call-in radio show asked me to answer questions from their listeners.

Me, I didn't want to go on radio or TV or give interviews. I just wanted to get back to work on the story. But the paper thought it would be great publicity; they said it would help sell newspapers.

So I did it. And that was how I became an overnight star. A media sensation. My fifteen minutes of fame. Of course, I told myself I never had any choice in the matter. I was just doing what I'd been told. It was all part of the job.

But somewhere along the line, a funny thing happened.

I started to like it.

I knew I needed a big follow-up story. And I got one.

First, I found the widow of the dead Wall Street executive. Diane Borelli knew who I was; she'd already seen me on one of the TV interviews. That seemed to make me all right in her book. So she told me about their four years of marriage, their new baby and their house on three acres of prime Westchester land. She said Joseph Borelli was a great husband, a wonderful provider and a terrific father. She made him sound like something out of an old situation comedy. Almost too good to be true. He was Ward Cleaver, Steve Douglas and Mike Brady, all rolled into one.

I didn't ask her what Ward Cleaver was doing out on a Saturday night in New York with a pretty young waitress.

Then I tracked down the mother of the slain girl, Susan Lansdale. She came from the Midwest—a little town outside Indianapolis. Mrs. Lansdale told me her daughter had gone to New York with the dream of becoming a ballet dancer. She'd been taking classes at Juilliard and making money by working nights at the Gotham City bar. "Susan was so beautiful and so talented," the woman sobbed. "Why would anyone want to kill her?"

I didn't have any answer for that one.

The *Blade* ran the story under my byline, with pictures of both Joseph Borelli and Susan Lansdale. Alongside it was a sidebar about the earlier victims, as well as pictures of them.

The headline said: **"Victims of the Killer."** Below that was another headline: **"Who Will Be Next?"**

When I was finished, Reagan and I decided to celebrate by going out for dinner and drinks. I don't remember how much we ate, but we sure drank a lot.

We started out at a place called Jim McMullen's on the Upper East Side. After that, we went to the bar at Elaine's. Elaine's is a big celebrity hangout on Second Avenue where they fawn all over you if you're famous and make you feel uncomfortable if you're not. I'd gone in there once when I first came to New York and got treated as if I had a case of leprosy. But now it was like my own private Cheers—everybody knew my name.

By 3 A.M. we were at Dorrian's on Second Avenue. Dorrian's would become famous a few years later in connection with another notorious killing. A young couple named Robert Chambers and Jennifer Levin met there, then went into Central Park to have sex. Afterward, Chambers strangled her to death. The newspapers called it "the Preppie Murder Case."

But something pretty damned important happened the night Reagan and I were there too.

That was when Loverboy was born.

There was a jukebox next to the bar playing '50s and '60s rock-and-roll hits. "Hound Dog." "Bye Bye Love." "Good Golly Miss Molly." The two of us kept pouring in quarters and telling the guy behind the bar to turn up the volume.

At some point we got out in the middle of the floor and started dancing to something by the Righteous Brothers.

"Why do you think he does it?" I asked.

"Who?"

"The killer."

Reagan shrugged. "It's a thrill. A kick. There probably is no reason."

"Sure there is. There's always a reason. The killer has to get something out of it."

"What?"

"I don't know."

"Maybe the reason is the key to catching him."

Another song came on the jukebox: "Love Is Strange" by Mickey and Sylvia. Patrick Swayze and Jennifer Grey fell in love to it in the movie *Dirty Dancing*. And so did Jack Reagan and I on that long-ago night in Dorrian's, I guess.

"What else do we know about this guy?" I asked.

"Not much."

"Well, he definitely seems to be an equal opportunity killer."

"What do you mean?"

"He kills both men and women."

Reagan shook his head. "It's the women he's after. The men just get popped because they're there. He never goes for a man by himself. Just women and couples."

Jack was right about that.

"He needs a name," I said.

"The killer?"

"Sure. Every serial killer worth his stuff has a cool nickname. Something catchy for headlines. Son of Sam. The Boston Strangler. Zodiac. What can we call this guy?"

"Son of Lucy." He smiled.

"How about the New York Strangler? Or Capricorn?"

"Most of the victims are single women, right?" he said. "How about the Singles Killer?"

"Not alliterative enough for headlines."

"The Singles Slayer."

"Better."

The song kept playing as we danced. I listened to the words of Mickey and Sylvia as they sang to each other.

> Sylvia . . . how do you call your loverboy?
> C'mere, loverboy.

That's when it hit me.

"Loverboy," I said.

"Loverboy?"

"Sure. He seems to be looking for love. Only when he finds it, he murders the lovers. So we call him Loverboy. What do you think?"

"I love Loverboy," he said.

He kissed me.

After that, we drank some more.

Then we went to bed.

And that was how Loverboy got his name.

Twenty-two

The first note came a week later.

It was in an envelope that was mailed to me at the *Blade* from somewhere in Manhattan. There was a return address in Brooklyn Heights written in the upper left-hand corner of the envelope. And a single word.

"Loverboy."

I'd used the name for the first time in a story after the night at Dorrian's with Reagan. And I'd kept on using it in every story since. The rest of the media picked up on it too. Television stations. Radio news. The other newspapers in town. Even the police put out a press release referring to the "so-called Loverboy killings."

So, of course, the envelope could have been just a practical joke.

But I didn't think so.

I knew it was the real deal.

I was even more convinced of that after I read what was inside:

Dear Lucy,

Congratulations on finding out my little secret.
I was going to go public with it very soon any-
way. Maybe have a coming-out party of sorts. You

know, like a debutante. I could have even used the body of some pretty little debutante as a kind of party gift. But this way is probably better.

First off, let me make something perfectly clear— I am not crazy.

Helluva opening, huh? Sort of like Richard Nixon saying, "I'm not a crook," or a guy proclaiming he doesn't beat his wife, or Sgt. Schultz insisting, "I know nothing," on Hogan's Heroes reruns. He doth protest too much, as Shakespeare put it.

Trust me on this, though. What I'm doing is totally sane.

I think.

At the very least, it's sort of like the old story about a patient who goes to see his psychiatrist and tells him, "All right, I may be paranoid, but that doesn't mean someone's not out to get me."

Lucy, I want you to deliver this message from me to all the women of New York City:

I love you.

I love you all. I really do.

I LOVE YOU TO DEATH.

Now it's time to go back to work.

For both of us.

Take a trip across the river to Brooklyn Heights.

You'll find your next story there.

Loverboy

Her name was Cheri Barnes, and she was a cocktail waitress at a restaurant near the Promenade, along the East River.

The manager said she'd worked from 6 P.M. to 2 A.M. the night before. Her time of death was somewhere between 3 A.M. and 5 A.M., according to the medical examiner's office. That meant Loverboy had probably followed her home. Or maybe he had waited for her. He could have even been stalking her for days, making records of her movements.

Who knew how a crazed murderer's mind worked?

The cops found her in the bedroom. She was wearing the same miniskirt, low-cut top, high heels and nylons she'd had on that night at work. People who knew her said she'd been very attractive. But the killer had shot her at close range in the face, making such a mess of it that her beauty was just a memory now. He'd also pulled her miniskirt up over her hips and written in lipstick on her thighs the word "Whore!"

Twelve years later, when I found Julie Blaumstein's body, I realized it was almost a carbon copy of the Cheri Barnes murder.

But why?

Was it the same killer all over again, trying to replay his greatest hits? Sending me a message that the nightmare had never really ended? That he'd only been resting for the past twelve years? Hello, Lucy—I've been away, but now I'm back.

Or was this a new monster, playing out a deadly game with someone else's hand?

I called Jack Reagan as soon as I got that first note about Cheri Barnes. We drove out to Brooklyn Heights together, and I hung around with him during the investigation of the crime scene. Lieutenant Ferraro showed up later.

Ferraro wasn't happy to see me.

"What's she doing here?" he wanted to know.

I just love being talked about in the third person.

"The killer sent her a note at the *Blade*," Reagan said. "Told us where to find the body."

"You got the note?"

I handed it to him.

"You realize, of course, that you've probably already destroyed any fingerprint evidence the killer left on it."

"I was very careful, Lieutenant. As soon as I realized what it was, I only held it by the top corner. If he left any fingerprints—which I doubt—they'll still be there. All you have to do is eliminate my prints and Detective Reagan's. And now, of course, yours too. Anything left belongs to our murderer."

He grunted. "So you're an expert on fingerprints, huh, Shannon?"

"I watch a lot of *Columbo* and *Perry Mason*," I said.

Ferraro looked down at the note, frowning as he read the message.

"Okay, thanks for your help," he said to me when he was finished. "You can go home now."

"I'm not going anywhere."

"What's that supposed to mean?"

"I'm a reporter. I have a right to be here."

We glared at each other.

"You have a right to report on whatever information we decide to disseminate to you through normal law enforcement communication channels," Ferraro said.

"Are those the same law enforcement communication channels that have kept these killings covered up for so long? Maybe if the public knew there was a killer running around out there, Cheri Barnes might still be alive today. Ever think about that, Lieutenant?"

Ferraro turned to Reagan. "Just keep her out of my way," he said.

He walked over to a group of other cops and medical people standing around the body.

"What's his problem?" I asked.

"The lieutenant's a real by-the-book kind of guy. Got that whole policeman's manual memorized. He can quote from it for you if you want—page by page."

"Good for him."

"Tommy's very ambitious too."

"Well, this case could make him—or break him."

"Yeah. As long as no one knew about it, he was pretty safe. But now there's going to be all this public scrutiny—and the head of the task force is going to take the heat if we don't catch somebody pretty soon."

"Big deal. So he doesn't make captain."

"Tommy thinks he's going to be police commissioner someday."

"No kidding?"

"Like I said, he's a real ambitious guy."

I called in the story to the paper. It was another big exclusive for me and the *Blade*. The editors were ecstatic. No other reporter in town had even heard about it yet. They'd all have to do follow-up stories the next day. I wasn't merely covering this story. I was a part of it now. I was on a roll.

Later, as they were taking Cheri Barnes's body out, Reagan whispered something to me. I don't remember exactly what he said, after all these years. But it was some sort of sexual innuendo about what he wanted to do to me in bed that night. I giggled loudly.

Ferraro heard it.

"You think this is all a big joke, don't you?" he said to me.

"I'm sorry, I just—"

"There was a woman murdered here tonight. Other people are dying too. Of course, to you it's a big story that's going to make you famous. You think it's going to turn you into a female Jimmy Breslin or Woodward and Bernstein, don't you?"

I didn't say anything.

"Well, that's real blood over there. And Cheri Barnes was a real person. I don't think there's anything funny about her death at all."

"C'mon, Lieutenant," Reagan said. "Back off on her."

Ferraro shook his head. "You think I don't know about you too, Jack?"

"Know what?"

"Shannon here didn't simply stumble onto this case. You handed it over to her."

"Hey, she's a reporter. She found out herself. . . ."

"She couldn't find Times Square without someone's help. She's a kid. She's been working at the *Blade* for about five seconds, and this is the first big story they've ever let her cover. I checked. I know how she got it, Jack. I'm not stupid."

He turned to me.

"Let me give you some advice, Shannon. You're young, you've got your whole life ahead of you. Don't get involved with someone like Reagan. He's a fucking lush. He's bad news. He's going to cause you nothing but trouble. Of course, from what I hear, you're pretty much a lush too. Maybe the two of you deserve each other."

Then he stomped away. I just stood there, too stunned to say anything back.

"Fuck 'im!" Jack Reagan said as we watched him go. "Let's get a drink."

Twenty-three

Look, it wasn't exactly a breaking news flash that I was doing a lot of drinking.

But Lieutenant Ferraro's remark that night really bothered me.

I used to think of myself as pretty tough back then. On the other hand, I was only twenty-four years old—and having a police lieutenant talk to me like that about my personal life shook me up.

Until then, nobody else had ever come right out and told me I had a drinking problem. Oh, I know people sometimes gave me funny looks at parties. Or made jokes at work about how far gone I was the night before. I'm sure now they probably talked about it behind my back too.

But before my confrontation with Tommy Ferraro, I'd somehow managed to convince myself that my drinking wasn't really all that big a deal—that I could handle it.

In those days I was a pretty good drunk.

I had my routine down perfectly. I never took the first drink until after noon. That was the magic hour. Lunchtime. I usually had a couple while I was eating, but no more. I was really good about that. Then it was straight back to work. Bright-eyed, bushy-tailed—without even a trace of alcohol on my breath.

I always kept a package of mints in my purse for just that purpose.

After work, I'd have a few drinks to relax, then get down to some serious drinking. I drank everything. Lots of beer. Martinis. Tequila. Bourbon. And vodka. Especially vodka. Vodka was my drink. My specialty. My own private poison, as one counselor called it later during one of my periodic visits to rehab. God, I loved it. At some point in the night, I'd always switch to vodka on the rocks or vodka martinis and then I'd be gone for good. There was no turning back.

Sometimes people would have to help me home at the end of the night, but most of the time I was okay. I'd fall into bed, sleep for five or six hours and wake up feeling fine. Then it was back to work, where I'd start the cycle all over again.

There were no hangovers back then. No nausea. No blackouts. No waking up in a hospital emergency room at 6 A.M. and wondering where I was and how I got there and feeling like I wanted to die.

That would all come later.

But back then I was having fun.

Loverboy was page 1 news during that entire summer.

For three months he prowled the night streets, gunning down young women or couples in parks or singles clubs or out on dates all over New York City.

By Labor Day the total stood at twenty-one. Thirteen dead, eight wounded. Most of those happened after I got involved in the case. The killer had worked slowly for the first six years, carrying out a number of attacks but doing nothing to call attention to himself. But now he had a name—and a mission. Loverboy struck time after time in quick succession, taunting the police and the public with notes to me about each victim.

Evil was in full bloom during that summer of 1984. And New Yorkers were terrified.

Most crime doesn't truly touch people. It happens before we realize it, or to someone else in another neighborhood, or to a specific targeted group like prostitutes or gays or drug addicts. But this was different. People knew this killer was out there before he struck. And he was targeting young, white, middle-class people. Most of them women.

Everyone out on a date or a night on the town was looking over his or her shoulder. People started staying home after it got dark. They bought guns for protection. The first few victims that summer all had long brown hair, so lots of women cut theirs very short or wore blond wigs in the hope they wouldn't be a target. (It didn't matter—the victims included several blondes and a redhead before the killer was finished.)

I suppose I should have been scared too. I mean, Loverboy had targeted me as the person to send his death notes to at the *Blade*. I was a young woman. I even had long brown hair. There was no reason to think he wouldn't turn on me at some point.

But I never worried about that back then.

To me it was all just a big game.

Even the victims didn't seem real. Oh, I knew there were people dying out there, all right. But when you're a reporter, you develop this ability to separate yourself from people's tragedies and traumas and deaths. You have to when you see them every day. All I knew was it was a great story—and I was right in the center of it.

In a few short weeks I'd gone from a lowly cub reporter to the most famous journalist in town. I was interviewed on TV. I was written about by all the other papers in town. *Time*, *Newsweek* and *People* did big articles on me. Even the police came to me for help—at one point they got me to write an open letter to the killer on the front page of the *Blade*, urging him to surrender.

Loverboy was my whole life that summer.

And Jack Reagan.

Jack and I spent all our time together working on the case. Wherever he went, I was there. Questioning witnesses. Looking for evidence. Checking out leads. We were a team. Probably more of a team than he and Ferraro, who didn't like either of us.

That was okay. I made Jack the hero of the investigation in my stories. And he was my pipeline for exclusive information that put me light-years ahead of every other reporter in town.

Then, of course, there was the sex. We spent hours in bed together; we tried out all sorts of different positions and techniques. I was twenty-four years old, I was from Ohio and I'd never had sex like that with anyone in my life before. Sex was always one of the strong points about my relationship with Jack.

That and, of course, drinking.

Looking back on it now, I find it difficult to think about Jack Reagan without thinking about the drinking too. We were doing it all the time. We weren't always drunk, of course. But we sure were high a lot—or at least had a pleasant buzz working for us.

I sometimes wonder what my romance with Jack would have been like without alcohol. Or if we would have even had one. I remember that on the rare occasions when he wasn't drinking, I didn't find him nearly as interesting. Maybe he felt the same way about me.

But alcohol fixed that. Alcohol was the answer to any problems in our relationship. It was the answer to everything in those days. Vodka always made everything better.

Jack Reagan and Lucy Shannon—a love affair for the ages.

A modern-day Romeo and Juliet.

A real fun couple.

Well, most of the time. But there were a few disturbing things starting to happen.

You see, Jack wasn't a happy drinker like me. He sometimes got ugly.

Once, we were in a bar on Staten Island and someone asked me to dance. It was no big deal, really. The guy was as drunk as we were, and I just said no. But Jack turned it into this big macho thing. He took out his detective's shield, waved his gun in the guy's face and threatened to arrest him and do all sorts of terrible things to him before they got to the police station. Then he made him apologize to us in a loud voice, in front of all his friends in the bar. Christ, all he'd wanted was a lousy dance.

Another night, we came out of a place in Queens and found a double-parked car blocking ours. Jack took out his gun and shot out the guy's side and front windows. Someone called the cops that time, but they just told us to go home and sleep it off, after they found out who Jack was. Cops always look out for other cops.

There were lots of other times—when he'd been drinking—that Jack would drive too fast or play music deliberately loud or just go out of his way to get into an argument with people over some trivial point.

You never knew when one of his rages would happen.

Like the night we were at my house, and he was watching a Yankees baseball game. He'd made a big bet on them winning. When a guy from the other team hit a home run, Jack went ballistic. He kicked in the screen of my television, sending glass flying all over. When I tried to calm him down, he hurled me against a wall. The next morning he sent me flowers at work, and a long note of apology. That night he took me dancing at the Rainbow Room and told me how much he loved me.

So there were definitely problems in the relationship.

But nothing I couldn't handle. No big deal. Just a few little blips marring the otherwise happy romance of Lucy Shannon and Jack Reagan.

Until the night at Finnegan's.

That was when it all started to go wrong. . . .

Twenty-four

By the end of August, Jack Reagan had become obsessed with catching Loverboy.

That was understandable, I guess. He'd been chasing him for a long time—from the time the police first figured out the killings were related. There'd been nothing but dead ends over the years. Witnesses who knew nothing. Leads that didn't pan out. Suspects who had airtight alibis. Meanwhile, the killer was still out there, taunting us all as he carried out his deadly business. No wonder Jack was frustrated.

Jack had another goal too. He not only wanted to catch Loverboy, he wanted to do it before Ferraro did. The two of them were partners in name only now. They hardly even spoke to each other. Jack did his work on the street with me, while Ferraro hung out at the task-force headquarters downtown—rubbing shoulders with the brass.

I guess it worked for him too, since he wound up being police commissioner. But Jack didn't care about that stuff. Jack was a cop, pure and simple. He just wanted to make the biggest arrest of his career.

Funny about him and Ferraro. You couldn't ask for two more opposite types. Ferraro was a by-the-book, spit-and-polish, "yes sir and no sir" guy. Jack was a rebel. A guy who never followed the rules.

Maybe that was why I identified with him. I'd been like that all my life too. Now I had a partner.

Sometimes we'd sit around and dream about what would happen if he caught Loverboy.

Jack said there'd never be anything he could do to top that. He talked about getting off the street afterward and taking a desk job. Or maybe retiring and buying a place upstate so he could go fishing. Or even going into business for himself as a security consultant or private investigator.

But I didn't think any of that was really going to happen. I couldn't see Jack Reagan ever being happy doing anything except being a cop—and drinking his nights away in bars.

Anyway, like I said, he was definitely getting more and more intense about Loverboy. Every lead, every tip that came along—he was convinced that was the one that was going to finally crack the case wide open.

There were a lot of tips and leads.

All the publicity surrounding the case had everybody looking at a friend or lover or neighbor as a potential Loverboy. A lot of these people meant well; others just wanted to cause trouble. But thousands of names poured in to the task force, and each name had to be checked out.

Some of the names came from women who wanted to get even with ex-boyfriends who'd jilted them. Or from mothers convinced that their sons were perverts because they'd never married. Other names in the task force's bulging files belonged to genuine nutcases. They just didn't happen to be our nutcase.

Whenever one of Jack's suspects didn't pan out, he got very depressed. Sometimes he didn't believe it. He'd say he should be the head of the task force— that Ferraro was bungling the whole investigation. Jack was convinced Ferraro would do anything to screw him. That Ferraro wanted to keep all the glory from the Loverboy arrest—whenever it finally happened—for himself.

I suppose I should have been worried about Jack a long time before I was.

The turning point came on the Friday night before Labor Day.

I was finishing up a story on deadline when Jack called. It had been a long day—I'd covered a press conference, done some interviews and spent a few hours at the task force headquarters—and an even longer night the night before. We'd closed some bar in Washington Heights at about 4 A.M. All I wanted to do now was go home to my bed and sleep.

"We're going to Finnegan's Bar," Jack announced.

"Where's that?"

"Queens."

I sighed. "Not tonight, Jack."

"I think he's there."

"Who?"

"Who? Loverboy, that's who."

"What are you talking about?"

"I've got a snitch who put me onto this guy. His name is Raymond Lyons. He perfectly fits the profile of Loverboy that we got from one of the shrinks—an angry loner, lives at home with his mother, uncomfortable with women. And he's been hanging around this bar, talking about the case. Saying all the dead girls had it coming."

"It's probably just another false lead."

"What if it isn't? Do you want to miss out on the arrest of the century?"

That was what did it.

Finnegan's turned out to be a place filled with a blue-collar crowd, a few construction workers and even some college kids. It was just another bar. It seems like I'd seen a thousand of them with Jack in the past few months. He was already drinking when I got there.

"Where's Raymond Lyons?" I asked him.

"Not here yet."

"So what do we do now?"

"We wait."

Jack was drinking bourbon. He finished it off and ordered another, along with a vodka martini for me. I didn't like the look in his eye. He seemed out of it, almost a little crazed. I realized he'd probably started drinking a lot earlier that evening. Maybe he'd been drinking all day.

It was three hours later before Raymond Lyons showed up. Jack was pretty well out of it by then. I was drinking a lot too, but I wasn't in nearly as bad a shape as he.

Jack walked over to Lyons, flashed his detective's shield and told him he was on the Loverboy task force.

"I understand you've been talking about the murders a lot in here," Jack said.

"Yeah," Lyons told him. "So what?"

He was a short, almost frighteningly thin guy with glasses, maybe in his early twenties. He didn't seem worried about why a cop wanted to talk to him. That was strange. It's not the right guy, I thought to myself. He's just another nut looking for attention. I wanted to drag Jack out of there, but it was too late for that now.

"You know anything about the killings?" he asked Lyons.

"I might."

"Like what?"

"That's for me to know and you to find out."

He laughed loudly at his remark.

"You think it's funny?" Jack asked.

"I think it's hilarious."

"Why?"

"They were all bitches. They deserved to die."

Jack stared at him. It was a scary look.

"Raymond, are you Loverboy?" he asked.

The kid just smiled. "What do you think?" he said.

Jack asked the question again.

Lyons gave the same answer.

You could tell Jack was about ready to explode. But Lyons didn't seem scared. He didn't seem worried. He still had this strange smile on his face, like it was all a big joke.

I walked over and stood next to the two of them. I was sipping on a vodka martini and watching nervously as this drama unfolded in front of me. I didn't know what else to do.

"Are you Loverboy?" Jack asked him again.

"What do you think?" Lyons repeated.

Then he looked over and saw me for the first time. I guess he realized Jack and I were together.

"Do you know what I'd do if I was Loverboy, Mr. Policeman?" he said.

Lyons nodded toward me.

"I'd take out my forty-four and use it on this bitch."

He was leering at Jack now. Taunting him.

"First I'd mess up her pretty face. Then I'd stick the gun between her legs and blow her twat from here to kingdom come. I guess that'd make fucking her a little difficult for you, huh?"

Everything turned into a blur after that.

Jack punched him in the face—and he went down. Then Jack hit him again. After that, he started kicking him. Jack was like a madman. Everybody else in the bar—including me—just watched in horror, afraid to try to stop him. Lyons's face was a mess and he was coughing up blood. Every time he hit him, Jack asked the question over and over again: "Are you the killer?"

Lyons wasn't answering anymore with "What do

you think?" He wasn't answering at all. I'm not sure he could.

Finally Jack picked him up and sat him down on one of the bar stools.

"Let's you and me play a game, Raymond."

He took out a revolver.

"Did you ever play Russian roulette?"

Raymond Lyons looked scared now. He must have realized at last that he was dealing with someone even crazier than he was.

Jack emptied all the bullets out of the gun. He held up one of them for Lyons to see. Then he put it back into the gun—and whirled the chamber.

"I'm going to ask you the question again. This time you're going to give me the right answer."

He put the gun up to the side of Raymond Lyons's head.

"Are you Loverboy, Raymond?" Jack asked.

The guy was crying now. He tried to shake his head no.

"Wrong answer," Jack laughed.

Then suddenly he pulled the trigger. There was a click as the hammer came down on an empty chamber. Lyons screamed. I looked down and saw a puddle of liquid forming underneath the bar stool. Raymond Lyons had wet himself from fear.

"Hey, you won that time, Raymond," Jack said.

He held up the gun again and whirled the chamber another time.

"Let's play again."

I have no doubt Jack would have killed him. He would have kept spinning that chamber and pulling the trigger until Raymond Lyons confessed he was Loverboy. But it didn't work out that way. Someone had managed to call the cops. A couple of them came through the door now with guns drawn.

They knew Jack. Cops never want to give another cop trouble. They tried to play it cool.

"What are you doing, Jack?" one of them said.

"Questioning a suspect."

"A bit unorthodox, isn't it?"

It was a tense moment. This could go either way. The cop was trying to diffuse the situation by treating it lightly. But if that didn't work, he was going to have to shoot Jack.

"You don't like Russian roulette?" Jack asked.

"Put the gun down," the cop told him.

"It's a fun game."

"Not for the victim."

Jack looked at the trembling man on the bar stool.

"Sure it is." He laughed. "Just ask him."

"C'mon, Jack . . ."

"Hell, I'll prove it to you. I'll play the damn game myself."

Jack took the gun, spun the chamber again and suddenly put it up to the side of his own head.

"Jesus, Jack!" the cop yelled.

"See, I'm not afraid at all."

He pulled the trigger. There was another click. The chamber was empty.

"Hey, I guess it's my lucky day too." He smiled.

They got the gun away from him after that. Everyone wanted to keep the whole thing quiet, so the cops eventually put me and Jack into a police car and took him home. Lyons was hospitalized for a week. I don't know if he ever told anybody what happened. As for the other people in the bar, I guess they didn't want to get involved, because Jack was never brought up on any charges.

That night I undressed Jack and put him to bed. I lay there next to him in the dark, worried about him and even more worried about me. At one point he woke up and reached over to hug me.

"What the hell were you thinking about back there in the bar?" I asked.

Jack smiled. "It was no big deal, Lucy."

"Russian roulette? No big deal? You could have killed yourself."

"There's a trick to playing that game."

I stared at him.

"What trick?"

"G. Gordon Liddy said it best. The Watergate guy. He used to do this gimmick in bars where he'd hold his hand over a lighted flame. Someone asked him what the trick was. He said the trick was, you had to not mind the pain."

I still didn't understand.

"That's the trick to playing Russian roulette," Jack said. "You just have to not mind dying."

Twenty-five

Jack Reagan was out of control.

I knew that now.

But what about me?

I was with him day and night. We worked together, ate together, drank together and—last but certainly not least—slept together. Was I the only voice of sanity and reason in his otherwise troubled life? Or was I part of the problem too?

The day after Finnegan's is when I made my first try at dealing with my drinking. I had nothing stronger than diet soda at lunch. That night after work I didn't do my usual barhopping. Instead I went home, made myself a quiet dinner and read a book.

I know it doesn't sound like much, but it was a start. A start at a normal life. There'd be a lot more of those kind of starts—mostly false ones—over the years until I finally faced up to my demons.

Of course, the first step in battling demons is figuring out who they are.

I desperately needed to sort out what was good and what was bad about my life.

I'd just witnessed firsthand what the pressures of the Loverboy case had done to Jack. Was the same thing happening to me?

I wanted to talk to somebody about it, but I wasn't sure where to turn to.

I was afraid to ask any of my editors at the *Blade* because I thought they might decide to take me off the Loverboy story.

I didn't have any real close friends to confide in—I'd been too busy working ever since I came to New York to make any.

So, in the end, I tried my parents. I didn't really think they'd have any answers for me. They'd never had in the past. But old habits die hard.

"I need help," I told my mother when she got on the phone from Ohio.

"How much do you need?" she asked.

"It's not about money, Mom. I make plenty of money. The *Blade* pays me well."

"What's wrong, then?"

I told her about all the pressures of the story I was working on, about my not-so-perfect relationship with Jack Reagan, about all my fears and insecurities that had come bubbling to the surface; most of all, I talked to her for the first time about my drinking.

I said that somehow all my problems always seemed to revolve around the drinking.

"So why don't you stop drinking?" she said.

"I—I can't. . . ."

"Then you should try harder."

Beautiful.

So instead, I decided to try to fight it on my own.

I tried to help Jack too. I really did. I asked him to go to a counselor with me or an Alcoholics Anonymous meeting, or to ask the police department for help. He wasn't interested. In fact, he got very angry when I suggested it and stormed out of my apartment.

I didn't hear from him for three days. When I did, it was pretty ugly. He woke me up with a phone call in the middle of the night. I could hear the sounds of a bar in the background. He sounded very drunk.

"Get your ass over here, Shannon!" he said.

"Where are you?"

"Duran's. It's in the fucking West Forties somewhere, way over by the river."

"I'm not drinking with you tonight, Jack."

"Are you still on that crazy kick?"

"It's not crazy. I'm just trying to take it easy for a little while. You should think about it too."

"When the hell did you become such a goddamned do-gooder? You used to be fun. Now you're as much a pain in the ass as my wife used to be."

He'd never mentioned a wife before. I wondered where she was.

"I found him," he whispered into the phone.

"Who?" I asked.

Even though I already knew what he was going to say.

"Loverboy."

"C'mon, Jack, you're not going to start that again. . . ."

"No, it's really him this time. I swear."

"How do you know?"

"I was in his house."

"You broke in?"

"Yeah, I know it's illegal. But so is killing people. Let me tell you, his place is a gold mine of evidence. Loverboy clippings pasted on all the walls, blood-stained clothes and even a forty-four. I'll bet we can match the gun up with the bullets found in the victims. This is the real deal, babe."

I wasn't so sure.

"How drunk are you, Jack?"

"Would you get off that kick and just meet me here at Duran's. I'm going to go arrest him—and I want you with me. You should be a part of it. We're a team. Shannon and Reagan. Together forever, right?"

"I think you should call this in to the task force downtown," I said. "Let them handle it."

"And let Ferraro get all the glory?"

"Is that what you care about?"

"I don't want to see that prick Tommy Ferraro standing up in front of the TV cameras taking credit for all the hard work we did. He'd just love that."

"I'm sure he'd give us part of the credit."

"Like hell he would. He'd see this as his ticket for a big promotion, his road to the top. Fuck him. I'm doing this my way. Are you in or not?"

"Let's talk about it in the morning."

"I'm not waiting until morning."

"The killer will still be there. We'll have breakfast together and then—"

"I'm going in right now."

"Don't do this, Jack."

"Are you in or not?"

I thought about it for a few seconds. But, of course, there was really no decision to make.

"Not," I said finally.

Jack slammed the phone down in my ear.

He called back a few minutes later. I knew he would. But I didn't pick up the receiver that time. My phone rang maybe twenty times. Then he hung up, and tried again. After that, he stopped.

My life changed a lot after that.

I didn't stop drinking. Far from it. Within a couple of days I was hitting the bottle as hard as ever. But now I knew what I was doing to myself. I wasn't kidding myself anymore. I was a drunk. Just like Jack Reagan.

And that was really the end of my relationship with Jack.

I saw him a few times after that. But it was never the same. I guess we just drifted apart, the way two people in a relationship do when they don't have anything in common anymore.

I never slept with him again.

So I guess you'd have to call that phone call with Jack Reagan a real turning point for me.

The first day of the rest of my life.

Twenty-six

"So what happened then?" Mitch Caruso asked me.

"Nothing."

"What do you mean?"

"Loverboy just went away. He stopped killing. And after a while the story died too."

"What about the suspect that Reagan thought he'd found?"

"There never was any suspect."

"But—"

"Jack just had too much to drink."

"So he never went back to that house he told you was filled with evidence?"

"No. He stayed in the bar most of the night. When he woke up the next morning, he'd forgotten all about it. He was pretty far gone at that point."

"And that was the end of the two of you?"

"Yeah. You know, I sometimes wonder what would have happened if I had gone to the bar to meet him that night. Would I have stayed with him— would I have gone down the same path of self-destruction he did? But I got out in time. Hey, I've had my problems. But I'm dealing with them."

We were getting close to the crime scene now.

There was still one question Caruso hadn't asked me.

I knew he would.

"How did Reagan die?" he asked.

"He committed suicide."

"How long ago was that?"

"About a year after we broke up."

I looked out the window. It was still early evening, and people were out on the streets shopping or going to the movies or out for a meal. Living nice, normal, sane lives. How did mine get so screwed up?

"I'd pretty much lost touch with him by then—we hadn't talked in a couple of months. I was dating an organized-crime cop working out of the Seventy-first Precinct in Brooklyn. I thought it was pretty serious, and I guess it was. He wound up being my first husband. Anyway, one night Reagan called me up out of the blue."

"What did he say?"

"That he was going to kill himself."

"Jesus!"

"He asked me if I remembered the game he played that night at Finnegan's. Russian roulette. I told him I did. Well, he said the trick to winning at it was still the same. You just didn't have to care about dying."

"What did you say?"

"I thought he was bluffing."

"But he wasn't."

I shook my head no.

"He put a bullet in the gun and spun it around. Then he pulled the trigger. I could hear the click of an empty chamber over the line. He did it a second time too. Another miss.

"That's when he told me he loved me. He said he didn't want to live anymore without me.

"The third time was the one that did it. I could hear the gun go off over the phone, and then the line went dead. I dialed 911. But when they got to Jack's place, he was already dead. He'd blown his head off, just like he'd said. There was a picture of me next to him."

Caruso let his breath out slowly. He looked like he was in shock.

"Is that why you kept on drinking so much?" he asked.

"God, I don't know. I'm not sure it's that simple. They say you can't blame other people for your drinking, you have to look at yourself. Mostly the reasons are inside you. But it hasn't been easy. I've had three failed marriages. I've been on and off the wagon for twelve years. My career hasn't exactly worked out the way I thought it was going to."

"There must have been some good moments along the way."

"You want to hear something really weird?" I said. "That summer covering Loverboy was the high point of my life. The only time I've ever had everything going for me. I was twenty-four years old. Maybe I just had too much too soon."

We pulled up in front of the stewardess's apartment house. There were police cars blocking the street and cops all over.

"That's some story," Caruso said as we got out of the car.

"Yeah, it is, isn't it?"

"And that's all of it?"

"The whole thing," I told him.

Then we walked inside to see Loverboy's latest victim.

I was lying, of course.

That wasn't the whole story at all.

Not even close.

But it was all I was going to tell Mitch Caruso.

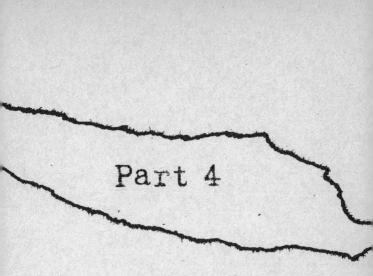

Part 4

READ ALL ABOUT IT!

Twenty-seven

LOVERBOY STRIKES AGAIN!

**Cops probe fourth new slaying—
note warns of more victims**

Exclusive
by Lucy Shannon

A 25-year-old stewardess was found shot to death outside her Queens apartment last night—apparently the latest victim in the infamous Loverboy slayings.

The killer left behind a taunting note addressed to this reporter which said: "There'll be a lot more—just like in '84!"

It also included his trademark phrase: "I love you to death."

Thirteen people were murdered in New York City from 1978 to 1984 by a person who called himself "Loverboy" and left similar notes during the summer of 1984.

If this is the work of the real Loverboy, he is now responsible for killing 17 people and wounding eight more over a period of nearly two decades.

Last night's victim was identified as Deborah

Kaffee, a stewardess for American Airlines who was returning home from Kennedy Airport after a cross-country flight from Los Angeles.

Her body was found by a neighbor who heard gunshots shortly before 7 P.M.

"I saw someone running away," the neighbor told cops. "Just a shadowy figure out of the corner of my eye. Then I saw poor Deborah. She was covered in blood.

"Who would want to do that? She was such a lovely girl."

Police say the pretty blond stewardess died instantly after being shot three times in the head at close range with a .44-caliber gun.

All the other victims also were shot with the same type of weapon.

Kaffee had arrived back in New York on a cross-country flight that landed at 4:40 P.M., and then went to a nearby bar called The Hangar, which police say is a favorite spot for stewardesses and pilots.

They believe the killer saw her there and then followed, or possibly even accompanied, her home.

"I know we think of someone jumping out of the bushes with a gun," said Detective Mitch Caruso.

"But there's also the possibility that the woman went with him willingly. Loverboy doesn't have to be a bogeyman—he could be a very charming fellow, just like Ted Bundy was."

The note found at the scene—the latest in a series addressed to this reporter—talked about "a summer of blood."

Like the earlier letters, it alternated between horrifying threats and dark humor.

"I will not rest until my job is done," the

writer says. "I am on a mission. A mission
from God."

At another point, he talks about sometimes
having difficulty choosing his victims.

"So many pretty girls, so little time (ha ha!)."

Police say they are still trying to determine if
the killer is the same one who terrorized the
city 12 years ago—and then disappeared.

"He says he's Loverboy," Deputy Police Commissioner Victor Pataglia told reporters at a
hastily called press conference. "And everything seems the same—the victims, the gun, the
notes. But it could be a very clever copycat."

Pataglia said Police Commissioner Thomas
Ferraro—the head of the original Loverboy task
force—had no immediate comment on the latest
round of killings.

But City Council President Peter Garwood—
who most political experts predict will be running against Ferraro in next year's mayoral
election—questioned the copycat theory as well
as Ferraro's handling of the case.

"All signs indicate that one person has done
all of the murders," Garwood said at a separate
press conference.

"This city, and Police Commissioner Ferraro,
have to finish what we started 12 years ago.
But this time let's do it right. We have to find
Loverboy."

There's nothing like a big story to energize a
newsroom.

Most of the things a paper covers are pretty dull.
City Council votes. School board crises. Stuff from
Washington or places like Bosnia or the Mideast that
nobody actually understands. People have to know
about all of it, I guess. But they don't really care.

This was different.

This was a story.

An in-fucking-credible story.

A once-in-a-lifetime story.

Except that it seemed to be happening twice in mine.

I realized that everybody was looking at me differently now when I walked into the *Blade* city room. I wasn't poor Lucy the office drunk anymore. I was Lucy Shannon the ace reporter. I'd used up my fifteen minutes of fame a long time ago. But now I was getting a second helping.

Suddenly everybody was my friend again.

Editors wanted to tell me about their stories. Copy-kids offered to bring me my coffee. Other reporters who had ignored me for years stopped by my desk to talk. Even Victoria Crawford smiled and said hello to me.

Maybe that had something to do with the fact that the *Blade*'s circulation was running dramatically higher than normal since our coverage of the new killings started.

Every morning now when I came to work, there was a growing stack of messages from other media people requesting interviews about my own role in the case. Newspapers. Magazines. TV news programs. Shows like *Inside Edition* and *A Current Affair* and *Geraldo*.

I tried to ignore most of them.

But one of the most persistent was Michael Anson, the woman who wanted me in her movie about Loverboy.

"It would be a natural, Lucy," she said. "Dogged woman reporter devotes her career to chasing the city's worst killer. How can you say no?"

"No."

"I could really beef up your part. Make you a hero. Maybe even get into some stuff about your personal life and . . ."

"I don't think that's a good idea," I said.

"Why not?"

"I'm a reporter. A reporter should report. Not act in movies or appear on talk shows or be the subject of other people's stories."

"Okay, we'll get an actress to play your role. But you can still make a cameo appearance—and then we'll do a big publicity campaign about the real-life reporter who's still trying to crack the case—"

"Good-bye, Ms. Anson," I said.

I hung up just as Janet Wood sat down next to me.

"Who was that?" she asked. "Oprah or Dave?"

"Hollywood calling," I said.

Janet shook her head in amazement.

"Now all you need is a sex life."

"I'm working on that too."

I told her all about Mitch Caruso.

"Another cop?" she said incredulously.

"Yeah, I know. . . ."

"Didn't you tell me you were finished with cops?"

"I think this one's different."

"They always are."

Barlow walked over. He was eating a corned beef sandwich. It looked good. It would look even better with a beer.

"News meeting this afternoon," he told me. "Victoria Crawford's office."

"You want me to go?"

"Yeah, Vicki wants to talk more about Loverboy."

"Is there a problem?"

"Hell, no. She thinks you're doing a great job. She loves you."

"Victoria Crawford hates me."

"Not anymore. You're selling a lot of newspapers. That makes you number one on her hit parade these days."

I looked over at Janet.

She just rolled her eyes.

"When you're hot, you're hot," I said.

Twenty-eight

"Do the police have any suspects yet?" Victoria Crawford asked me at the meeting.

"Not that I know of."

"How are your sources with the investigating cops?"

I thought about me and Mitch Caruso.

"Pretty good," I said.

"But not as good as last time?"

"I'm not sleeping with any of them, if that's what you mean."

"That never was part of the job description, Lucy."

"You know me—I always like to go that extra mile."

Everyone laughed—even Vicki.

We were really hitting it off these days, me and the Vickster. I remembered what Janet had told me about the divorce rumors. If they were true, Vicki was playing for big stakes here. She needed this story, and the big circulation boost it gave the *Blade*, to try to hold onto her job.

Suddenly Loverboy was as important to her life as it was to mine.

Fate sure works in strange ways sometimes.

Vicki's next question was the obvious one. I knew it was coming, but I still wasn't ready for it.

"Did the police have any suspects last time?" she asked.

"Yes," Barlow said.

"No," I said.

Vicki smiled at both of us.

"Well, that seems to cover most of the possibilities," she said.

Barlow cleared his throat and gave me a funny look.

"Maybe you forgot, Lucy. But I've spent the morning going through a lot of your old clips. There were three suspects back in 1984. The cops looked at all three of them pretty carefully, but they never came up with anything substantial."

"Who were they?" Vicki asked.

"Their names were David Gruber, Albert Slocum and Joey Russo."

"So where are they now?"

"Gruber's in jail. He got busted about ten years ago for molesting some little girl in a school playground. Slocum's dead. He overdosed on heroin in some flophouse down on the Bowery. No one's heard from Russo in years."

"He's probably dead too," I said.

"What makes you think that?" Vicki wanted to know.

"Just a guess."

"Well, he seems like the hottest prospect we've got."

I didn't say anything.

"Anybody got any ideas on where to look for him?" she asked.

"The last known address we have is his mother's on the West Side," Barlow said. "It's way over near Tenth Avenue—in Hell's Kitchen."

"You might as well start there, Lucy," Vicki told me.

"It's not him," I said.

"What?"

"He's not Loverboy."

"Why not?"

"The real Loverboy is dead."

Everybody stared at me.

"You still don't believe this is the same guy doing all these new killings?" Vicki asked.

"No, this is a copycat."

"The City Council president seems to think it's the same person. Did you hear Garwood's press conference?"

"I think he's wrong."

"So what happened to the real Loverboy?"

"How the hell do I know? Maybe he blew his brains out. Maybe he got hit by a bus. Maybe he died of a brain tumor. But something happened. He's not alive anymore. He didn't do these new murders."

"You keep saying that."

"Look, I've worked with homicide cops for years—I've learned a lot about how a killer's mind works. It's real hard to kill someone for the first time. It goes against everything we've all been taught since we were kids. But then, once the killer's done it, well, it's not such a big deal anymore. The second time is easier. And the third time even easier than that. I think Loverboy found that out. He liked to kill. So he never would have stopped for twelve years. Ergo, he's dead. And we should be looking for a different person."

Vicki tapped a pencil nervously on the desk as she listened. I noticed she wasn't wearing a wedding band on her left ring finger. Maybe that was some sort of statement. *I'm my own woman. I'm still the editor here—with or without my powerful husband.*

On the other hand, maybe she just forgot to put the ring on this morning.

Or maybe she never wore one—I really didn't remember.

Sometimes I think about stuff like that too much.

"Well, let's check out this Russo character anyway," she said to me. "If it turns out he really is dead, then we can eliminate him from the equation. Anything else, Lucy?"

"Yeah. I'm still intrigued by this movie they're making here about Loverboy."

"You figure that might have sparked the new killings?"

"It sure seems like one hell of a coincidence, doesn't it?"

I went through everything about my visit to the movie set. I told her about how Michael Anson wanted me to be in the film. And I related how I had pointed out to Anson that maybe even she could have committed the murders to get publicity for it.

"That sounds pretty far-fetched," Vicki told me.

"Yeah, I know."

"But you really think it's possible?"

"Anything's possible."

"What about Thomas Ferraro?" Barlow asked.

"What about him?" Vicki wanted to know.

"Well, he was the head of the Loverboy task force twelve years ago. Now he's the police commissioner, running the entire investigation."

"It's an interesting connection," I agreed.

"He hasn't had much to say about the case, has he?" Vicki said.

"No."

"I wonder why."

I didn't know what to say.

"Maybe Police Commissioner Ferraro's got something to hide," she said.

Hell, we all had something to hide.

Thomas J. Ferraro.

Me.

Maybe even Vicki Crawford.

Twenty-nine

I was sitting in the *Blade* cafeteria drinking coffee with Patrick Avery.

Avery was the senior police reporter at the *Blade*. He had been covering crime in New York City for thirty-eight years, and he'd worked on every big story from Kitty Genovese to Son of Sam. He hung around police stations so much he looked, talked and acted just like a cop. Everyone at the paper called him "the Inspector."

Sometimes, when he was the first reporter at a crime scene, he managed to pass himself off as a detective by muttering to a young patrolman: "I'm Avery from downtown. Where's the stiff?" Other times, on the phone, he got reluctant witnesses or victims to be quoted in his stories by saying: "This is Inspector Avery. I just need to ask you a few questions. . . ."

When he'd started as a cub reporter for the *Mirror* in the 1950s, there were thirteen newspapers in New York City. After the *Mirror* folded in 1962, he went to the *Journal American*. That went down in 1965 and became the *World Journal Tribune*, which stopped publishing in 1967. Since then, he'd been with the *Blade*.

He was a classic newspaperman, reminiscent of the old-time reporters of *The Front Page* era. The glory years of newspapers. Before TV, $2-million-a-year anchormen, ex-beauty queens doing the news, demographic surveys, sound bytes and sweeps weeks.

I liked Patrick Avery a lot.

"Did I ever tell you how I found out the *Journal American* was closing?" Avery asked. "I'm at my desk working on this murder in Murray Hill when my phone suddenly goes dead. I look down, and I see a guy from New York Bell on his hands and knees on the floor, unhooking the cord from the wall. So I start screaming at him. The telephone guy looks up at me and says: 'Hey, buddy, this paper just folded. Didn't anyone tell you?'"

He leaned back in his seat and smiled. "And that's how I found out I was out of a job."

I smiled too. I'd heard that story maybe a hundred times, but it always made me laugh.

"So what's happening, Lucy?" Avery asked.

"What do you mean?"

"Well, I know my old newspaper stories are fascinating, but I figure you brought me down here and treated me to coffee for another reason. What are we here to talk about?"

"Loverboy," I said.

"Ah, yes. I read your story. He's back, huh?"

"I don't think so. I think this is a copycat killer."

"Either way, it's a great story."

I nodded. "Tell me what you know about Tommy Ferraro."

I was intrigued by what Vicki had said about his low profile around this case.

"Our esteemed police commissioner? Well, I'll bet he never met a mirror he didn't like. He does love those TV cameras."

"How about his political ambitions?"

"He definitely wants to run for City Hall. The Mayor's retiring next year, and Ferraro and Peter

Garwood, the City Council president, are the two leading candidates to replace him."

I nodded. "Do you think Ferraro's any good as a cop?"

"I've seen better," Avery said, "and I've seen worse. But he's very good at the police public relations bullshit. And that's what it's all about these days. I wouldn't underestimate him."

"For a guy who loves to see his face on the six o'clock news, he's been awfully quiet about these new Loverboy killings."

"Yeah, I noticed that too."

"Why?"

Avery shrugged. "He was the lead detective on the Loverboy task force. They never caught anybody. Maybe he thinks a botched investigation isn't a very good image to project for a man who's running for mayor. Or maybe . . ."

"Maybe what?"

"Maybe he's got something bigger to hide."

That was the same thing Vicki had said.

But what could Tommy Ferraro have to hide about Loverboy?

"There are a few other people—not just Ferraro—who have a lot at stake in this story," I said.

"Like who?"

"Michael Anson. The movie producer. I went to see her—she wanted me to be in her movie. I even suggested that she might have done the new killings to hype the movie. She said that was ridiculous."

"Well, that *is* pretty far-fetched, Lucy. But I hear Anson does need a hit."

"You mean, to stay on top in Hollywood?"

"More than that. The word is Anson suffered a series of financial reverses on her recent movies. The woman's got a real cash-flow problem. She's tapped out. Bankruptcy City."

"So where is the money for this film coming from?"

"She borrowed it."

"Where? From a bank?"

Avery shook his head. "The banks wouldn't help. She didn't have any collateral. So she went to Vincent Gionfriddo."

"The mob guy?"

"That's right. Vincent Gionfriddo financed the whole picture. Gionfriddo doesn't care about collateral. Of course, his rates are extremely high. And the penalty for not paying . . . well, let's just say it's a lot worse than bankruptcy."

"Jesus!"

"Michael Anson's gambling all she's got—maybe even her life—on this movie raking in big money at the box office."

I'll do anything to make it a hit, Anson had told me.

Did that include murder?

"And then there's Vicki," I said.

"Our Vicki?"

"Sure. I assume you've already heard about the impending breakup of her marriage. It could be a doozy of a divorce battle. And one of the things at stake will be control of the *Blade*. What could be better than a big story that would send circulation soaring under her editorship? Loverboy could do that. It succeeded before. So did Son of Sam. People buy newspapers to read about mass killers. And they keep buying them until the killers are caught. Or until they stop killing people."

"Are you suggesting Victoria Crawford is doing these new murders to hype circulation?"

"Wouldn't that be something?" I said. "I could solve the case, be a hero and put Vicki in jail all at the same time."

Avery laughed. "That's your fantasy, Lucy."

"Well, it's a nice fantasy," I said.

We were finished with our coffee. We stood up and began walking back toward the newsroom.

"You know, I've always had a funny feeling about the Loverboy case," Avery said. "Even back when you first covered it in 1984. It just seemed . . . unfinished."

"Of course. They never caught anybody."

"No, it was more than that. There was something else going on there. Something I could never quite put my finger on."

I didn't say anything.

"This is a big story, Lucy."

"I know that."

"I've got a hunch it's gonna be even bigger than you realize."

Thirty

The address for Joey Russo's mother was a run-down six-story tenement in the West Forties. I walked up the stairs into a small, dimly lit vestibule. There was no doorman here. No closed-circuit-TV security system. No welcome mat saying "Our Happy Home." Just a few battered mailboxes with names on them.

One of them said: Mary Russo, Apt. 6B. Joey Russo's mother. Next to the front door was a sign: BUZZ FOR ADMITTANCE. I pressed the buzzer.

"Who's there?" someone said over the intercom.

It sounded like an elderly woman's voice.

"Mrs. Russo?"

"Who wants to know?"

"My name is Lucy Shannon. I'm a reporter with the *New York Blade*."

There was a long pause.

"A reporter? What does a newspaper reporter want to talk to me about?"

"It's about your son, Joey—"

"I don't have a son," she said and broke the connection.

I sighed and buzzed again. There was a long wait this time. I looked through the window of the door at the street outside. There was a bodega across the street with a sign that read SE HABLA ESPAÑOL and a big German shepherd asleep on the steps. In front of it was a green Buick with two men in Panama hats listening to loud music and tapping their hands to the beat on the sides of the car. Other than that, the block was quiet. Finally the speaker crackled again.

"Please go away," the old woman said.

"I don't want to harass you, Mrs. Russo," I said. "But I do need to talk to you. So I am going to wait until you open the door to let me in. It's very hot down here, and I'm not particularly wild about the neighborhood. I'd appreciate it if I didn't have to stand here a long time. Okay?"

There was another pause.

Finally the buzzer sounded and the door opened.

"Thank you," I said into the intercom and walked upstairs to her apartment.

The woman who answered the door was about seventy. She had unkempt white hair, walked with a cane and looked to be about fifty pounds overweight.

She invited me inside.

The living room was furnished with the kind of stuff you'd expect to find at the Salvation Army. Of course, I hadn't exactly been expecting *House Beautiful*. On the wall was a large crucifix. Next to it was a picture of Jesus Christ hanging on the cross. On the coffee table was another picture of Jesus, this time at the Last Supper.

We sat down on a couch that had seen better days.

"So tell me," Mrs. Russo said, "why are you coming to see me after all these years?"

"I want to find Joey," I said.

She smiled. Not a friendly smile, but a sad one. "You want to find Joey? Well, I'm sorry. I can't help you."

"Why not?"

"No one's heard from Joey for twelve years."

"I know that. But I thought that, since you are his mother, maybe he'd called or—"

"Mother!" Her cane smashed down on the floor with such force that it rattled the picture of Jesus on the table. She carefully straightened it as if she had offended him personally.

"Don't call me his mother. Don't remind me of that affliction the Almighty gave me to bear in this world. May the Devil take him, wherever he is."

"You don't have any idea what might have happened to him?" I asked softly.

"Who cares? Dead, probably. No loss. The boy was evil."

"How was he evil?"

"He rejected the Lord. He did not accept the Lord Jesus Christ as his personal savior."

"Uh-huh," I said. "Listen, a lot of people don't do that, Mrs. Russo. That doesn't necessarily mean . . ."

"He had the Devil in him, that boy. Just like his father. I threw his father out. And I did the same with the boy after I found his filth in this house."

"Filth? What kind of filth?"

"The pictures."

"Pictures?"

"The women. Naked women. One day I even caught him doing stuff to himself while he looked at them."

"Doing what?"

"Dirty things."

"You mean he was masturbating?"

"Yes." She nodded. Her face flushed a bright red. "I took a cane and beat him when I found him doing that perversion, but it did no good. The boy was just bad."

"How old was he when this happened, Mrs. Russo?"

"Twenty-four," she said. "He was twenty-four."

I looked down at the floor. I wasn't sure what to say. I wanted to tell Mrs. Russo that there was nothing wrong about a young man of twenty-four looking at pictures of naked women. That there was nothing wrong about masturbating. That there was nothing wrong with sex. But I didn't do any of those things. Because all I wanted to do was find out what Mrs. Russo knew about her son and get the hell out of there.

"When's the last time you saw Joey?" I asked.

"I told you. Twelve years ago."

"Do you remember exactly what happened?"

"Yes," she said. "I was sitting here when the doorbell rang. He answered it and there was a man there."

"What happened?"

"He talked to this man for a few minutes, then said he was going out. When I asked him where, he wouldn't say. He just said, 'When the man says you gotta go, you gotta go.' That was the last time I saw him."

"Do you have any idea who the man at the door was?" I asked.

She shook her head.

"I never saw him before. And I never saw him again."

"Could he have been a friend?"

"My son had no friends."

"A co-worker?"

"Joey didn't work. He tried a few different things, but they didn't work out . . ."

Her voice trailed off and she shook her head sadly. As if anything her son ever did in this life could work out.

"Do you think you'd recognize this man if you ever saw him again?" I asked.

"I don't know . . . it's been such a long time."

"But you might?"

"I suppose so."

I took a deep breath.

"Mrs. Russo, I assume you know your son was a

suspect in a series of killings of young women and their dates before his disappearance twelve years ago."

She nodded.

"And that these killings have started again."

She looked over at the picture of Jesus. Like she was looking for some sort of divine guidance.

"Yes, I've read about them." She sighed.

"Do you think Joey is capable of doing something like this? Do you think he could have done it twelve years ago? And do you think—if he is alive—he might still be doing it?"

Mrs. Russo clasped her hands together and looked me straight in the eye.

She didn't need Jesus's help anymore.

"Yes," she said, "I do. The boy has the Devil in him."

Thirty-one

Albert Slocum was definitely dead.

I made sure of that.

I mean, I didn't dig up his body or anything. But I went to see his old lawyer, a civil liberties crusader named Stuart Endicott. Endicott showed me the death certificate, an autopsy report and a small newspaper clipping about his client's sad demise.

"Albert killed himself," Endicott said. "That is, he technically pulled the trigger. But it was society that put the gun in his hand."

I yawned loudly.

"You don't believe me?" he asked.

"Sorry, but I'm a little busy, Mr. Endicott. I'm not into social revolution this week."

"I blame the police. The education system. The government. They all failed Albert."

"Albert Slocum was a drug addict, a pervert and a sadist," I said. "He raped six women and held one of them captive for ten days while he did sick stuff to her. That's why the police had him listed as a suspect in the Loverboy murders."

"I'll admit, Albert did have some problems," Endicott said.

"He was a creep. The only thing I want to know is if there's any possibility he could have been Loverboy."

"Of course not. Everybody seems to think Loverboy is still doing the latest killings. My client is dead."

"Do you think he might have been capable of doing them if he were alive?"

Endicott hesitated before answering that one. Just for a second. But it was enough for me to know what he was thinking.

"No comment," he said finally.

I sighed. "Yeah, I think so too, Stuart."

David Gruber was serving a twenty-year sentence at Ossining, in upstate New York. The police arrested him with a five-year-old girl in his apartment. She'd been brutally beaten and sexually abused. They also found naked Polaroid pictures of other little girls who'd been abducted. Those cases were still pending.

I went to visit him and told him what I wanted to know.

"Are you Loverboy?" I asked.

Gruber just laughed.

"Of course not," he said. "I certainly didn't do these recent murders. I've been in here. Besides, I was in jail, too, when three of the original killings happened. You can check that out if you want."

He was right about that. I had already checked him out.

"Anyway, that's not my style."

"What do you mean?"

"I'm not into women."

"Just little girls?"

"Exactly. Women are loathsome creatures. Arrogant, demanding, nagging—always complaining about something." He shuddered. "I put my mother in that category too, which gives the psychiatrists here a real field day. Now, little girls—they're completely different. So pure, so innocent, so delightful.

Especially when they're afraid. Do you understand what I mean, Miss Shannon?"

I shook my head.

"You're sick, Gruber."

"That's a subjective opinion."

"It's a fact."

He smiled.

"So how goes your search for Loverboy? Not well, I imagine. That's why you're here."

"We'll find him," I said.

"Do me a favor. If you ever do catch up with this gentleman, tell him I admire him. Tell him I respect his work. I don't understand him—like I told you, grown-up women just don't seem worth all that much work to me—but I'm still a great fan of his accomplishments. Will you make sure to pass that on to him, Miss Shannon?"

"Fuck you," I said.

He smiled. "Sorry, but I'm not interested in that. Not with you anyway. I'm afraid you're much too old. But I wish I'd known you a long time ago. Perhaps you have some baby pictures you could send me. It gets very lonely in here."

By the time I got back to the city, it was late afternoon. I went over to the West Side Precinct to see if they'd come up with anything new in the investigation. Caruso wasn't around. But Lieutenant Masters was.

I told him what I'd found out about David Gruber, Albert Slocum and Joey Russo.

"We just got the ballistics report back on the Kaffee woman," he said. "The bullet that killed her matches the ones we found in the other three shootings. The same guy did all four."

"What kind of gun?"

"A forty-four-caliber Bulldog revolver."

"The same thing Loverboy used to use."

He nodded. "It's a powerful gun. A real cannon."

"What about the original Loverboy killings?"

"A different forty-four."

"So this is a copycat."

"Maybe."

"But . . ."

"Look, everything else is the same as the original Loverboy. And he's not going to be stupid enough to carry around the gun all this time that he used to kill all those people. He threw it away twelve years ago, and now he's got a new one. That makes sense. Right?"

"I guess so," I said.

"You don't seem convinced."

"I still figure this one for a copycat."

"Me, I'm putting my money on the single Loverboy theory."

"Then who is he?"

"Well, Slocum is dead and Gruber's in jail. So that leaves . . ."

"Joey Russo."

"I just issued an arrest warrant for him. He's our only suspect."

"If he's still alive."

"Yeah, if he's still alive."

I called the story in to the *Blade* city desk, billing it as another *Blade* exclusive. That ought to make Victoria Crawford happy. I also threw in some of the stuff I found out about Russo from his mother. As I hung up the phone, I saw Mitch Caruso coming into the squad room.

He waved and walked over to me.

"Are you interested in dinner?" Caruso asked.

"You mean, like a date?" I said.

"Sure." He smiled.

"This is really our first date," I reminded him. "The first one didn't count. It got called on account of murder."

"No dead bodies this time," he said.

"Always a good idea on a first date."

So, as you can see, it turned out to be a pretty good day for me.

Another big exclusive.

A budding romance.

All in all, I felt pretty good.

I probably would have felt even better except for Joey Russo.

Thirty-two

"You don't look like a cop," I said.

"What's a cop supposed to look like?" Caruso asked.

"Jack Webb."

"That's it?"

"Maybe Clint Eastwood."

"So who do you think I look like?"

I studied his face for a minute.

"Jackson Browne," I answered.

"The singer?"

"Yeah."

"He doesn't have a mustache."

"Okay, a hairy Jackson Browne."

He laughed.

"Well, I've got some good news for you," he said.

"What's that?"

"I like Jackson Browne."

"Me too." I smiled.

The two of us were walking down Park Avenue South toward my apartment house. We'd eaten dinner at the Gramercy Tavern on East Twenty-first Street. The Gramercy Tavern is a celebrity hot spot; you have to wait six months to get a reservation. Mitch Caruso got us right in, though. I'm not sure how. I guess it has something to do with being a cop and carrying a gun and a badge. People tend to listen to what you have to say. Even maître d's.

It had been a nice dinner.

The last time I'd been with him I'd poured my heart out about Loverboy, my drinking and a lot of the troubles in my life for the past decade or so. I figured now it was a good idea to lighten up a bit. Maybe it was finally time to have some fun. Maybe it was time to open up to someone. Maybe it was time to get laid again.

"So how did you wind up being a policeman?" I asked.

"Oh, I tried a bunch of other stuff first. I was in a rock band. I dabbled in acting. I waited on tables for a living. I even hitchhiked across the country to Los Angeles and got a few bit parts in some movies and TV shows. But when it came time to settle down, I decided to be a cop."

"Why?"

"I guess I always liked playing cops and robbers when I was a kid."

"And you were always one of the good guys?"

"I still am," he said.

"Do you come from a police family?"

"Sort of."

"Was your father a cop?"

"My uncle."

"Is he still on the force?"

He smiled at the question. I wasn't sure why. "Yeah, I guess you might say that."

"He must be proud of you."

"Well, actually, I don't think he understands me very well. We're from different generations. He's very old school—a real by-the-book police traditionalist. Me, I think the police have to keep up with the times. Relate better to the communities, to young people, to minorities. Some of the things we've been doing for a long time don't work so well anymore. So maybe it's time to make some changes."

"And you're going to be the one to do that?"

"I'm going to try. I'm going to college at night. Taking courses in criminal justice, urban affairs, even a bit of philosophy. I don't want to be a homicide detective all my life."

"Wow!" I told him. "An ambitious cop."

"Everybody's ambitious, Lucy."

"Not me."

"Sure you are."

"I used to be," I said. "A long time ago."

We were standing at a light at Eighteenth Street, where I lived. As the light turned green, we started to cross the street. He put his arm around me to guide me past a double-parked car. He didn't take it away. I slipped mine around his waist. It felt comfortable.

"How about you?" he asked. "How did you become Lucy Shannon, newspaper reporter?"

"Did you ever see a movie called *Deadline U.S.A.*?" I said.

He shook his head.

"It stars Humphrey Bogart as the managing editor of a New York newspaper that's about to go out of business. On its last day of publication, a young guy comes to the paper looking for a job. Bogart tells him: 'Kid, let me tell you something about the newspaper business. It may not be the oldest profession in the world. But it's the best.' "

I sighed. "I loved that movie."

"Do you still feel that way about newspapers?"

"I guess it's sort of like a love affair. The first few weeks or months together are really magical. I mean, you love everything about the person, warts and all. But then time goes by and you get married and after a while the magic wears off. Finally, one day you look over across the room at your husband—and it's like he's a stranger. You don't know why in hell you're even together. That's sort of the way I feel about the newspaper business."

"Gee, it sounds depressing."

"It is. Most of the time. But every once in a while . . ."

I let my voice trail off.

"What?"

"Well, even in a bad marriage, there are these moments. You look at the other person lying next to you in bed, and suddenly it all comes back. It doesn't last very long, maybe only for an instant. But you remember how you once felt about them. What you used to have together. And you wonder if there's any way to ever get that feeling back again."

"Does that happen to you often?"

"Oh, now and then," I said.

We were at my apartment house now. We stood at the front door.

"I guess this is the turning point of the date," I said.

"Huh?"

"This is when I either say good night to you or ask if you want to come in for some coffee."

"Coffee," he said.

"Yeah. Only you and I both know coffee is not what we're talking about here. That's just a code for how the date went. If the date bombed, you make some sort of excuse—you have to get up early or you don't like coffee or something—but you promise to call me again soon. If the date was a success, you come in with me."

"For coffee?"

"Whatever."

There was a long silence. But not an uncomfortable one. Nothing seemed uncomfortable between us.

"So do you want to come up for some coffee?" I asked.

He smiled. "I love coffee."

"Me too," I said.

Then we went upstairs.

Thirty-three

My apartment is what you'd call functional.

There's one bedroom, a big living room with an alcove that I turned into a study, and an eat-in kitchen.

There are no beautiful prints on the wall. No expensive rugs on the floor. The furniture is nothing special—most of it comes from department stores, the rest from garage sales or friends who moved out of town. I've got lots of books and stacks of newspapers around the place, because I do a lot of reading.

I don't figure to ever wind up on the pages of *Good Housekeeping*.

But it's comfortable and it's cheap, at least by New York City standards.

I made Mitch Caruso and myself some coffee in the kitchen—all that talk about it had made me want a cup—while he watched the eleven o'clock news on TV in the living room.

Anyway, that's what he said he wanted to do.

But when I came out with the coffee, there was no sign of him. It wasn't that big an apartment. I didn't think even I could have lost a man that quickly. So where was he?

"Come out, come out, wherever you are," I said.

There was no answer.

I looked around the living room. Then I started to

walk down the hall toward the bedroom. Just as I did, I saw him coming out of there. My bedroom, that is.

"Sorry," he said. "I was looking for the bathroom."

He seemed a bit flustered.

"Over there," I said, pointing to the other end of the hall.

I went back in the living room, sat down on the couch and waited for him to come back.

When he did, he seemed different. More distant than earlier in the evening. He sat down in an EZ Boy chair across from me, even though there was plenty of room left on the couch. Not a good sign.

"You got any more theories about Loverboy?" he asked.

"You want to talk about Loverboy?" I asked.

"Sure. Why not?"

"I kind of thought we might want to forget about that for a while and concentrate on other stuff."

"It's kind of hard to forget about. But sure, we can talk about something else, if you want."

"Whatever."

He drank some of his coffee.

"You still don't think it's the same guy, huh?" he said.

"No, I don't."

"Why?"

I gave him my "killers just don't stop for twelve years" theory.

"Maybe he had no choice," Caruso said. "Maybe he's been in jail. Or in a mental hospital."

"That's a possibility."

"But you don't buy it."

"Like I told you before, my guess is we're dealing with a copycat. A very clever copycat. But somebody totally new."

He nodded. "So how do we find this copycat?"

He probably thought I didn't have any answers for that. But he was wrong.

"Doesn't it seem more than just a little strange to you that a movie on the case is being shot at the same time as the new killings occur?" I said.

He stared at me. "You think there's a connection between the movie and the murders?"

"I think at the very least the movie spurred the killer to start up. And it could be even more sinister than that."

"Such as?"

"What if someone with the movie company is doing these murders?"

"Who?"

"Michael Anson, for instance."

"The director?"

"Uh-huh."

"That's absurd."

"I checked her out. She's got big-time money troubles. She's in deep shit with loan sharks and the mob. She desperately needs this movie to be a big hit. Everything's riding on it for her."

"Okay, so she's got a few debts. That doesn't make her a murderer."

"Everybody's talking about this movie now because of the murders. You couldn't buy better publicity."

"Are you saying . . . ?"

"I'm just saying you should check Anson out. Her and her amazon bodyguard. Especially the bodyguard. Now, *there's* someone that definitely looks like a killer to me."

I sipped on my coffee.

"Anybody else?" he asked.

"Yeah," I said. "Thomas Ferraro."

"The police commissioner?"

"That's right."

"What about him?"

"Where is he in all this? He's not holding press conferences. He's not answering questions. He's not going on TV. He's never even shown up at any of the crime scenes."

"Maybe he's busy with other things."

"Loverboy is the biggest story in years. What could be more important than Loverboy? Besides, it's his story. Twelve years ago, Ferraro was the lead detective investigating this case. Now he's avoiding it like the plague. Why?"

"There's lots of reasons he might—"

"I think he's hiding something."

Caruso shook his head in amazement.

"Let me get this straight, Lucy. You think that the police commissioner of New York City is somehow involved in these murders?"

"I didn't say that. I said I thought he was acting strangely. I just want to know why. You can't ignore the fact that he was very involved in the first string of murders. . . ."

"So were you."

"Okay, I was. But there's a difference."

"What?"

"I know I'm not the murderer."

Caruso smiled at me now. A funny smile. Not ha-ha funny. More like he was laughing at a private joke that I wasn't in on.

"Do you remember how I told you before that I had an uncle who was a cop?" he said.

"Sure."

"Do you know his name?"

I shook my head no.

"Thomas J. Ferraro," he said.

Gulp.

"The police commissioner?" I asked softly.

"There's only one Thomas J. Ferraro on the force that I know of."

"And you're Commissioner Ferraro's nephew?"

"Uh-huh."

"So . . . so I guess you'd probably know if there was—was anything funny going on about him and Loverboy," I stammered.

"I think so."

"Well, it was just a theory," I said.

There was an uncomfortable silence. I wasn't sure what to do next. I didn't want to talk about Thomas J. Ferraro anymore. I didn't want to talk about Loverboy. I wanted Mitch Caruso to kiss me, hold me and go to bed with me. It had been a long time.

He stood up.

"I've got to go," he said.

"Already?"

"It's getting late."

"It's not that late."

"I've got a meeting first thing in the morning."

I walked him to the door.

"I had a nice time," I said.

"Me too."

He leaned down and gave me a perfunctory kiss on the cheek.

Then he was gone.

Damn! Something had gone very wrong with the evening. But I wasn't sure what. I wanted to know why. I wanted Mitch Caruso to come back. I wanted a drink. Yeah, that was what I needed. A drink. Just one vodka martini. Or maybe two. That'd sure make me feel better.

I shook my head and—in a second or two—the feeling went away.

I walked down the hall into the bedroom. The closet door was open. I was pretty sure I'd shut it the last time I'd been there. I pulled out one of the drawers in my dresser. A few of the things inside were out of place.

Somebody had been going through my stuff.

But why?

Was Mitch Caruso really a sneak thief who'd been trying to rob me? Of course not. He was a policeman, not a robber.

Was he some sort of pervert who just liked going through women's clothes?

Or was there something else going on here that I didn't know about?

Thirty-four

Norm Malloy told me someone was waiting for me when I got to work in the morning.

"See that guy standing in front of your desk?" Malloy said in between answering phone calls.

I nodded.

"His name is Elmer Lutz."

"So?"

"He says he's Loverboy."

I was—to put it mildly—a tad skeptical. Elmer Lutz was a short, pudgy man of about sixty. There was almost no hair on his head. He spoke with a stutter and in a high, squeaky voice. He didn't look like Loverboy to me. Actually, he looked more like Elmer Fudd than an Elmer Lutz.

I walked over, introduced myself to him and listened politely to what he had to say. Then I went back to Malloy at the city desk.

"You don't seem to be in mortal danger," Malloy said.

"I face death in the eye every day."

"Did this guy really confess to all the killings?"

"Among other things."

"Huh?"

"He also confessed to kidnapping Jimmy Hoffa, bombing the World Trade Center and helping Charles Manson kill Sharon Tate."

"Oh, Christ!"

"No kidding. You think the authorities want to clear up any other unsolved crimes on the books? How about the Kennedy assassination? I don't think he's got an alibi for that."

Malloy shook his head.

"Whenever a mass killer gets a lot of publicity, this kind of thing happens."

"Yeah, the fruitcakes really come out of the woodwork."

"What do you want to do with him?"

"Let's call the cops."

He made the call. While I waited for them to show up, I gave Elmer some coffee. He was very polite.

A short time later, two EMS cops came to get him. A young guy who looked like he didn't need to shave yet and a woman with long blond hair she bundled up inside her hat. The older I get, the less cops look like cops.

They started to lead him away, but he suddenly began to protest violently. He said they were supposed to put handcuffs on him.

"Other people get handcuffs," he said in a whiny voice. "Why can't I?"

The two young cops looked at each other and shrugged. Then the blond-haired woman took a pair of handcuffs out of her belt and cuffed Elmer's wrists behind his back. Then they took him away.

He looked happy.

It was definitely becoming crazy season in New York City.

A midsummer heat wave had settled in, and the near-one-hundred-degree temperatures—plus the daily headlines about a mass killer roaming the streets again—turned the town into a tinderbox ready to explode at the slightest provocation.

There were some like Elmer Lutz who wanted to take credit for the murders. But most wanted to put the blame on somebody else. It didn't really matter on whom: ex-boyfriends; bosses who'd fired them; neighbors they didn't like; loan sharks they owed money to. The police department's files were soon bulging with reports from people who claimed they knew who Loverboy really was. None of them did. But the cops checked everyone out.

Meanwhile, all the people who weren't claiming to be Loverboy—or trying to say someone else was—were worried about becoming the next victim. The same pattern as last time was happening all over again. New Yorkers stopped going out so much at night. Attendance at singles bars and dance clubs and movies dropped off dramatically. Gun sales were up. Women learned how to shoot at pistol ranges and took self-defense classes.

Things were getting pretty wacky at the *Blade* too.

In our effort to sell more papers, we were pulling out every tired crime cliché and gimmick to keep the story going. Psychics. Psychological profiles. Front-page appeals for Loverboy to surrender. You name it, we shamelessly tried it.

The psychological profiles were pretty funny. We went to a bunch of so-called experts and asked them to speculate on what Loverboy was really like.

Some said he was a loner, had a domineering mother, hated women, and probably seemed quiet and withdrawn most of the time, but was prone to sudden outbursts of violence.

Others disagreed. They said the same thing Caruso had said in the article I'd done about Deborah Kaffee's death.

Maybe Loverboy was a fine, upstanding citizen. Maybe he had a big job and a beautiful wife and family. Maybe he was handsome and charming and had a real way with the ladies.

"I think he probably picked some of these girls up," one of the shrinks said about the victims. "Or they let him into their homes voluntarily. Loverboy doesn't have to be a bogeyman. He could be anybody. We might be very surprised at his identity when we finally catch him."

The truth was, nobody really knew the answer.

"Jesus, what a bunch of crap," I told Barlow as I read through some of the medical mumbo jumbo. "I could have made this up myself."

"Yeah, but you're not an expert," he said.

The psychics were weird too. A lot of would-be Jeane Dixons who went to the murder sites or touched a piece of one of the victim's clothing and tried to conjure up a vision. Most of the visions were pretty much the same. Loverboy would eventually be caught, but there'd be more killings first. Brilliant, huh?

Finally, there was the oldest newspaper chestnut of all—the appeal to the killer to give himself up. It's been done with every mass murderer. I wrote this one myself, just like I did the first time, back in 1984. It was in the form of an open letter. The headline in the *Blade* said: **"Loverboy Reporter to Killer: Give Yourself Up to Me!"** He didn't.

But people were buying the *Blade* in record numbers.

Newsstand sales were zooming. Every paper in town was selling better because of the case, but none as well as the *Blade*. We were the leader. The brand name. The paper with the hotshot reporter to whom Loverboy actually sent his deadly messages.

Me.

It was turning me into a star all over again. Even bigger than the last time. Ricki Lake called me up and asked me to be on her show. *People* magazine sent a reporter over to do a profile piece. I made page 1 of *USA Today* one morning.

I was hot.

I was the woman of the hour.

Just the same as it was twelve years ago.

Like Yogi Berra once said, it was déjà vu all over again.

Thirty-five

The movie company had moved to Times Square.

They were doing a scene about the murder of a nineteen-year-old college student named Karen Whitcomb, who was shot outside the Port Authority Bus Terminal. She'd been on her way home to Tenafly, New Jersey, after working on a term paper at the New York Public Library on Forty-second Street.

It was one of the early killings, before people knew about Loverboy. So at first everyone assumed she'd been a victim of random violence. There were pimps, prostitutes, drug dealers and quick-buck artists all over the neighborhood. It was easy to figure the Whitcomb girl had just crossed paths with someone like that. One newspaper even used her murder as part of an editorial campaign to push for a cleanup of Times Square.

But it really had nothing to do with Times Square. It was Loverboy. Loverboy never cared what kind of neighborhood it was. Hell, the police task force twelve years ago had spent hundreds of hours trying to figure out some sort of pattern to his attacks. They never succeeded. Maybe he didn't have one. Maybe he just killed whenever the urge came over him.

Times Square has changed a lot since Karen Whitcomb's murder.

A lot of the strip joints, X-rated movie theaters and

porn bookstores are gone now. They've been re-
placed by office buildings and parks. It's part of an
urban renewal project that people call progress. I
suppose it is. But I still remember how much I used
to love the excitement and electricity of Times Square
when I first came to New York. I don't feel that excitement anymore. Of course, that probably has more
to do with me than with Times Square.

Michael Anson was sitting in a director's chair in
one of the Port Authority offices. A makeshift movie
set had been set up nearby in the terminal. Anson
was talking with a young woman who looked
vaguely familiar to me. I suddenly realized why. It
was the actress who was going to play Karen Whitcomb—and she looked remarkably like the pictures
I'd seen of the real Karen in old newspaper clips.

Anson saw me now and waved. She was wearing
a T-shirt, jeans and cowboy boots today. I guess it
was her *Midnight Cowboy* look for Times Square. I
walked over to her.

The young actress had gone outside, back to the
movie set for today's scenes. Micki was there,
though. Standing guard next to Anson. She was still
scowling too. Miss Congeniality.

"Hi. I was glad to get your call," Anson said. "I've
been reading a lot about you lately."

"Yeah, I'm front-page news."

"We both are," she said and smiled.

"Isn't life grand?" I asked.

I looked out the door at the actress she'd been
talking to.

"That's an amazing similarity," I told Anson. "She
looks just like the real Karen Whitcomb did."

"Yeah, it's eerie, isn't it? I was lucky to find her."

"Can she act?"

Anson laughed. "All she's got to do is look scared
and play dead."

"So we're not talking about an Oscar-winning performance here?"

"My pictures aren't made to win Oscars, Lucy. They're made because people want to see them."

"And they generally stress realism more than anything else, don't they?"

Anson smiled. "Yes, that's my own brand of movie magic."

I glanced at Micki again. She still hadn't moved.

"Can you and I talk alone?" I asked Anson.

"You mean without Micki?"

"Yeah. I was hoping she might take her sunny personality outside for a few minutes."

"Why?"

"I've got something to tell you."

"About being in the movie?"

I shook my head.

"This is private. I don't think you're going to want anybody else to hear it."

Anson nodded and gestured to Micki to leave. Micki didn't like it. But Michael Anson was the boss, no question about that. Micki glared at me one more time. Then she headed for the door.

"So what's so damned important?" Anson said after she was gone.

"Vincent Gionfriddo."

She was surprised. I'd caught her off-balance. But she tried her best to recover.

"Who?"

I laughed. "That's good. That's very good."

"Vincent Gionfriddo? The name does sound familiar. . . ."

"Let me refresh your memory. Gionfriddo is a mobster. A big-time underworld figure both here and in L.A. He deals in extortion, drugs, prostitution and loan-sharking. He maims and murders people who make him mad. And—oh, yes, one more little thing—you owe him a great deal of money."

Anson didn't say anything right away. She took out a cigarette and lit it. I looked to see if her hand was shaking. It wasn't.

"You don't know much about Hollywood, do you, Lucy?" she asked finally.

"No."

"It's a strange place. Sometimes directors make movies that bomb at the box office, but still earn tons of money from cable or foreign film rights or some complicated tax write-off. Other times a filmmaker does everything right and still takes a financial beating. When that happens, we have to look for a short-term infusion of cash. It's just business."

"So Vincent Gionfriddo gave you the money to make *Loverboy*?"

She nodded.

"And how are you going to pay him back?"

"From the profits."

"What if there are no profits?"

"There will be. It's going to be a hit."

"And I'm helping to make it one. Me and *Loverboy*."

"As a matter of fact, you are."

She took a drag on her cigarette and laughed. "I can see where you're going with this, Lucy. You still think that maybe I'm killing all these recent victims just to get publicity for my movie."

"Are you?"

"No. But it is an intriguing idea."

"It's working too."

"Yeah, maybe I should try it as a plot in my next film. Anyway, like I said before, I could say the same thing about you, Lucy. Maybe you're killing people to help get your newspaper career back on track. That's working too, isn't it?"

I didn't say anything.

"I checked you out for the movie," Anson said. "Lucy Shannon, wunderkind reporter at twenty-four and washed up at thirty-six. Married and divorced three times, in and out of alchoholic rehab—it's not a pretty picture. The only thing good that ever happened to you was Loverboy. So maybe you just decided to bring him back so people would remember you again."

"I would never do anything like that."

"Of course you wouldn't. Neither would I. That's my point."

She ground out her cigarette on the bottom of her boot. She leaned close to me.

"Can I ask you a personal question, Lucy?"

I nodded.

"Do you ever get tired of men?"

"What do you mean?"

"Well, you've been married three times. If a person eats steak every day and it's not good for them, they switch to something else. Chicken. Fish. Or even become a vegetarian. Maybe you should change your diet."

She smiled.

"I like you, Lucy. I like your energy. I even like your smart mouth."

Jesus Christ, she was coming on to me. I wasn't sure how to react. This had never happened to me before. I was in uncharted waters here.

"We're not talking about vegetarianism, are we?" I asked her.

"No."

I looked over at the door. "What about Micki?"

"What do you mean?"

"I thought she was your girlfriend."

"Don't worry about Micki. I can handle her."

I stood up. I was getting very uncomfortable.

"I've got to be going," I said.

"What about being in my movie?"

"I don't think so."

She shrugged. "Well, call me if you change your mind."

"Sure."

"Or just call me anyway, sometime."

On my way out, I passed Micki. She was standing just outside the door. She glared at me even more unpleasantly than she had before—if that was possible. From inside the room I could hear Michael Anson pick up the phone and call someone. I could make out most of what she was saying.

I wondered if Micki had heard any of our conversation.

I hoped not.

Thirty-six

"Let's do the greatest," I said.

"The greatest now or of all time?" Janet wanted to know.

"Of all time."

"Cool!"

We were sitting around a round table at Headlines, waiting for that evening's edition of the *Blade* to come off the presses. Me, Janet, Barlow, Brian Tully, Karen Wolfe and Norm Malloy. There was a big pitcher of beer in the center of the table. Not for me, of course. I was drinking water. No problem.

Our table was right underneath what is known as the Wall of Fame. That's a display of pictures at Headlines, featuring some of the legendary people who'd worked for the *Blade* over the years.

"The greatest obit writer ever on a newspaper in this town was Daniel Fullerton," Malloy said as he looked at one of the pictures.

Malloy knew almost everything there was to know about the history of the *New York Blade*.

"An obit writer?" Wolfe asked.

"Not *an* obit writer. *The* obit writer. Fullerton turned obit writing into an art form. It was the only thing he did. You knew him, didn't you, Walter?"

Barlow nodded. "He even looked like an under-taker. He was really pasty-faced, he talked very softly and he always wore black. The guy was truly strange."

"Fullerton hated it whenever they took the death of someone famous away from his obit page and turned it into a front-page story," Malloy said. "On the day John F. Kennedy was assassinated, Fullerton came into the city room and saw everyone racing around, stripping wire copy and putting new leads on the assassination stories. So he walked over to the managing editor and said, 'Does this mean you'll be taking the Kennedy story for page one?'"

Everyone laughed.

"Toughest editor?" Janet asked.

"Eddie Slotnick," Barlow replied.

We all shrugged. No one knew him.

"He used to be executive editor here a long time ago. Back when I was just a young reporter."

"You a young reporter?" I said to Barlow. "God, that really is ancient history."

"Was Slotnick any good?" Tully asked.

"Yeah, but he was a real ball buster. He used to write these brutal memos. One time a columnist's wife died. The guy did a column titled 'My Wife' that was a long, personal memory of the woman. It really had no place in the newspaper."

"Slotnick killed it?" Wolfe said.

"No, he let it run."

Barlow took a sip of his beer as we all waited to hear what had happened next.

"Anyway, a couple of days go by and now it's time for the guy to turn in his next column. This one's titled 'My Wife—Part Two.' Slotnick kills this one. Then he sends the guy a memo. Know what it said?"

We all shook our heads.

"'One wife, one column.'" Barlow smiled.

The table erupted in laughter.

"Who was the most colorful reporter?" I asked.

"Larry Morrison," Malloy said. "The greatest re-write man of all time."

"Why?"

"Because he'd do anything to get a front-page story. Even though sometimes he went too far."

"Such as?"

"Well, one time there was this big hostage drama and Morrison told the city editor he'd gotten an exclusive telephone interview with the gunman. The paper put it on page one: '**They'll Never Take Me Alive, Gunman Vows.**' The next night the guy gives up—and it turns out he's a deaf mute. The city editor demands an explanation. Morrison says: 'Gee, boss, he never told me that.' "

Everyone laughed again.

"Yeah, I think that's going too far," Tully said.

"Just a little bit," Wolfe agreed.

"It's a tough call sometimes," Barlow mused. "How far do you push a story before you cross over that line? The one between aggressive reporting and doing something really unethical."

I didn't say anything. Suddenly I didn't like where this conversation was headed.

"Give us an example of something really unethical," Janet asked him.

"Janet Cooke."

"Who's Janet Cooke?" Wolfe asked.

"She was a reporter for *The Washington Post*," I said. "She did a series of articles a few years ago about an eight-year-old drug addict that won her a Pulitzer Prize. Only it turned out there really was no kid. She'd made him up. They had to take the Pulitzer back and she lost her job."

"Where is she now?"

I shrugged. There were blank looks all around the table. No one knew.

"I guess that really *is* crossing the line," Janet said.

A copyboy came in carrying a stack of *Blades* and

handed them to Malloy. He passed them around the table. My latest Loverboy story was right there at the top of page 1.

I was reading it to myself when I realized the copyboy was standing next to me.

"You're Lucy Shannon, aren't you?" he asked.

"Yeah."

"My name's Dick Sievers."

"Hi, Dick," I said.

We shook hands. He was very young, and—I suddenly realized—handsome in a dark, brooding kind of way.

"It's really an honor to meet you, Miss Shannon. I've been reading all your stuff. I want to be a reporter, too, someday. Just like you."

Janet snickered next to me. I ignored her.

"Have you done much journalism?" I asked him.

"Well, I'm taking a course in it now at NYU. Basic newswriting."

"That's a start."

"And, of course, I'm working at the *Blade* nights as a copyboy."

I nodded. I wasn't quite sure what to say.

The kid looked very nervous.

"The thing is . . . well, I was wondering . . . maybe sometime we could talk about it. Like over coffee or a drink or something. I mean, I know you're probably really busy—but I've got a lot of questions. And I think I could learn a lot more in twenty minutes with a real reporter like you than from a whole semester of journalism classes."

"Sure." I smiled. "I'd be happy to talk with you."

After he left, everybody at the table started ribbing me.

"God, he's got a crush on you," Janet said.

"Why you?" Wolfe wanted to know.

"Yeah, you're old enough to be his mother," Tully joked.

"Here's to you, Mrs. Robinson," Barlow said, holding up his beer glass in a toast.

I picked up the *Blade* and pointed to my story on page 1.

"Everybody loves a star," I said.

It was a little after eleven when I left Headlines that night. I was by myself. The rest of them were staying there to drink some more. That's one of the benefits of being sober. Not so many late nights closing bars down. It's great for getting sleep.

There was some construction going on next door when I got out onto the street. They'd built one of those temporary walkways—a sort of tunnel made of metal and wood—that you had to go through to get to Seventh Avenue. I started through it, wondering if I'd have much trouble finding a cab.

There were still plenty of people on the street. That was why I didn't get worried when I heard the footsteps behind me. I felt safe. I was in the middle of the Village and it wasn't that late and danger was the last thing on my mind.

I was almost to the end of the walkway when it happened. Another few feet and I probably would have been all right. In full view of many passersby. Just get in a cab and go home and jump into bed. But I never made it.

An arm suddenly went around my neck, and I felt somebody grabbing me from behind.

I struggled, but whoever it was was really strong. A hand clamped over my mouth as I tried to scream for help.

"This is just a little reminder that no one is safe from Loverboy—not even you, Shannon," a voice whispered in my ear. "I'm always out there watching all you bitches."

There was an alley next to me. I felt myself being dragged into it. It was dark and hidden and no one would ever see me in there.

I knew I had to fight back. I summoned up every ounce of strength I had. I bit down hard on the hand across my mouth. There was a scream of pain and I heard something fall to the sidewalk.

Someone hit me then.

There was a blinding flash of pain in my head, and I remember hitting the sidewalk as I fell.

After that, everything went black.

Thirty-seven

I was probably unconscious only for a minute or two.

When I woke up, I was lying on the pavement in the alley. My head hurt and so did my throat where the guy had grabbed me. I checked my purse. Nothing was taken. Plus, I was still alive. All in all, it could have been worse.

I wasn't sure how badly I was hurt, though.

I slowly made my way back out to the street. No one else there seemed to have noticed what had happened. I thought about asking for help or hailing a cab or going back to Headlines. But then I saw St. Vincent's Hospital, just a few blocks away. I walked to the emergency room.

They X-rayed my head and checked out my bruises. While I was waiting, I called the *Blade* from a pay phone and told them what had happened. The night editor put me on with a rewrite man. He said they were going to do a story on it. After a while, the doctor came back with some X-rays which showed nothing on me was broken or missing. He advised me to go home and get a good night's sleep.

Instead I walked to the nearest police station, on West Tenth Street, where I filed a report on the attack.

The desk sergeant seemed bored as he wrote down

the information. Until I told him the part about Loverboy. And said my name was Lucy Shannon.

"You're the reporter, aren't you?" he said.

"Yes."

"I think they want to talk to you."

"Who?"

"The detectives."

He led me to a small room and asked me to wait there. The room had a small rectangular table and three folding chairs. I sat down in one of the chairs. I hoped the detectives weren't too busy. This was turning into a very long night.

Five minutes passed. Then fifteen. Then close to an hour.

This was stupid, I thought to myself. The cops weren't ever going to catch anybody anyway. I was ready to get up and leave when two detectives finally came through the door. They weren't the detectives I had expected, though.

Masters and Caruso entered, carrying a cardboard box. They laid it down on the table in front of me.

"What are you guys doing here?" I asked.

"We heard about what happened," Caruso said.

"Gee, it's nice you were worried. But I'm okay. Honest."

I flashed him a reassuring smile. He didn't smile back.

That was my first sign that something was wrong.

The second was when Masters took out a Miranda card and began reading me my rights.

"You have the right to remain silent, you have the right to consult a lawyer . . ."

I looked at Caruso. "What the hell's going on here, Mitch?"

He reached into the cardboard box and took out a newspaper. He put it in front of me. It was a late edition of the *Blade*. The story of my attack was on page 1. There was a picture of me too. The head-line said:

LOVERBOY SHOCKER
Blade Reporter Attacked;
Cops Seek Link to Slayings

"That's some story," he said.

"What's your point?"

"You wrote it before you came to the police."

"I wanted to make it in time for the next edition."

"So how could you say we were investigating a link between what happened tonight and the slayings?"

"I just assumed you would—it seemed obvious. The guy who attacked me talked about Loverboy."

"The story's not true," Masters said.

"When did you become a journalism critic?" I asked.

He cleared his throat. He seemed uncomfortable too, just like Caruso. "We canvassed the area, Lucy. No one saw any attack. There's no evidence in the alley. No sign of a struggle anywhere."

"I was there, Lieutenant, remember?"

He grunted. "Yeah. Just you and this imaginary assailant."

I couldn't believe this was happening.

"Are you saying I made this up?"

"It's starting to look that way."

"Why would I do that?"

Masters pointed to the newspaper article. "To get on the front page. To keep this whole Loverboy thing going for you."

"That's ridiculous."

I looked over at Caruso. "Is that what you think, Mitch? That I made it all up just to get my name in the paper again?"

He shook his head. "I don't know, Lucy. . . ."

"Maybe you didn't do it deliberately," Masters said. "Maybe you really thought you were being attacked. People who drink a lot sometimes have delusions—"

"I don't drink anymore."

"You'd just left a bar."

"I was drinking Perrier. You can ask anyone there."

"We did," Caruso said.

"What did they say?"

"The bartender told us you sometimes sneak drinks. He says the last time you tried to quit, you kept a flask in your pocket—and poured it into your glass under the table. Nobody knew anything about it. Until you passed out."

"That was a long time ago."

"Is that what happened tonight?"

"No!"

"Look, Lucy," Caruso said softly, "if you want to call a lawyer now . . ."

"I don't need a goddamned lawyer," I snapped.

"I think you do."

"Why? Even if I was drinking—which I wasn't— when did that become a crime?"

Masters reached into the cardboard box and took out some other things. A scrapbook. A few letters. A vodka bottle.

"Where did you get those?" I wanted to know.

"Your apartment."

"What were you doing in my apartment?"

"We had a warrant to search it."

"Why?"

Then it dawned on me. Of course. That was why Mitch Caruso had been looking around my bedroom. He'd been trying to find out if there was anything there to come back for later with a warrant. He hadn't been on a date at all. He'd been on the job the whole time.

I glared at him. He looked away.

"You son of a bitch!" I said.

Masters picked up the vodka bottle he'd taken out of the box.

"Why does a woman who isn't drinking anymore have an empty vodka bottle in her apartment?"

"Beautiful memories," I said.

"That's bullshit."

"I don't have to answer these questions."

He glanced down at the rest of the stuff he'd taken out of the box.

"The scrapbook is filled with every article that's ever been written about Loverboy. You seem obsessed with him, Shannon."

"I'm a reporter. I keep clippings."

"How about the letters? They're Loverboy's letters. The ones he left at murder scenes."

"So what? They were written to me. Why wouldn't I keep copies so—"

"These aren't copies," Masters said. "They're originals. And they weren't the same as any of the letters from previous murders. These were new. What were you going to do—put them at the next crime scene?"

"And why would I do that?"

"To make sure you got another big story."

"That's crazy."

"Then how do you explain this?"

He reached into the box one more time and took out a gun.

Not just any gun.

A Bulldog .44 revolver.

Just like the one Loverboy used.

"We found this in your apartment too," Masters told me.

That was when I knew I was really in trouble.

"I want to talk to a lawyer," I said.

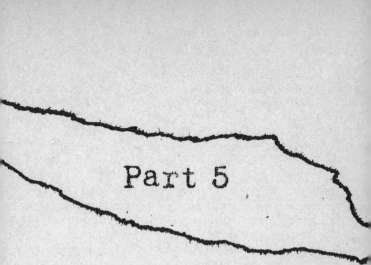

Part 5

TANGLED UP IN BLUE

Thirty-eight

They say there's nothing like the fury of sharks turning on one of their own.

I remember watching a documentary about it once. Most of the time a school of sharks works in perfect union. Constantly moving through the water looking for its next prey. Relentless. Deadly. Nature's perfect killing machine.

But then, if something happens to one of the sharks, everything changes. Maybe the shark cuts itself on a jagged rock. Or it's shot or harpooned by a passing boat. Whatever, the sight of blood whips the other sharks into a frenzy. There's no sympathy there. No effort to help their crippled cohort. No 911 calls in the world of sharks. They just go after it with a gusto even fiercer than that applied to any of their innocent victims.

Reporters are a lot like that.

We really are all sharks, I realize now. I mean, we talk about freedom of the press and the public's right to know and all sorts of lofty goals. But when you get right down to it, we feed off other people's misery. Murder. Scandal. Tragedy. That's what news is really all about.

Sometimes critics talk about how there should be more good news reported by the media. But that's never going to happen. News—by its very nature—is inherently almost always something bad.

I knew all that. I'd just never seen it from the other side before. Suddenly I was the hunted, not the hunter. I was the wounded shark. And the rest of them were after me. They smelled blood.

There was a crowd of them waiting for me when I came out of the station house. Newspaper reporters. Television crews. Radio stations. Someone at the precinct must have tipped them off. Why not? I'd gotten a million tips like that myself.

I was wearing handcuffs. Masters and Caruso had seemed almost apologetic when they put them on me, but they'd said it was official procedure. The two of them were on either side of me now and led me toward a waiting police car.

"Is it true that you wrote the new letters from Loverboy yourself?" a TV reporter yelled.

"Are you Loverboy?" someone else wanted to know.

"Have you been charged yet with a crime?"

I didn't answer.

I knew all the faces. Many of them were my friends. How many times had I done the same thing they were doing now? Yelled out questions at suspects, badgered them, followed them down the street.

That was a reporter's job. To get the quote or sound byte or headline that would make all the difference for the news. I always thought it was fun. But it wasn't much fun being on the other side.

Cameras were pointed at me. Flashbulbs went off. Sometimes I've seen cops put their coats over suspects' heads to keep them hidden in situations like this. No one put a coat over my head. But I didn't care. It really didn't make any difference.

When we got to the police car, Masters and Caruso

pushed me into the backseat, with both of them getting in alongside me.

Then the driver turned on the red light and siren and we headed downtown to police headquarters.

Caruso never said anything to me, and I didn't speak to him. We just sat there in silence for the entire ride. Masters was nicer, asking me several times if I was all right and if there was anything I needed. I'd known him for a long time, and I think he was kind of embarrassed by the whole situation. I appreciated his concern and compassion. My opinion of him went up considerably. I don't want to tell you what I was thinking about Detective Mitch Caruso.

They kept me in a holding cell until my lawyer arrived.

It was the middle of the night, so it took the *Blade* a while to track one down. I spoke to Barlow first, then to Vicki herself at home. Both were totally shocked by what had happened.

One of the cops I knew brought me a cup of coffee and a turkey sandwich from an all-night deli next door. I drank some of the coffee, but I didn't touch the sandwich. I tried to close my eyes, but I couldn't sleep either. My head hurt. My neck ached.

I finally managed to drift off for a little while, though it was a fitful nap. I woke up with a start, confused and disoriented. At first, I thought I was having another nightmare. Then I looked around and remembered where I was.

This was no dream. This was really happening.

There's an old saying: "You should be careful what you wish for, because it may come true."

A long time ago, I'd wished for a big story.

Now I was the story.

It was dawn—I could see the first rays of sunlight breaking through a window—when one of the cops came to see me again.

"Your lawyer's here," he said.

"Good."

"I thought you might be interested in this too."

He laid a newspaper down in front of me. It wasn't the *Blade*. It was the *Daily News*. My picture was on the cover. The headline said:

REPORTER QUIZZED
IN LOVERBOY SLAYINGS

Yep, I was definitely big news.

Back on page 1 again.

Just like I always wanted.

Thirty-nine

The lawyer's name was Kate Robbins.

I asked for her—instead of some of the more senior partners at the firm the *Blade* uses—because we'd worked together before and I liked her.

I'd been sued for libel by a high-profile lawyer who constantly advertised his services on television. I did a series of investigative articles questioning many of his claims of legal victories as untrue. The article was accurate, but he asserted that parts of it violated his privacy because he did not qualify as a public figure, like a politician or a movie star. Kate argued that he'd forfeited his right to privacy with the aggressive TV ad campaign. I won the case—and even got an award from the American Bar Association for exposing him as a corrupt lawyer.

"Lucy, I'm not a criminal lawyer," she said now as she sat down.

"I know that."

"Libel, plagiarism, copyright law—those are my specialties. Not murder."

"Okay."

"I think you need a criminal lawyer."

"I'll get one later."

"So why am I here?"

"Right now I really need a friend."

Kate sighed and opened up her briefcase. She took

out a yellow legal pad and a pen. The legal pad had writing on several pages. She'd been taking notes even before she saw me.

Kate was about forty, with long dark hair and piercing brown eyes. A strand of hair fell into her eyes now. She pushed it back. I imagine she didn't have much time to comb it and get dressed this morning. She lived on Long Island with her husband and two young children. Probably had to wake up the husband, make sure someone looked after the kids and then grab a train or cab into the city before she could even deal with my problems. Kate Robbins lived a normal life. Like most people. I wondered what that was like.

"I talked to the arresting officers before I came in here," she said. "This is what they've got:

"One, a scrapbook filled with clips from the case. Which doesn't mean anything, because you're a reporter and you keep clips of a lot of stories.

"Two, three Loverboy letters which were never found at the scene of any of the crimes. They say that's proof you were leaving the letters yourself. But we claim you were just trying to get into the killer's mind, or writing a book about the case, or some shit like that."

"Three, there's the gun. A Bulldog forty-four revolver. That's not a real problem if it doesn't match up with any of the murders, but big trouble if it does."

I felt light-headed. It was getting difficult to breathe. For a second, I thought I might faint. I couldn't believe that any of this was happening to me.

I was scared—really scared—for the first time in a long while.

"So where does that leave us?" I finally managed to ask her.

"Best-case scenario—they get you for tampering

with evidence or maybe even planting evidence because of the letters. They also nail you for possession of an unregistered gun. That works out to a prison term of anywhere from between four and seven years.

"Worst-case scenario—the gun matches the Loverboy killings and they've got you dead bang for murder. That's an automatic life sentence, with no possibility of parole for at least thirty years. You could even go to death row. There's a death penalty now in New York State."

I let my breath out slowly.

"I'm not wild about either option."

"Me either."

"Any other alternatives?"

"Yeah, we get all their evidence ruled inadmissible."

"How?"

"Well, they had a warrant to search your apartment. That seems legal enough. But why did they get the warrant? Did they have probable cause? That's the big question."

I told her about learning Mitch Caruso had been nosing around my bedroom.

"He probably found the stuff, told Masters, and they came back for it with a warrant," I said.

"Did you invite Caruso into your apartment?"

I thought about our conversation on the sidewalk in front of my building.

"Yeah, I guess so."

"But not to search it?"

"No, for a cup of coffee. We were on a date. Or so I thought anyway."

"Okay, that's good. We can argue that he obtained entry to the premises by misrepresenting himself. As far as you were concerned, he was not acting in his capacity as a police officer. He was a private citizen when he went through that door. It might work."

I nodded.

"Kate, can I ask you another question?"

"That's what they're paying me for."

"Aren't you going to ask me if I did it?"

She shrugged. "That's none of my business."

"Don't you want to know?"

"Look, if you want to discuss your guilt or innocence, that's up to you. But I cannot do anything about it. And I can't let it affect the way I defend your case. That's my obligation as a lawyer. Do you understand?"

"So even if I tell you I'm guilty, you can't tell anyone?"

"That's right."

"It's lawyer-client privilege?"

"Yes."

I thought about it for a long time before I decided. But I really had no choice. I never did.

"I want to talk about it," I said.

I told her everything. It was the first time I'd ever done that with anybody, and once I started, it just came pouring out. Kate didn't speak, she didn't move, she didn't take any notes. When I was finished, Kate reached over and put her hand on top of mine. She squeezed it softly.

"Is that all of it?" she asked.

"Everything."

"Jesus Christ!" she said.

That was when I began to cry. I hadn't cried since I was a little girl. I'm not a weeper. I didn't cry when Jack Reagan died. I didn't cry when my marriages broke up. I didn't cry when I was in rehab. But now it all came out like a tidal wave, years of it bottled up inside me so much that I thought I would never stop.

"Lucy, I think you should see somebody about this," Kate said.

"You mean a psychiatrist?"

"Yes."

"I already am."

"For how long?"

"Twelve years," I said.

Forty

" **I** need help," I remember telling Dr. Collett. "I'm a mess."

"You mean your drinking?" he said.

"My drinking. My relationships. My life."

"Do you like drinking?"

"Like it? Yes, I like it. Actually, I love it. When I'm drinking, I'm on top of the world. I'm funny. I'm perceptive. I'm sexy. I'm not worried about missing a big story or the state of my love life or any of the things that eat me up inside a lot of the time. When I'm drinking, I've got it all. I'm superwoman. My favorite place in the world, except maybe a newsroom, is a bar. Any time is good. But the best times are the quiet times. Late afternoon, before the evening crowd arrives. Or the early-morning hours, after most of them have gone home for the night. Sitting there with a vodka in my hand—well, that's just heaven for me. It's the answer to all my problems."

"I thought drinking was your problem," Dr. Collett said.

"Sometimes it's the answer too."

"Do you want to talk about your other problems?"

I went silent. How could I answer a question like that?

"Not right now," I finally replied. "Maybe another time."

*   *   *

That was my first session with Dr. Collett.

It happened right after I broke off my relationship with Jack Reagan, and I tried to deal with my drinking for the first time. I'd been going to see him ever since. Once a week, fifty-two times a year, for the past twelve years. I'm not sure it's done me much good. But I keep going because I don't know what else to do. People who are drowning don't complain about the lifeline someone has thrown to them. They just hold onto it for dear life and hope to be rescued.

Dr. Collett was my lifeline.

We talked about a great deal of things.

My marriages, for one. He was fascinated that I always seemed to be attracted to police officers.

"They call us cop-fuckers," I said. "Women who get turned on by men in blue."

"Is that what you are?"

"People say so."

"What do you think?"

I pondered that.

"I cover cops for a living. I'm around them all day and night. They're pretty much the only men I spend time with. So I hang out with them. I drink with them. Sometimes I date them. And sooner or later, I usually wind up marrying one of them."

Husband Number One was a real by-the-book, "I bleed police blue" detective. He came from a family of hero cops, and he was the exact opposite of Jack Reagan. Which I guess was why I married him. Husband Number Two was almost a carbon copy of Reagan, so that was doomed to failure. Husband Number Three was somewhere in between and lasted the longest—three years.

There were lots of things wrong in all of the marriages, but the one constant was my drinking. In the end, that was what made it impossible for anybody to live with me. I generally had the drinking under control at the beginning of the relationship, but then it got progressively worse.

Was it my drinking that made the marriages go bad?

Or was I drinking because the marriages were bad? Which comes first—the chicken or the egg?

Dr. Collett and I also talked about my career.

I told him how I agonized over every story. How I fretted that whatever I did wasn't good enough. How I tossed and turned at night, replaying every assignment. How I would wait by the newsstand for the delivery of the other papers—terrified they would have something I didn't. Dr. Collett said I was very driven and compulsive when it came to my newspaper career. He seemed to think that was significant.

He wanted to know about my childhood. So I told him about my parents, Joseph and Rose Shannon; growing up in Garfield Heights, Ohio; feeling alienated because I was still gawky in those formative teenage years and never seemed to fit in with the popular kids' crowd; and how I was compulsive about success even back then—always determined to get the best grades and join the most extracurricular activities to prove that I was better than anyone else.

"Did you have boyfriends?" Dr. Collett asked me.

"Not until my senior year."

"What happened in your senior year?"

I smiled. "I got pretty."

"Pretty?"

"One morning I looked in the mirror and I wasn't gawky anymore. I'd grown up. Guys that never even looked at me before suddenly were pestering me for dates."

"So things got better for you after that?"

"No."

"But you just said . . ."

"Not better. Different."

But despite all our hours together—all the conversations over the entire twelve years I'd been seeing him—Dr. Collett and I never talked about my real problem.

The reason I'd finally decided I needed to start seeing him.

The closest we came was on the day I brought up the blackouts.

They were getting worse. I'd started waking up in strange places without any memory of what had happened the night before. Once I drove twenty miles in my car and didn't remember a bit of the trip. Another time, I woke up alone in a hotel room without any idea how I'd gotten there. And then there was the morning I found a used condom in my bed. I'd had sex with someone the night before, but I didn't know who. For days afterward, I was afraid to meet the gaze of men in the office or on my police beat, wondering if it might be one of them.

I sometimes wondered what else I did during these blackouts.

Did I sit in my apartment and write letters from Loverboy to myself?

Did I leave them at murder scenes and then pretend to find them?

Or did I do things even worse than that?

I talked about it this one time with Dr. Collett.

"The thing I want to know," I told him, "is whether it's possible I might do something bad during one of these blackouts."

"Define 'bad.' "

"Unpleasant. Harmful." I paused. "Violent."

"You mean, hit someone with your car and then flee? Or have sex with your father or somebody with AIDS, or be a mass killer? Something like that?"

I nodded.

"The rule of thumb for behavior during blackouts is pretty simple," he said. "You don't do anything during them that you wouldn't do while you are conscious. If you're the type of person who likes to take their clothes off and dance naked on top of barroom tables, you might do the same thing during a blackout. Otherwise, your moral inhibitions will stop you. It's like hypnosis. A hypnotist can't make you do something you feel is morally wrong. Our moral compasses keep working even when the rest of the brain shuts down."

"So you're saying I would never do anything bad during a blackout?"

" 'Bad' is a relative term."

"Okay, really bad."

"Give me an example."

I pretended I was thinking about it.

"Let's take a totally extreme example," I said. "I couldn't murder anybody during a blackout. Right?"

"Not unless you ever murdered anybody while you were conscious." He smiled at me. "You haven't, have you?"

I smiled back. Then I changed the topic in a hurry.

That wasn't what I wanted to hear.

You see, I knew the answer to his question.

And that was my real problem.

Forty-one

A hearing was set for later that morning.

I wasn't sure what to expect. That's pretty funny, actually. I mean, I was a goddamned criminal-justice reporter. I'd covered a million court appearances like this. I could recite the routine from memory.

But this wasn't just another case or another story. This was me. This was real life. So I sat there in the courtroom with Kate holding onto my arm for support as I waited nervously for my fate to be decided, the way thousands of others before me had sat and waited.

"How are you doing?" Kate asked.

"I've been better."

"Just remember, you don't say anything except for two words. What are they?"

" 'Not guilty.' "

"Say them again."

" 'Not guilty.' "

She leaned closer to me and spoke right into my ear.

"Now, if the judge asks you any other question, you let me handle it. If the prosecution says anything, you let me handle it. If you've got to go to the bathroom, you tell me and I'll handle it. If you see a fire break out in the courtroom, don't say anything. Just tell me and . . ."

"You'll handle it."

"I'll yell 'Friggin' fire,' " she said.

I smiled.

"Now, do you have it all straight?"

"I think so."

The courtroom was packed, mostly with reporters and TV crews. Barlow and Janet were there in the *Blade* section. So was Victoria Crawford, which was a surprise. And Norm Malloy. I was a real piece of *Blade* history for him now—the first reporter ever to be arrested as a serial-killer suspect.

No question about it, I was definitely a media event. I thought about how strange it was to be sitting at the defense table instead of back in the press section. One thing was for sure—if I ever covered another court hearing, I'd never see it the same way again. *If.*

My arraignment was before Judge Russell Fuchs. I knew Judge Fuchs. I'd been to a few political dinners with him, and I think we even danced together at one of them. Of course, he was pretty drunk, and so was I.

Not that any of that mattered, though. He'd had acquaintances and even celebrities pass through his courtroom before. A few years ago, he sentenced a former chief judge to prison for extortion. There was also a city councilman brought up on corruption charges, I believe. So he wasn't likely to get too rattled by a reporter whom he maybe danced with once a long time ago.

"What happens when this is over?" I asked Kate.

"We ask for bail," she said.

"Will I get it?"

"Not if they charge you with murder."

"Do you think they will?"

"I don't know. This whole case is screwy. I'm not sure they know exactly what they have, or why they've got it. Maybe we can use that to our advantage."

"What do you mean?"

"Just wait." She grabbed my arm again. "Okay, here we go."

The bailiff stood up.

"Criminal Case Eighteen-Nine-oh-six," he called out. "The people of New York versus Lucy Shannon."

I got up and walked toward the judge. Kate was right behind me.

The prosecuting attorney was named Garrity. He was about thirty-five, with an expensive pinstriped suit and a great haircut. He looked like a young hotshot on the way up. This was his lucky day. A high-profile event to cut his teeth on. He must be really happy, I thought.

Only he didn't look happy. He looked confused. He seemed to be having an argument at the prosecution table with somebody from his office. I could hear raised voices, but I couldn't make out what they were saying.

"Anytime you're ready, Mr. Garrity," Judge Fuchs said.

He didn't answer right away.

"Mr. Garrity?"

"Sorry, your Honor."

I glanced behind him. Masters and Caruso were there. Masters was reading something out of a notebook. I wondered if he'd be called to testify against me today. Caruso caught my glance and smiled. A sad smile. I looked away.

Judge Fuchs gazed down at me. If he recognized me, he didn't show it.

"Miss Shannon, you have been charged with possession of an unregistered weapon, filing a false police complaint and obstruction of a criminal investigation. There are also potentially more serious

charges pending against you, depending on the outcome of ballistics tests involving the weapon. How
do you plead?"

I looked over at Kate. She nodded.

"Not guilty," I said in a loud voice.

Fuchs nodded. This was all pro forma stuff.

"Is there a bail request?"

"We make a motion that the defendant be freed
immediately on her own recognizance," Kate said.
"Failing that, we request that bail be set at a reasonable amount—taking into account Miss Shannon's
reputation as a respected journalist and responsible
citizen with no previous criminal record."

Fuchs turned to Garrity. "Counselor?"

But Kate wasn't finished.

"But before we even talk about bail, I move that all
the charges against my client be dropped," she said.

Fuchs rolled his eyes. "C'mon, Miss Robbins. You
know the purpose of this hearing is to accept a plea
and decide on bail. You'll have a chance to argue
your client's case at a later date."

"There are unusual circumstances in this case," she
said, "that I feel need to be addressed right now."

"What unusual circumstances?"

"The police had no reason to go into my client's
apartment. They did so only because Miss Shannon
was out on a date with the arresting officer. He later
took out his personal animosity toward her by—"

Fuchs slammed his gavel down. "Miss Robbins,
that's enough!"

"He couldn't screw her in bed, your Honor," Kate
finished, "so he decided to screw her any way he
could."

Fuchs shook his head and looked over at the prosecutor. "Mr. Garrity?"

Garrity didn't respond right away. Instead he
walked over to the prosecution table for another dis-
cussion. This one didn't seem to go any better than

the first. When he came back, he had a peculiar expression on his face.

There was something really strange going on here. I had no idea what it was.

"Your Honor," Garrity said, "we agree to withdraw the charges against Miss Shannon."

There was an audible gasp from the crowd in the courtroom.

The judge was as surprised as anyone.

"You're dropping the case?" Fuchs asked.

"Yes."

"Let me get this straight. The State of New York spent a good deal of time and taxpayers' money to get a warrant—which may or may not have been legal—to search this woman's apartment. In it you found a collection of evidence allegedly linked to a mass-murder case. Then, after arresting Miss Shannon and holding her overnight and getting us all in this courtroom to deal with whatever it is you think you've got, you say: 'Whoops—never mind!'"

Garrity's face turned bright red. This case wasn't going to give his career a boost after all.

"That's right, your Honor."

"Why?"

"I can't say at this time."

Judge Fuchs impatiently slammed his gavel down again.

"All right, case dismissed," he said. "All charges against the defendant are dropped."

He looked at me. "Miss Shannon, the court officers will return any of your belongings, and you are free to go." Then he turned to the bailiff. "Next case."

There was bedlam in the courtroom.

The reporters were shouting out questions and trying to get to talk to Garrity or to me and Kate. She pulled me through a side entrance, then out into the hall and toward a service elevator. We just made it out of there. A pack of reporters descended on us as the elevator doors were closing.

I thought maybe Kate had some answers, but she didn't. She was as confused as everybody else.

"What the hell just happened in there?" she said.

Forty-two

Everybody cheered when I walked into the *Blade* newsroom.

I hadn't been exactly sure how the people there would react. It made me feel good. I didn't have anybody waiting for me at home. I really didn't have a family back in Ohio anymore. The newsroom was my only family.

For the first time in a long while, I remembered how good I used to feel when I walked into the place. I remembered the magic. The electricity. All the reasons that I wanted to be a newspaperwoman in the first place.

Maybe you can go home again.

Barlow came over to my desk.

"Congratulations," he said. "I think."

"Thanks."

"I've got a lot of questions, Lucy."

"I don't have many answers."

"Let's try."

We went through it all. I assured him that I hadn't been drinking the night of the attack in the alley—and hadn't made it up or imagined it.

"What about the vodka bottle in your apartment?" he asked.

"I keep it there as a reminder," I told him.

"A reminder of what?"

"How shitty I felt after the last time I drank."

I said the clippings were from my scrapbook. I said I'd written the letters—and even tried to make them sound like Loverboy—because I was thinking of writing a book about the case. That was what Kate had suggested as a possibility in court. It seemed as good an answer as any.

"And the gun?" he asked.

"I bought it a few years ago."

"Why?"

"For protection."

"Against who?"

I shrugged. "Burglars. Sex maniacs. Escaped mental patients. It seemed like a reasonable idea at the time."

"Where'd you get it?"

"From some cop."

"Do you remember his name?"

"No." I smiled sheepishly. "It was a long time ago."

"And the fact it happens to be the same kind of gun that Loverboy uses—that's just a coincidence?"

"Yeah."

There was a flaw to the story, of course.

A big flaw.

But no one—not the cops, Garrity the prosecutor or even Walter Barlow—had figured that out yet.

At least I didn't think so.

Because if they had, I'd have never walked out of that courtroom a free woman.

"We need to write a story on this," Barlow was saying. "And it has to be objective. We can't look like we're slanting anything just because you work here. Janet will do the piece. She'll talk to you first. Then she'll get the police side of it too. All right?"

"No problem," I said.

Janet.

Janet was doing my story.

Hey, don't get me wrong. I like Janet. Janet was probably my best friend at the paper. We sat next to each other, we swapped newspaper stories, we talked about each other's love lives. No doubt about it, Janet was one fine human being.

But this was supposed to be my story.

I went through it all again for her, just like I did with Barlow. She seemed embarrassed at having to interview me. I guess she was worried about offending me. Or maybe she was worried that I really was a murderer.

"What do you think happened in court this morning?" she asked when we were done.

"Some sort of technicality, I guess," I said. "Even my lawyer can't figure it out."

"That looked like a lot more than a technicality going on at the prosecution table. Those guys were seriously stressed out. Something blew up in their faces."

"Yeah, I need to find out what it was."

"You?"

"It's my story," I said defiantly.

"There are other stories, Lucy."

"Not for me there aren't."

A commotion broke out in the newsroom. Everyone was suddenly gathering around a television set in the center of the office. Barlow gestured for me to come over too. I looked at the screen. Ronald Mackell's face was on it. The owner of the *Blade*.

"You better listen to this." Barlow grunted.

Mackell was talking to reporters in the lobby of the Mackell Building on Park Avenue. That was the headquarters for the Mackell Corporation, a far-flung conglomerate of properties and businesses that stretched around the globe. The *Blade* was one of them.

". . . and so I was appalled and shocked," Mackell was saying, "to learn that one of my own employees was implicated in connection with this horrifying series of murders."

"The charges against Miss Shannon were dropped," one of the reporters told Mackell.

"Only because of some fast talking by a high-powered lawyer."

"But that was your lawyer," the reporter pointed out. "She worked for the *Blade*."

"I never authorized anyone to represent Shannon. I believe that the police department of New York City does not arrest people for no good reason. They obviously had clear and convincing evidence of wrongdoing. I fully support their actions. And I believe this was a travesty of justice that took place in court today."

Barlow shook his head. "Jeez, his buddy could have written that for him."

"Who's his buddy?"

"Ferraro."

I stared at him. "The police commissioner?"

"Sure."

"Ferraro and Mackell are friends?"

"They have lunch together, they play handball together, they belong to the same country club. I think Ferraro even vacationed this year at Mackell's house in the Hamptons. Hell, Mackell's one of the main people pushing Ferraro for mayor."

"Jesus Christ!" I said.

"What's wrong?"

"Thomas Ferraro just keeps turning up in the strangest places in this case."

Mackell was still talking:

"And so I have notified the editor of the *Blade* that Ms. Shannon's employment should be terminated immediately. There is no place for her in my organization. She is a disgrace to fine journalists everywhere."

I heard a gasp of surprise from behind me. It belonged to Vicki Crawford. She was standing there watching her husband's performance with the rest of us.

"You son of a bitch," she said out loud to the screen.

Then she looked at me.

"Get back to work," she said.

"I've just been fired."

"Not by me you haven't."

"But your husband—"

"My husband is a very important man. My husband is worth eight hundred million dollars."

She'd raised her voice now and was almost shouting.

"My husband also has a very young blond-bimbo mistress that he's screwing twice a week in a suite at the St. Regis Hotel. We'll be discussing all this in divorce court soon, and those are going to be the most expensive fucks in history for him. In the meantime, I'm still the editor of this newspaper. Now get busy. You've been working on this goddamned murder case for twelve years, and you still haven't gotten it right. Don't screw it up this time."

She strode off toward her office.

"Does that mean I'm still on the story?" I called out after her.

"You're still on the story."

Way to go, Vicki!

Forty-three

I needed some answers.

A lot of weird stuff had been happening to me over the past twenty-four hours.

I wanted to find out why.

I wasn't exactly sure how to do that, but I figured there was only one place to start.

Back at the alley in Sheridan Square where I'd been attacked.

My reasoning was pretty simple. I didn't know how to find the killer. I didn't know what was going on between the police and me. So I'd start in the alley. If I could prove that someone really had attacked me—and track down whoever did it—then maybe the rest of the pieces of the puzzle would fall into place.

Sheridan Square looked much different in the daylight than how it had looked at night.

The alley was still there, of course. But a construction crew was working on the sidewalk in front of it and a street peddler was selling his wares and lots of people were walking by. Looking at the place now, I thought it seemed unbelievable that someone had dragged me in there and tried to strangle me.

But it had happened.

I knew it had.

I entered the alley and started searching for clues.

Of course, the police had already been over it and found nothing. They certainly would have seen anything obvious. On the other hand, they probably hadn't done that thorough a job, especially if they didn't believe me. Besides, it had been dark, and Masters and Caruso hadn't had that much time before our confrontation at the station house. So all I had to do was look for something that wasn't so obvious.

I walked slowly up and down the alleyway, going over every square foot of it the best I could. It was maybe sixty feet long, with some trash heaped up along one wall and a pile of construction debris toward the front.

I didn't find anything.

When I was finished, I started from the beginning and did it again. I must have retraced my steps a total of ten times in all. The effort took me a couple of hours.

That's the only way I know how to do things. I cover stories the same way. I may not be the best reporter in the entire world, but no one is more diligent than I am. I don't give up. I just keep going until I find an answer.

The answer to the riddle of my attack turned out to be buried underneath some of the garbage. It was almost completely covered, probably because somebody had piled more garbage on top since I'd been there. That was why I had missed it at first.

It was tiny and white, maybe only an inch or so in length. And it probably wouldn't have meant anything to the police, even if they had found it. They'd never seen it before.

But I had.

And I knew where.

Michael Anson didn't look so pretty this time. Her face was bruised, she had a bandage on her forehead and one of her lips looked swollen.

"What do you want, Shannon?" she said when she saw me.

"Is that any way to talk to the woman you want to make the star of your movie?"

"Fuck you."

I guess the bloom had gone off our relationship.

"Problems in paradise?" I asked.

"Yeah, but my problems are none of your business."

"*Au contraire*," I said.

"What are you talking about?"

"I've got another problem for you."

I took out the white object I'd found and placed it down in front of her.

"Ever seen that before?"

She had, but she didn't want to tell me.

"It's an animal's tooth."

"So?"

"You and I both know someone who wears animal teeth around their neck, don't we, bunky?"

"Micki," she said grimly.

"Bingo."

Anson sighed. "Look, Micki came and told me how she'd attacked you. I couldn't believe it. I tell you—I was completely flabbergasted. No way I knew anything about it."

"Why did she do it?"

"She heard us talking the last time you were here. I said something about all the publicity for the Loverboy case helping the movie, and she jumped to conclusions. She did it for me. She thought she was helping by making it look like Loverboy came after you. Micki's not too bright, but she means well."

"How'd you get the bruises?" I asked.

She grimaced.

"Gionfriddo?" I asked.

She shook her head. "Like I said, Micki heard us talking. She was upset about what I said to you—

well, about wanting to get together. We had an argument. It got out of hand."

"I thought you said you could handle her."

"I was wrong."

I picked up the tooth and dropped it back inside my purse. I was going to need it. It was evidence.

"Where are you going with that?" Anson asked.

"To the police."

"Do you really think that's necessary?"

"Miss Anson, your pal Micki attacked me because she thought it would be good publicity for the movie. I know that doesn't make a lot of sense, but that's what she did. Okay, so maybe she thought murdering a few people—and making it look like Loverboy did it—would help the publicity for the movie too. Did you ever think about that?"

"Micki would never kill anybody."

"How can you be sure?"

"I know her. . . ."

"You were wrong about the beating," I said.

Then I went to find Mitch Caruso.

I had a lot to talk about with him.

Forty-four

Mitch Caruso was surprised to see me. But happy. I think.

"I was going to call you," he said.

"Why?" I asked. "Did you want to come over and search my bedroom again?"

"I'm really sorry about that. I was just doing my job."

"Don't worry, I'm just glad I found out you were looking for evidence. Otherwise, I would have figured you for some pervert sniffing through my underwear drawer."

I smiled at him.

"You seem to be taking this surprisingly well," he said.

"I'm trying to put the most cheerful spin on it that I can."

"Why?"

"Because I need your help."

"To do what?"

"Prove you guys were wrong about me."

I took the tooth out of my purse and laid it down in front of him.

"This fell off a necklace," I said.

"So?"

"The person wearing the necklace was the one who attacked me in the alley."

I told him about Micki and Michael Anson and the movie. How Anson was in big trouble with the mob if her movie wasn't a hit. How Micki decided she could help her lover if she created a lot of publicity for the movie. Maybe by attacking the reporter covering the story—and making it seem like Loverboy did it. Or maybe even by doing something worse.

"You actually think she might have committed these murders to help the Anson movie?" Caruso asked.

"It's possible," I said.

"Is she that crazy?"

"You thought I was that crazy, didn't you? That I was going around shooting people to help my fading newspaper career. Whose idea was that anyway? Yours? Masters's? Wait, don't tell me—it was your uncle's, wasn't it? My old friend Police Commissioner Tommy Ferraro."

Caruso grimaced.

"Look, you fit the profile," he said. "Then, when we found that stuff in your bedroom . . ."

"What profile?"

"Loverboy's. We had a group of top psychologists come up with a whole list of characteristics for the killer. Someone obsessed with the case. Someone mentally unstable. Potentially a substance or alcohol abuser . . ."

"And that reminded you of me."

"There have been similar cases. Remember you were telling me about another serial-killer case you'd read about, where the murders just stopped too; then years later, the newspapers started getting notes from the guy again. And it turned out they were written by one of the cops in the original investigation who became so caught up in it that he started to think he was the killer. Well, we figured maybe the same thing had happened to you."

"So that's why you asked me out?"

"I asked you out the day we found Barry Tischler and Theresa Anne Vinas. That was before any of the new notes. I really wanted to date you."

"Gee, that worked out conveniently, then, didn't it? You got a potential girlfriend and a prime suspect, all wrapped into one package. Neat."

Caruso shook his head. "It wasn't like that, Lucy."

"Why me?" I asked. "How the hell could I be Loverboy? I was eighteen goddamned years old and in high school back in Ohio when the first killings happened."

"We don't think it's the same guy," he said.

"A copycat?"

He nodded.

"That's what I've been saying all along. But no one agreed with me."

"They do now."

"Why?"

"I'm not sure."

"Why don't you tell people that?"

"They want to keep it a secret. They think it will help us catch the real killer if he thinks we're still looking for the first guy."

"Who they are now convinced is dead."

"Yes."

Interesting.

"Why were the charges against me dropped?" I asked.

"I'm not sure. I was surprised, too, when it happened."

"I'll bet your uncle—our esteemed Police Commissioner Ferraro—was pretty unhappy when he heard the news."

"Not exactly."

"What do you mean?"

"He was the one who told the prosecutor to back off on you."

Tommy Ferraro!

It was goddamned Tommy Ferraro who got me released from jail.

But why?

And what the hell was his involvement in all of this?

"Anything else?" I asked.

"Yes. The ballistics tests came back negative."

"On the gun you found in my apartment?"

He nodded. "It didn't match the bullets in any of the four bodies."

"Four."

"Right. Barry Tischler, Theresa Anne Vinas, Julie Blaumstein and Deborah Kaffee."

"You didn't check them with the original Loverboy killings."

"No."

"Why not?"

"Like I said, they told me they were convinced the original Loverboy was dead."

Which explained a lot.

"Look," I said, "I want to make a few things clear to you. I really was attacked in that alley. I have not had a drink in six months. I was not the original Loverboy. I did not commit these new murders in an alcoholic haze, or because I was obsessed with the case, or in a desperate effort to rescue my failing newspaper career. Do you believe me?"

"I want to."

"But you're still not a hundred percent sure, are you?"

He shrugged.

"What will it take to convince you?"

He thought about it for a second.

"How about we put you on the box?"

"A lie detector?"

"Yeah. It's not admissible as evidence, either way it comes out. But a bad test result isn't going to do you any good. I don't think your lawyer would want you to take it."

"If I pass, will you help me find this new Loverboy?"

"We'll both find him."

"Okay, let's do it," I said.

Forty-five

"Is your name Lucy Shannon?"

"Yes."

"Do you reside at One-fifty-five East Eighteenth Street in Manhattan?"

"Yes."

"Are you thirty-six years old?"

"Yes."

"Are you a newspaper reporter in New York City?"

"Yes."

"Are you employed by the *New York Blade?*"

"Yes."

"As a reporter at the *Blade*, have you ever been involved with the news coverage of a series of murders known as the Loverboy killings?"

"Yes."

"Have you written stories about them?"

"Yes."

"Did you ever knowingly fabricate any of the facts in those stories?"

"No."

I was hooked up to a lie detector at police headquarters. The guy asking the questions said them all in the same monotone voice. I guess this was part of the procedure.

I couldn't see the lie detector apparatus from

where I was sitting. But I remember the way it always looked in the movies. There was a roll of graph paper and a metal needle drawing a line of ink across it. Most of the time it was level. That meant the person on the machine was telling the truth. But every time there was a lie, the needle jumped violently across the graph.

I wondered if many of my answers would make the needle jump.

"Did you ever write a note purporting to be from Loverboy in order to advance your newspaper career?" he asked.

"No."

"Did you ever plant such a note at a murder scene?"

"No."

"Have you ever planted any evidence at a murder scene?"

"No."

"Are you Loverboy, Miss Shannon?"

I smiled. "No."

"Did you have any involvement with Loverboy in any of the killings?"

"No."

"Have you ever killed anyone?"

"No."

The test took about twenty minutes.

When it was over, I took an elevator downstairs and walked outside to wait. Caruso said he'd meet me there as soon as he got the test results.

It was a beautiful summer day, with the temperature in the seventies and a breeze blowing in off the water. There were lots of people out enjoying it— eating their lunches, sitting on park benches, or laughing and joking with friends. I sat down on one of the benches, outside police headquarters. Sometimes I wished I had a job like other people. Nine to five every day, a leisurely lunch, then straight home after work. I wouldn't have to worry about police searches or mass murderers or newspaper deadlines. I wouldn't have to tell any more lies. Maybe then I could be really happy. Maybe.

I felt a hand on my shoulder. It was Mitch Caruso.

"How'd I do?" I asked.

"Pretty good."

"I passed with flying colors?"

"You only missed one question."

A warning bell went off in my head. Uh-oh, I thought.

"Which one?"

" 'Have you ever killed anyone?' "

"My answer was no."

"That's right."

"And the machine says I lied?"

"The needle went right off the chart."

I looked at Caruso's face.

He was staring at me as if he suddenly realized he had no idea who I was or what I was really about. But that was all right. Sometimes I felt the same way about myself.

"Look on the bright side, Mitch," I said. "At least you know from the other questions that I'm not Loverboy, right?"

He didn't say anything.

"Lucky for you too. I mean, that probably would have put a real damper on our relationship. How could we ever date or sleep together or maybe get married someday? You'd never know when I might pull out my trusty forty-four and blow your brains out. That's no way to live—"

"Cut the crap, Lucy."

"Yep, you sure are one lucky guy."

"Who did you kill?"

I thought about the secret I'd been holding onto for so long. It was time to let it go.

"Joey Russo," I said softly.

"The Loverboy suspect from twelve years ago?"

"Yes."

"How?"

I made an imaginary pistol with my thumb and forefinger, and pretended to pull the trigger. "Boom-boom, right in the head."

"You did this?"

"Me and Jack Reagan."

"When?"

"On our final adventure together."

"Do you mean that night he called and told you to meet him at the bar?"

"Yeah. It was one hell of a last date."

"But you told me you didn't go."

"I lied."

It's funny about keeping a secret that big. I'd held onto it for twelve years, never breathing a word to friends, husbands or even the psychiatrist who was paid to pull stuff like that out of me. But now that I'd finally told one person, Kate Robbins, it didn't seem like that big a deal anymore. The second time around is easier, I guess. Just like they say about murder.

"Tell me everything," Caruso said.

"Okay."

And so I did.

Forty-six

Jack Reagan said he was going to play Russian roulette again.

Unless I agreed to meet him, he would put a gun to his head and pull the trigger. If it didn't go off, he would hang up and call back. Then—if I still said no—he would spin the chamber and try it again. He said he would keep doing it until I changed my mind or he was dead.

I thought he was bluffing.

The first time anyway. I told him to play his stupid games by himself and hung up. But by the second phone call, I decided he was serious. I heard the click of the gun on an empty chamber over the line. And I remembered the look on his face that night at Finnegan's.

So I went to him. I knew it was a terrible mistake. But I didn't know what else to do.

Maybe that's why I drank so much that night.

Once I got to the bar where Jack was, there was no stopping me. I really put it away. I still remember most of it only in bits and pieces. But I know that by the time we went to see Joey Russo, I was royally blitzed.

We drove to Russo's mother's apartment house in the West Forties, the same place I'd gone back to a few days ago.

I didn't go inside that first time, though.

I waited in the car while Jack went upstairs. He was gone for a long time. I was so drunk I fell asleep at some point. The next thing I remembered was Jack opening the door and shoving Joey Russo into the backseat.

Russo looked terrible. There was blood on his face and he didn't say anything. I guess he'd passed out.

"He resisted arrest," Jack explained.

"Jesus, Jack . . ."

"We got the right guy, though."

He took out a .44 and some Loverboy letters and showed them to me.

"I found these with him."

I read the letters. They were addressed to me. The prose, the jokes, everything about them was the same as the ones I'd been getting. They were from Loverboy, all right.

"Some of them are new ones," I said. "Not just copies of any we've seen before."

"He was probably saving these for his next victims."

"What about the gun?" I asked.

"A Bulldog forty-four. Loverboy's choice of weapon."

I looked at the unconscious figure lying in the backseat.

"What did Russo tell you?"

"He admitted it."

"He said he was Loverboy?"

"Damn right. He laughed about it too. Boasted that I'd never be able to stop him. Said I'd seized all this evidence illegally. That I'd violated his constitutional rights. He told me a lawyer would get him off, then sue me and the city for millions in damages. After that, he'd go back to killing again. And I couldn't do a damn thing about it."

Reagan shook his head. "What a sick fucking world."

He took out his gun and pointed it at Russo.

"I should blow this motherfucker away right now. Save the taxpayers a lot of money. Maybe save some innocent lives too."

I was really getting scared now. Even drunk, I knew this was bad.

"Stop it, Jack!"

"Why?"

"You've already screwed up the bust. Don't make it any worse."

"Shit. Are you worried about this slimeball's rights? Hell, I'll read him his rights."

He took the barrel of the gun and pressed it into Russo's mouth.

"You have the right to consult your attorney, asshole. You have the right to remain silent." Reagan laughed. "And you sure as hell seem to be doing that. You have—"

I got out of the car.

"Where are you going?" Reagan asked through the open window.

"To call the police."

"I *am* the police."

"I don't want to be involved in this, Jack."

There was a pay telephone on the corner. I started walking toward it.

I was halfway down the block when I heard a shot from inside the car. Then there were two more. I ran back and looked inside.

Jack Reagan was still holding the gun in Russo's mouth. What was left of it, anyway. Most of Russo's face had been blown away and there was blood all over the backseat.

"The kid was right, you know," Reagan said softly. "He would have walked. The evidence was dirty.

And he would have killed more people. This was the only way, Lucy."

I don't remember a whole lot of what happened after that. I know we drove around for what seemed like hours with Russo's body in the car. A couple of times we stopped because I was sick. I hung my head out the window and vomited, while Jack looked around for a place to hide Russo's body. Finally we wound up at an abandoned pier along the Hudson River. Jack weighted the body down with stones and then rolled it into the water.

By this time it was nearly dawn, so we went back to my place and crashed.

That was the last time I ever slept in the same bed with Jack. We sure as hell didn't do anything, though.

At one point Jack reached over and touched my shoulder. I pulled away. I didn't have any more illusions about us. I hated him now. I hated what he'd done. Worst of all, I hated me for being a part of it.

When I woke up in the morning, he was gone.

At first, I thought the whole thing was all just a bad dream. But then I found Russo's .44 and the letters he'd written.

Reagan had left them in my apartment.

"And that's what we found?" Caruso asked.

"Yes."

"Why didn't you ever throw it all away?"

"The thing is," I said slowly, "there were times when I thought that Reagan really had done the right thing."

I tried to put it into words as best I could.

"I mean, the Loverboy killings did stop after that night. We got the right guy. Joey Russo had done horrible things to other people, so this was truly justice. An eye for an eye. But then, whenever I started feeling that way, I took out Russo's stuff again. The

gun and the letters. And they made me remember
the night he died. And the way I'd felt when I saw
his bloody head inside that car. And I realized that
what Jack and I had done—well, it made us no better
than the Joey Russos of the world. In the end, neither
of us could live with that. Jack killed himself. I never
had the guts to do that. Not with a gun, anyway."

I started to cry again. Just like I did when I told
the story to Kate Robbins.

"Something in me died, too, that night we killed
Joey Russo," I said. "I know I didn't pull the trigger,
but I was there. I could have stopped it. I should
have stopped it. Maybe if I'd said something different to Jack. Maybe if I'd tried to take the gun away
from him. Maybe if I hadn't left him alone in the car
with Russo . . ."

I replayed in my head the events of the night that
had changed my life so irrevocably—just like I had
done so many times for the past twelve years.

"Jack was out of control. He was an explosion
waiting to happen. I knew that for sure when he
played Russian roulette at Finnegan's. I should have
demanded he get help. I should have gone to Ferraro
and told him about it. I should have done something.
But I didn't. I did nothing."

I shook my head.

"Except doing nothing is an act in itself, isn't it?
Inaction is a decision that has its own consequences.
In this case, it resulted in a man being murdered. A
terrible man. But it was still murder. No matter how
hard I tried to rationalize everything over the years,
I could never change that.

"But do you know what the worst thing was? It's
what I did after Joey Russo was dead. I didn't tell
the cops. I didn't tell my editors at the *Blade*. I didn't
tell anybody. Again, I did nothing. I kept it all bottled
up inside me, my own horrible secret from the world
that ate away at me bit by bit like a cancer.

"I thought I was saving my own life. That if people knew the truth, I'd lose everything that was important to me—my job, my reputation, maybe even my freedom. But I didn't really save my life at all. I lost it. All I did was create my own private prison.

"You see, I didn't like myself much anymore. Before Joey Russo, I always figured—deep down, no matter what happened—I was a pretty good person. But after that night I wasn't sure. And I didn't know how to live with that.

"And the thing I loved to do best—be a newspaper reporter—well, I couldn't do that the same way anymore either. A newspaper reporter is supposed to uncover the truth and tell the public about it. That's what I used to do. But now it was all a big lie. I mean, there I was uncovering other people's truths, while at the same time I was hiding the biggest secret of all for so many years.

"Everything I'd done in my whole life, everything I'd worked so hard to achieve—first back in high school in Ohio, then at the newspapers in New Jersey and finally during those heady, exuberant early days at the *Blade*—everything was meaningless because of the one thing I didn't do."

"Lucy," Mitch said softly, "I think the fact that you agonized with the guilt all these years means you really are a good person. A truly bad person wouldn't have cared so much about another person's death. Especially someone like Joey Russo. You do care. Passionately. It's too late to change the past, but you can still do something about the future. In the end, you're doing the right thing. You're telling the truth. You've punished yourself over Joey Russo for twelve years. That's enough. It's time now to forgive yourself and move on."

"Yeah, I've tried telling myself that, too, over the years," I said.

"Maybe it's the truth."

"It's a nice theory, but I'm still not sure it works."

"Why not?"

"Because, in the end, Joey Russo is still dead."

I tried to explain what it was like to Mitch.

"Sometimes, even now, I still think that I see Joey Russo," I said. "I'll be walking down the street and catch a glimpse of somebody that looks a bit like him. And for one fleeting instant, I imagine he's still alive. Or at least some sort of evil spirit of him is. Taunting me, torturing me, making sure that I'll never have a moment of peace because of what I did to him. But, of course, it's never really Joey Russo. The real Joey Russo is somewhere at the bottom of the Hudson River.

"Then there are the nightmares. I have a lot of them—they've gotten worse since I started covering the story again—but the dream I remember the most is the one with the electric chair. It's like a scene from an old prison movie. The prisoner is strapped into an electric chair with a black hood over his face, and the warden is standing nearby, ready to turn on the current. I'm watching it all like a spectator. But then suddenly I'm a part of it. I walk up to the prisoner in the electric chair—the one condemned to die—and pull off the hood. The ending is always the same. It's me I'm looking at in the chair."

I shook my head sadly.

"Every day of my life for the past twelve years, I've been expecting someone to find out about me. Waiting for the knock on the door when the police come for me. When they take me off in handcuffs and charge me with Joey Russo's murder and my nightmare comes true. Sometimes I even thought it would be a relief. But even that wasn't my biggest fear. Do you know what my biggest fear was, Mitch?"

"What?"

"That it would never end."

He nodded in understanding.

"I didn't want to live with all the guilt anymore," I told him. "But I didn't know how to live without it."

Mitch leaned over and took my hand. He squeezed it gently.

"And you never told anyone else about this during all that time?"

"No."

"Not any of your ex-husbands, not your parents, not even a close friend?"

I shook my head. "Nobody."

"Why not?"

"I guess I never knew anybody I trusted enough."

"Until now," he said.

I looked into his eyes. They were kind, gentle eyes. Just like him.

"Until now," I repeated.

He helped me to stand up.

"Let's go," he said.

"Where?"

He looked over at the police building. "Back inside."

"Am I under arrest again?"

"Someone wants to talk to you."

Forty-seven

It had been a long time since I'd been face-to-face with Thomas Ferraro.

I'd seen him at press conferences and on TV and even during a political dinner or two. But we never spoke. I sure as hell didn't want to talk to him, and he seemed to feel the same way. It was as if we both wanted to forget about the people we used to be back in the old days.

We'd both come a long way since then. Only we were moving in different directions.

Ferraro was an up-and-coming police lieutenant during the original Loverboy investigation, and I was a hotshot young reporter. Now he was the police commissioner. And me? Well, let's just say I wasn't a hotshot young reporter anymore.

Ferraro was sitting behind a big desk in his office, talking on the phone to a deputy commissioner about a future parade on Fifth Avenue. There were pictures of his wife and children in gold frames in front of him. Hanging on the wall were awards and plaques he'd won during his time on the force.

He hung up and looked across the desk at me.

"Long time no see, huh, Shannon?" he said.

"You've done really well for yourself," I told him, glancing at the awards.

"Thanks."

"Jack always said you were going to make commissioner someday."

"How about you?" Ferraro asked. "How's your life?"

"My life's shit."

"I'm sorry to hear that."

"That's okay, Tommy. You have enough ambition for both of us."

Ferraro shook his head sadly.

"Don't you ever get tired of it, Lucy?"

"Tired of what?"

"Being such a know-it-all."

"Hey, I don't know everything."

"You don't know anything," he said.

He and Caruso had talked before I came in. So he was already aware of everything I'd told Mitch about Joey Russo. I figured he must have been really surprised. Now I was waiting for the other shoe to drop.

But when it finally did, it turned out I was the one who was surprised.

"Can we talk off the record?" he said. "Just you and me."

"Why?"

"Because I don't ever want to read any of what I'm about to tell you in the newspaper."

"What's in it for me?"

"We've both got a lot to lose here, Shannon."

I wasn't sure what he was talking about, but I had a feeling he was right.

"Okay. Off the record."

"I don't even want you talking to Mitch about what I'm going to tell you. Is that clear?"

"Okay."

"I've got your word on that?"

"Yes."

Ferraro took a deep breath.

"I knew about it," he said.

"You knew about Joey Russo?"

"Yeah."

"How long?"

"I figured it out about six months later. When they started to disband the task force."

I couldn't believe this. "How?"

"I kept wondering why Loverboy had stopped killing. The only explanation was, he was dead. But how? I started going back over everything again and that led me to Russo's mother. She told me about the man who came to the door that last night. 'I've got to go with the man,' Russo had told her. I thought about that for a long time, and then it dawned on me. 'The man' is street lingo for someone in authority. Like a cop."

"Jack Reagan."

"I went back with a picture of Reagan and showed it to her. She definitely ID'd him as the one her son had left with. So I confronted Reagan with what I knew. I even said we'd found Russo's body with bullet wounds from his gun. It wasn't true, but he didn't know that. I told him we were going to bring him up on a whole slew of charges, so he better come clean. He confessed everything. Not long after that, he killed himself."

I swallowed hard. "I always thought Jack killed himself over me."

"Maybe that was part of it too."

"How come none of this ever came out before?"

There was a pained expression on Ferraro's face.

And all of a sudden I realized I was wrong about him.

He wasn't out to get me at all. He didn't want me to go to jail. He just wanted the Loverboy case to go away.

Ferraro hated dragging up the past as much as I did. We both had plenty of secrets to hide. The difference was, he was running for mayor. The stakes for him were much higher.

And now here I was again, sitting in his office, telling him about a murder he didn't want to hear about.

"That's why you pushed to get the charges against me dropped so quickly, isn't it?" I said.

He nodded.

"Because if my story came out, then yours might too."

"Jack Reagan was my partner on the Loverboy task force. We were supposed to be working hand in hand. If people find out he murdered Loverboy—and that I knew about it, but did nothing—I will not be elected mayor. I won't be police commissioner anymore. I don't want that to happen."

"You could have gone to Internal Affairs twelve years ago with what you had," I said. "Why didn't you?"

"I would have been committing career suicide. You know all about the police code of silence. Cops don't like cops who squeal on other cops."

"Yeah, the Serpicos of the world don't become commissioner, do they?"

"There are lots of other people out there besides cops who probably would say Jack Reagan did the right thing. Reagan meted out old-fashioned justice. An eye for an eye. No lawyers. No appeals. No mercy. And the killings stopped as soon as Russo was dead. Hard to argue with that kind of logic, isn't it? The thing we all have to decide is how far we're willing to go to maintain law and order in our society. Are we ever justified in breaking the law to maintain the law? If we fight monsters like a monster, do we not become monsters ourselves?"

"That's pretty philosophical stuff for a cop," I said.

"I've had a lot of time to think about it."

"And worry about it messing up your political future."

He didn't say anything.

"So what do we do now?" I asked.

"Well, we never had Russo's gun. Now we do, so we'll run a ballistics check on it with the earlier murders. But I know how it's going to come out. They'll be a match. Which means Russo was Loverboy. Loverboy is dead. And someone else is doing all these latest killings."

"Who?"

"I don't know."

Damn.

I didn't have many suspects left.

Ferraro was out of the picture now—he had plenty of secrets, but they were mostly like mine.

Russo was long dead.

There was still Micki, of course. Sooner or later, the cops would track her down. But I didn't really think she'd turn out to be the murderer. Or Michael Anson either.

"We've got to forget about the old Loverboy," Ferraro said. "This is somebody new. This is happening now."

"There still has to be some sort of connection," I insisted.

"Like what?"

"I'm not sure."

He shook his head. "I don't even know where to start looking."

I did.

Back at the beginning.

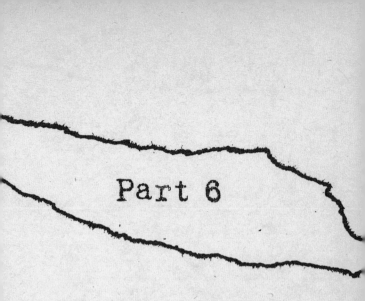

Part 6

THE LONG GOOD-BYE

Forty-eight

The same doorman was on duty at Emily Tischler's apartment house.

He was wearing the same get-up as before too. Black doorman jacket and pants. White braids hanging from the shoulders. White gloves. And a white hat with a black peak.

The doorman said Mrs. Tischler wasn't seeing anybody. He said she was still in mourning for her husband. He said he didn't think it was right to intrude on her grief by telling her I was there. He said he was sure I understood.

I didn't understand.

I wanted some answers.

"Does that help you pick up girls?" I asked him.

"What are you talking about?"

"Women just love a guy in uniform," I told him.

"Fuck you," he said.

I smiled. Now we were getting down to it.

It was childish to pick a fight with him. I knew that. But it made me feel better.

"Tell Mrs. Tischler I'm going up to see her," I said. "Tell her I have some questions to ask about her husband's murder. Tell her if she doesn't feel like answering them for me, I'll bring the police with me next time. Tell her that, will you?"

A few minutes later, Emily Tischler opened the door for me.

She had on a simple black dress and her eyes were red, as if she'd been crying a lot. The perfect widow. I wondered if the grief was for real or if it was just a look she'd gotten out of a catalog, like the *Town & Country* outfit she'd worn last time, or the modern furniture in the apartment.

"I know you mean well, Miss Shannon," she said, "but I'm really not ready for visitors right now."

"I'm not a visitor."

"Why are you here?"

"I want to find your husband's killer."

We went inside and sat in the same seats as last time.

"It wasn't Loverboy who murdered your husband, Mrs. Tischler," I said.

"But the police told me they thought it was."

"The police were wrong."

"Who else would want to kill him?"

"Maybe you."

She was shocked.

"I loved Barry. He was a wonderful man."

"Barry was a shit."

It was like I had slapped her across the face. Her lip began to tremble and her eyes teared up.

"Your husband liked young girls," I said. "You knew that. So maybe you followed Barry to the bar, tracked him and the Vinas girl to their parking spot and then—pow, pow, pow!"

It could have happened that way.

Then, because she realized she would be an obvious suspect, Emily Tischler went out and committed two unrelated murders to throw us all off the track by making it look like Loverboy did it. A sly one, that Emily Tischler. I had her now, though. She was going to confess to me, and then . . .

But even as I thought this, I realized how ludicrous it was.

"Do you really think I could do something like that?" she asked.

"No." I sighed. "Probably not."

She relaxed a bit.

"Look, do you have ideas about anyone else who might have wanted your husband dead, Mrs. Tischler?" I asked.

She thought about it for a second.

"Maybe a business associate?" she suggested.

"I don't think so."

"Why not?"

"This was too emotional a killing."

"What about about one of the other . . . ?"

She hesitated. It was difficult for her to say.

"The other women in Barry's life," she finally managed.

"Possibly."

I could go through Barry's little black book. Talk to all the women listed in there. Maybe one of them knew something. Maybe one of them did it. Maybe that was where the answers were.

Maybe.

But I still had a feeling I was missing something important.

"How about Barry's family?" I asked.

"What about them?"

"Any skeletons there?"

"Barry's father is head of Tischler's Department Store. He's very wealthy. Barry always got everything he wanted. He was certainly born with a silver spoon in his mouth."

"And your family?"

"My parents run a small drugstore in the Bronx— Carpenter's Pharmacy."

"So you weren't born with a silver spoon in your mouth?"

She smiled.

"Actually, I'm adopted."

"Really."

I found that interesting. Not because of anything to do with the case, but because I'd done a series about adoptions for the *Blade* a while back. One thing I learned was how many adopted children become obsessed in later years with finding their birth parents. When they did, it often worked out badly. I told that to Emily Tischler.

"Did you ever try to contact your real parents?" I asked.

"No."

"Why not?"

"My mother died when I was very young. That made my father put me up for adoption. I don't remember very much about them."

"But aren't you curious?"

"The Carpenters are really the only parents I ever had," she said.

She shook her head sadly.

"I just realized something. I started out life as Emily Malandro, became Emily Carpenter and then Emily Tischler. Three name changes already. Not bad, huh? Of course, now that I'm a widow, I'll have to decide which name to use again."

I wasn't sure what else to say, so I thanked her for her time, wished her well and said I'd get back to her if I found out anything about her husband's death.

Maybe I'd have better luck with the families of the other three victims.

Forty-nine

I tracked down Julie Blaumstein's parents by using a nationwide phone directory we have at the *Blade*.

You just stick a CD-ROM disc into a computer, punch in the name and area you're looking for, and the program gives you a list of possible matches. Then you can narrow it down even further with more specifics. Victor and Helen Blaumstein lived in Silver Lake, Wisconsin. No problem at all.

After that, though, came the hard part.

"Mrs. Blaumstein, my name is Lucy Shannon and I'm a reporter with the *New York Blade*," I said. "I'd like to talk to you about your daughter—"

She hung up.

I called right back. This is a point of professional pride with me. How many broken connections I can handle and still come away with a story. I once knew a reporter who made it up to fourteen. My personal high is nine. Of course, sometimes the person on the other end takes the receiver off the hook. And eventually you reach the point of diminishing returns, where they get so mad at you they wouldn't give you the story if you were the last reporter on earth.

Helen Blaumstein talked to me after the fourth time I called.

"Please stop calling," she begged. She was crying. "My daughter is dead. Someone did horrible, unspeakable things to her. My little baby. And now you want to sensationalize it so you can sell newspapers."

"I'm not sensationalizing anything," I said.

"Then what do you want?"

"I'm trying to catch the person who did it."

That was the right thing to say.

"What's your name again?" she asked.

"Lucy Shannon."

"I read about you in *People*. You're the one who's been covering the case for so long."

"It looks now like your daughter's death is not directly related to the earlier murders. So I'm trying to find something about Julie's life that might help me. A reason the killer did what he did to her and the other victims."

"Are you making much progress so far?"

"Absolutely."

Actually, I didn't have a clue.

"Well, I'll do anything I can to help, Miss Shannon."

She told me all about her daughter. How Julie got the job at the public relations firm. Her move into the new apartment. Even her trying to meet someone through the dating service because she said she was lonely in the big city.

"Julie was always very popular," Mrs. Blaumstein told me. "She never had any trouble meeting boys here. I warned her not to do this dating service. I said it sounded dangerous. But she told me I was just old-fashioned. She said she'd be fine—and that I was wrong to worry."

Mrs. Blaumstein started to cry again. "It's terrible to be right about something like that."

I checked out everything she told me. Julie's boss said she had done her work quietly and never caused any trouble. The dating service said it never monitored any of the on-line meetings—it was strictly one on one in cyberspace. The super of her building had never noticed anyone going in or out of Julie's apartment.

I took notes on everything. By the time I was finished, my notebook was nearly full.

But none of it meant anything.

The next victim, Deborah Kaffee, had a boyfriend named Brad Weber, who worked as a bartender at a Queens restaurant not far from the neighborhood where she lived.

I went out there to see him.

"The police asked me all these same questions after Debbie was murdered," he told me.

"I'm sure they did."

"So what are you doing here?"

"They could have missed something."

"And you're going to figure it out, even if they didn't?"

"Maybe."

Weber shook his head disgustedly. It was early afternoon and there was only a handful of people in the bar. An old guy down at the end. A middle-aged woman by herself at a table. Two young guys drinking beer by the jukebox. And me. I was nursing a diet soda.

"The least you can do, if you're going to tie up my time with this, is have a real drink," Weber said. "You want a glass of wine or something?"

"No, thanks," I said.

"What's the matter—you don't drink?"

"I did."

"So what happened?"

"I stopped."

"An alkie, huh? I should have figured."

"Why?"

"You've got the look."

"What look is that?"

"Like you want a drink."

He laughed at his own joke.

"I can see you're an astute observer of human behavior," I said. I looked around the deserted bar. "I guess that's why you've made such a success out of your own life."

Weber just grunted and walked down the bar to see if the old man wanted another drink. He did. Weber poured it for him, then came back to me.

"Where were you on the night your girlfriend was murdered?" I asked.

"In other words, do I have an alibi?"

"Never answer a question with a question. It sounds defensive."

"I was home watching television."

"Alone?"

"Yes."

"Weren't the police suspicious about that?"

"A little bit, maybe, at first. But it didn't matter once they linked Debbie's death to the previous murders."

He leaned across the bar and smiled at me. If my questions were bothering him, he didn't show it. He seemed more amused.

"You're missing the whole point, Shannon. The police say Debbie and the others were killed by the same person. Okay, let's say it wasn't Loverboy and it wasn't totally random. If there is a reason for it, that reason has to be in the first murder—not the last. It's not very likely our guy killed three people to set up the one with Debbie. It makes more sense that he got rid of the intended victim first, then did the others to cover up the real motive. The first murder, Shannon. That's where you should be looking."

He was right.

Barry Tischler and Theresa Anne Vinas.

I thought about that during the ride back to Manhattan.

I was going to have to go and talk to the Vinas girl's mother. And Emily Tischler again too. I still couldn't make up my mind about her. Was I missing something there? Was that wide-eyed, innocent routine all an act with Mrs. Tischler? Or Ms. Carpenter, or whatever the hell she was calling herself these days.

That was when I suddenly remembered something.

Emily Tischler had said, "I started out life as Emily Malandro, became Emily Carpenter and then Emily Tischler. Three name changes."

Malandro.

The name had sounded familiar to me when she said it, but I didn't think much about it.

I found a pay phone and dialed Emily Tischler's number.

"Do you know how your mother died?" I asked when she came on the line. "Or anything about your father?"

"No. I was very young when it all happened. Why? Is it important?"

"Emily," I said, "I think I know who killed your husband."

Fifty

" The original Loverboy is dead," I told Mitch Caruso. "So what are we looking for, then?"

"Someone with a different motive."

"Exactly. Now, if you had a daughter whose husband was cheating on her, how would you feel about it?"

Caruso thought about that.

"I suppose I might want to kill him."

We were in the squad room and I was leaning over Caruso's desk. I know I probably sounded crazy, but I wasn't. I'd finally figured it out.

"The Reverend Robert Fowler, who was Loverboy's first victim a long time ago, had a daughter with his girlfriend, Linda Malandro. Linda died in the shooting. Afterward, he gave up the little girl for adoption. Are you with me so far?"

He nodded.

"Barry Tischler's wife was adopted. Her real name is Malandro. She says her mother died when she was a little girl."

"It could be just a coincidence," Caruso insisted.

"I don't believe in coincidences."

"Neither do I," he said.

A little while later, I was with Caruso and Lieutenant Masters as the police converged on Fowler's church in Queens. Sirens wailed and flashing red lights lit up the evening sky. But the church was dark. There was no sign of Fowler.

"He's not in there," a cop said.

"Are you sure?" Masters asked.

"Yes, sir."

Another officer suddenly ran up. He was very excited.

"Lieutenant, I think you better see something."

"What?"

"It's in the basement."

We followed him downstairs. There were two other cops standing in front of an open door.

"It's a storage room," one of them said. "It looks like Fowler kept it locked. We had to break the door down."

Masters went in first, followed by me and Caruso.

"My God!" Caruso said as soon as he saw what was inside.

Clippings about Loverboy from over the years—the '70s, '80s and now—plastered the walls. They were all there. Linda Malandro. Danny Girabaldi. Kathleen DiLeonardo. Barry Tischler. Theresa Anne Vinas. Julie Blaumstein. Deborah Kaffee.

The killer's trademark greeting—"I Love You to Death"—was painted in huge letters on the walls over the gruesome display.

There was also a big picture of Fowler crouching in a marksman's stance and pointing a bulldog .44 revolver at the camera.

No one spoke at first.

We just stood there, transfixed by the bizarre scene and the picture of the Reverend Robert Fowler.

"Loverboy," I said softly.

Fifty-one

**MANHUNT ON FOR
'LOVERBOY' SUSPECT**

Exclusive
by Lucy Shannon

Police today were searching for a former victim of the infamous serial killer known as Loverboy—who they now believe has carried out a series of copycat murders.

He was identified as Robert Fowler, 44, minister of the Resurrection Baptist Church in Kew Gardens, Queens.

Fowler and his girlfriend, Linda Malandro, were the first victims of the original Loverboy, who opened fire on their car during the summer of 1978 at a secluded spot in upper Manhattan. Ms. Malandro died in the attack.

"Robert Fowler is now the prime suspect in the murders of Barry Tischler, Theresa Anne Vinas, Julie Blaumstein and Deborah Kaffee," said Lt. William Masters of the newly re-formed Loverboy task force.

"We believe he has been killing people himself—and trying to make it look like Loverboy—

as some sort of revenge for what happened to
him during the 1978 shooting.

"A warrant has been issued for his arrest on
four counts of murder."

The stunning announcement in the case came
after a series of bizarre developments over the
past few days, including the jailing and questioning of this reporter as a potential suspect.

The Blade has also learned that police now
believe the original Loverboy, who murdered 13
people and wounded 8 others between 1978 and
1984, is definitely dead. Sources within the department confirmed this, but did not say how
authorities were able to obtain the information.

Police converged last night on Fowler's
church, where they found a secret room filled
with newspaper clippings, pictures and other
materials about the Loverboy case.

"Fowler was clearly obsessed with Loverboy," Lt. Masters said.

"Something inside him snapped, and it
changed him from a Loverboy victim to a Loverboy clone. We won't know why until we
catch him."

Police acted after a Blade investigation revealed that Fowler is the father of Emily
Tischler, the widow of one of the new victims.
Barry Tischler was naked in a parked car with
teenager Theresa Anne Vinas at the time of
his death.

Cops suspect that Fowler's anger at Tischler
over his infidelity—combined with his obsession
about the Loverboy killings—is what set off the
new wave of terror. . . .

I sat in the *Blade* newsroom reading my story, feeling pretty good about myself for the first time in a
long while.

I'd cracked the case. Sure, I'd made a lot of mistakes along the way. And I could never undo what I'd done that terrible night with Jack Reagan twelve years ago. But in the end, everything was finally turning out all right. I'd confessed the secrets of my past to the police commissioner, who had some pretty heavy-duty secrets of his own. I'd figured out who the new Loverboy was. And I'd scooped the world with the story. Now all I had to do was wait until the police caught Fowler, and it would all be over.

Time to move on with the rest of my life.

"Best story ever?" Janet Wood said in a loud voice.

I looked over at her at the next desk. She was with Brian Tully and Karen Wolfe.

"Best since we've all worked here or best of all time?" Tully asked.

"All time."

"Son of Sam," he said.

"The preppie murderer," Karen suggested. "Or maybe the Central Park jogger?"

"I vote for Loverboy," Janet announced.

No one disagreed with her.

"There's never been a story like this one," she said to me. "Jesus, Lucy, you could win a Pulitzer for it. Even better, I think you deserve a place on the Wall of Fame at Headlines."

"Me?"

"Absolutely."

"Speech, speech!" Tully yelled.

I tried to think of something clever to say.

"I'll drink to that," I said finally.

They all stared at me.

"I'm just kidding."

Barlow came by a little later to congratulate me too.

"I still don't really understand why Fowler did it," he said. "I mean, the guy was one of Loverboy's victims, for chrissakes. How could he go out and cause the same kind of pain and anguish to other people as he suffered? It doesn't make sense."

"Who can understand what goes on in the mind of a mass murderer? Son of Sam. Dahmer. Bundy. Any of them. Fowler's entire life was turned upside down by what happened to him that night in 1978. It ate at him for years, and finally pushed him over the edge. They say cops sometimes identify with the criminal they're chasing. Or hostages with their kidnappers. Hell, the cops even thought that was what happened to me—that I'd become so obsessed with the case that maybe I was Loverboy. So why not one of the victims? Maybe it's a very thin line between sanity and insanity for all of us."

Barlow shook his head.

"It's a sick, crazy world we live in, Lucy."

I smiled. "If it wasn't, it would make filling up a newspaper every day a lot tougher, wouldn't it?"

I hung around for a while after that, even after nearly everyone else had gone home. I wanted to savor the moment. The feeling of triumph. It had been a long time. Too long.

I looked around the city room. There was only a handful of people there now. A few copyeditors. A night rewrite man on the city desk. Someone answering the phones. But I swear I could feel the magic of the place again. Just like I did that first day when I walked in there as a wide-eyed kid from Ohio.

Maybe my love affair with newspapers wasn't dead after all.

Not yet.

I heard somebody walk up behind me. At first I thought it was somebody else who wanted to congratulate me. Or maybe one of the copyeditors with a question about my story for the last editions.

But it wasn't.

It was Robert Fowler.

He was standing at my desk. He had a crazed look on his face, a copy of my front-page article in one hand and a Bulldog .44 revolver in the other. The gun was pointed right at me.

"You screwed it up, Shannon," Fowler said. "You really screwed it up."

Fifty-two

"The police are hunting everywhere for you," I told him.

I tried to keep my voice as calm as possible.

"That doesn't matter now," he said.

Then the Reverend Robert Fowler smiled. A scary smile.

A familiar old expression suddenly ran through my head: I'm locked inside a room with a madman.

"We're going to do an interview," Fowler said.

"What kind of an interview?"

"For your newspaper."

I still wasn't sure what he meant.

"I'm giving you the story, Shannon."

"Why?" I asked.

"For posterity."

"And after that?"

"We wait."

"For what?"

"The will of God."

The handful of other people still in the office realized something was wrong now. They were staring at Fowler and me.

"Are you all right, Lucy?" someone asked.

"Not exactly."

"What's going on over there?"

"This is the Reverend Robert Fowler."

"You mean the one who . . . ?"

"The Loverboy killer," I said.

Fowler kept the gun pointed at me. He paid no attention to any of them. It was like he and I were the only two people in the world at that moment.

"I'm calling the police," one of the guys on the copy desk said.

"That's a good plan," I told him.

Fowler said he wanted me to use a tape recorder. I kept a small microcassette in my purse. I dug it out now and set it up on my desk. I pressed the record button.

"Now what?" I asked.

"We do the interview," he said.

"You'll tell me everything?"

"I have nothing to lose anymore."

And that was just what we did.

An interview.

The interview of a lifetime.

"Did you kill Barry Tischler?" I asked him.

"Barry Tischler was a creep."

"So you murdered him?"

"Yes."

"And Theresa Anne Vinas?"

"She was in the car with him."

I took a deep breath.

"Did you do it because Tischler was cheating on his wife—your daughter, Emily?"

Fowler's face curled up in disgust. "Tischler was a rich, spoiled punk who used people up and threw them away."

"I know that," I said.

"Well, I wasn't going to let him do it with my daughter."

I shook my head.

"Emily's barely your daughter—she doesn't even know you exist."

"That's not true!"

"You haven't seen Emily since you gave her up for adoption eighteen years ago."

"She doesn't know about me, but I've followed everything that's happened to her. She's all I have left that matters to me in this world. All that's left of Linda. Of our love . . ."

I still didn't get what he was saying. It didn't make sense.

"But why kill the others?"

"They had to die."

"Why? Tischler was the one you wanted to kill. Why didn't you just stop with him and his teenage girlfriend?"

"I thought you'd understand," he said. "You of all people."

"What do you mean?"

"I wanted the publicity."

He leaned closer to me now. The gun was only inches away.

"Eighteen years ago, a lunatic called Loverboy shot me and killed the woman I loved," Fowler said. "He was never caught or punished. The case was eventually closed, and people went on with their lives. Nobody cared about it for years. Nobody but me. I had no life to get on with. Loverboy took that away from me. Then one day they started doing a movie about it here. All of a sudden, people were writing stories about Loverboy and talking about him again. That gave me the idea. I knew what I had to do."

"Kill Barry Tischler and blame it on Loverboy," I said.

"Exactly."

"And you knew the media would make a big deal out of it again."

"That's what you do, isn't it? You sensationalize everything. Well, I wanted it sensationalized. I wanted people to start looking again for the guy who took away my Linda—he's gotten away with it all these years. And I wanted that bum Tischler dead. So I killed two birds with one stone."

"But you're a minister," I said. "A man of God. You're supposed to pray for people, not murder them."

"I tried prayer for a long time. It didn't work."

He gestured toward the gun in his hand. "This did."

"What about the other victims besides Tischler?" I asked.

"The Vinas girl was in the wrong place at the wrong time. And Julie Blaumstein . . . well, that was the will of God."

"How about Deborah Kaffee, the last one you killed? Was that God's will too?"

"I told you—I had to make it look like it was Loverboy."

"But you did that with the Blaumstein woman. Why kill again?"

"I had to make sure the cops thought . . ."

"I don't think that's it," I said.

"What are you talking about?"

"People say it's very difficult to kill for the first time," I told him. "But it gets easier after that. I think you found that out."

Fowler didn't say anything.

"You enjoyed murdering people, didn't you? It gave you a feeling of power. I bet you really got off on it, Reverend."

Then I started to laugh.

"But you did it all for nothing," I said. "I've got a breaking news flash for you. Loverboy died twelve years ago."

"How do you know that?"

"I know."

"But the police never found him. He disappeared. All the newspapers said that. The police . . ."

"We lied," I said.

"I don't believe you."

I picked up the copy of the *Blade* on my desk and pointed to the paragraph in my article which cited police sources as confirming Loverboy was dead.

"What—what happened to him?" Fowler asked.

"He was murdered."

"Who killed him?"

"I did."

He started to laugh. But he stopped as soon as he saw the expression on my face.

I guess there was something there that made him realize I wasn't kidding. For the first time in a long while, I was telling the truth. Loverboy was dead.

And, at that moment, the Reverend Robert Fowler suddenly realized that everything he'd been doing to avenge the death of his girlfriend eighteen years ago had been for nothing.

Suddenly I heard the click of a gun bolt being pulled back.

But not Fowler's.

"Drop the gun right now, or I'll shoot!" a voice said from behind me.

I turned around.

It was Mitch Caruso.

Fifty-three

It all happened in a matter of a few split seconds.

Caruso standing there with the gun. More police behind him. And then, before any of them could do anything to stop him, Robert Fowler grabbing me from behind, putting his arm around my neck and holding the gun to my head.

"No, you don't move!" he shouted at them.

No one did.

"Everyone stay back—or I'll kill her."

"Don't do it," Caruso said.

"I've got nothing to lose."

"Let's talk."

"About what?"

"Maybe we can work something out."

Fowler laughed. "I don't think so. I murdered four people. I know what I did. Now I just want to try to tell people why I did it."

I wasn't sure if Fowler meant to kill me or not. But I knew that getting the story out seemed very important to him. And I was the person who could do that. I decided it was my ace in the hole.

"Mitch, I don't think he wants to shoot me," I said.

I twisted my head around to look back at Fowler. "Isn't that true, Robert?"

He nodded. "She's right," he yelled to the cops.

"So what do you want?" Caruso asked.

"I want Shannon to write a story."

"What kind of story?"

"My story."

I've hung around a lot with cops who've been in hostage situations like this. They say there's always a critical moment at the beginning where a decision has to be made whether to go in with guns blazing or back off and play it cool. The upside to the blazing-guns scenario is it's over quickly. The downside is the person in the middle—the hostage—sometimes gets caught in the crossfire.

I didn't want that to happen to me.

"Let me do it, Mitch," I said.

"Are you crazy?"

"He's already given me the interview. I'll sit down at one of the computers and write it up."

"We're all supposed to just stand here and wait while you do this?"

"No," Fowler said. "We do it alone. Everybody else leaves the room. You wait outside. This only involves me and Shannon."

"And then what?" Caruso wanted to know.

"You print it in the *Blade*. When it comes off the press, you bring me a copy. I read it. If it says what I want, I'll let her go."

Caruso shook his head. "I don't like that deal."

"It's the only deal I'm offering."

"What if we say no?"

"Then I shoot her."

"Maybe we can talk about some other options."

"I'm all out of options."

In the end, the cops agreed to it. They really had no other choice. They backed out of the newsroom and into the hall outside. Now Fowler and I were alone. The cops couldn't get at him. But he couldn't get past them to escape either. It was a standoff, I guess.

I sat down at a computer and wrote the story. The

story of my life. Literally. Fowler watched me the whole time with the gun pointed at me. But I didn't think he was going to use it, not then anyway. No point in killing me right now. He wanted the story. After it was done, well . . . I wasn't sure about that.

The funny thing is, I wrote a terrific story. Adrenaline pumping through you does that in the newspaper business. Of course, that adrenaline usually comes from a deadline or an anxious editor looking over your shoulder. But a gun is an even more powerful incentive. My fingers flew over the keyboard, and I was finished in less than thirty minutes.

Then I pressed a button on the computer and sent the story to a file to be printed. Someone outside would retrieve it from there, then get it ready to put in the paper. They were going to have to do a complete replate. That meant stopping the presses to put a new plate on them with my story for page 1.

I smiled at the thought of it.

One way or another, I was going to go down as a legend in *Blade* history.

Meanwhile, Fowler and I waited.

"Is that really true what you said before about Loverboy being dead?" he asked.

"Yes."

"Who was he?"

"His name was Joey Russo. He was a real loser. A misfit of society."

"And the police know all about this?"

"The commissioner does."

"Why didn't they ever say anything?"

"There were . . . uh, extenuating circumstances."

"Tell me about them."

And so I did.

I'd told the story a lot in the past few days. To Kate Robbins. Mitch Caruso. Commissioner Ferraro. Now to the Reverend Robert Fowler. I was getting pretty good at it.

"So everything I did was for nothing," Fowler said when I was finished. "I wanted the police to do something about Loverboy. But they already had. A long time ago."

"That's right."

"I wish I'd known this before."

"Life works in strange ways."

He smiled sadly.

"I guess I should be grateful to you, Miss Shannon. You did it. You and your policeman friend. You did what I wanted to do."

"I'm still not sure we did the right thing."

"Of course you did. This Joey Russo was a sick, vicious killer. A man who brought misery to so many people. A monster. An animal. He murdered people. You murdered him. An eye for an eye. What could be fairer?"

There was a knock at the door. It was Mitch Caruso. The first papers were off the press. He brought a copy of it in and laid it down in front of us. He looked at me as he did so. I nodded to him that everything was all right. Then he took one more look at Fowler, who was still holding the gun on me, and walked back outside.

Fowler read the story on page 1. Then he turned to the jump on page 2. When he was finished, he started at the beginning and read it all over again. Finally he put the paper down.

"That's very good, Miss Shannon."

"I'm glad you like it."

"Thank you," he told me. "Thank you for everything."

I wasn't sure what was going to happen next.

"Does that mean you won't kill me?" I asked.

"I'm not going to hurt you."

He looked down at the gun in his hand.

"I've hurt too many people," Robert Fowler said softly.

Then he stood up from the chair he'd been sitting in across the desk from me. He walked toward a door in the back of the city room. It led to a photo studio and storage area. Neither of them had an exit.

"You can't go that way," I told him. "There's no way out."

He smiled at me. A sad smile.

"Tell me something I don't know," he said.

I guess it was always going to have to end this way for him ever since that terrible night when the shootings started back in 1978.

He had everything then. The woman he loved. His baby girl. His life. And Loverboy took it all away.

Oh, the doctors fixed him up physically afterward. But mentally he was never the same.

You know what I think? I think Robert Fowler thought he should have died eighteen years ago in that car with Linda Malandro.

That's what he couldn't live with.

So when he did what he did in the end . . . well, I think he was just sort of putting things in order.

I heard a loud gunshot.

I jumped up, ran through the door he'd gone through and found Fowler lying there. There was blood all over his face. He was dead. The .44 was still in his hand.

A few seconds later, the police burst in with their guns drawn.

And it was over.

Fifty-four

I was sitting in Victoria Crawford's office again.

The awards and pictures of her were still on the wall. So were the famous front pages from *Blade* history. But this time there was a new addition. It said, **"LOVERBOY'S LAST INTERVIEW—Copycat Killer Confesses, Then Shoots Self."** My byline was underneath the headline.

"You did a great job, Lucy," she told me.

"Thanks."

"You're a star again."

"Yeah, I got a call from an agent this morning who wants me to write a book about the case. He says he thinks it can be a best-seller. Maybe even a movie too."

"A movie?"

"Yeah, I was thinking about getting Michael Anson to direct it."

She smiled.

"So what do you really want to do now, Lucy?"

"I want to be a reporter."

She nodded. It was the answer she wanted to hear.

"Being a reporter is all I ever wanted to be in life. I used to be a really good one. Lately, well . . . I know I haven't always done as good a job for the paper as I'm capable of. But this story made me remember all over again how exciting it is to work for a newspaper. I feel like I did the first time I walked into the city room. I miss that feeling."

I had some other stuff I needed to say too.

"I realize you and I have had our differences in the past. Maybe a lot of that was my fault. Actually, I know it was. I was jealous of your fame, power and money.

"A long time ago, we used to be friends. I'd like to try that again. I don't mean like we have to go to the movies or shop at Bloomingdale's or throw parties together. Actually, we don't even have to really be friends. I just don't want to be enemies with you anymore.

"You saved my job. When your husband wanted to fire me, you stood up for me. I couldn't have done this story without you. I expect support like that from people who are my friends—like Janet and Walter. But when it comes from totally unexpected places—like you—well, it makes it even more special. Thank you, Vicki."

She shook her head. "I didn't do it just for you, Lucy."

"I know."

"I did it because I wanted the story. I thought you were my best chance to get it. It was a business decision, not a personal one."

"I take that as a compliment."

"And," she said slowly, "I suppose I also thought that maybe it was about time you deserved a break."

Victoria Crawford and I looked at each other across the desk.

"I also did it," she said, "because I wanted to stick it up my husband's ass and show him he can't tell me what to do anymore."

We were talking about Ronald Mackell now.

"How's that going?" I asked her.

"Ron's moved in with his girlfriend. She's young,

blond and has a body like Pamela Anderson, with an IQ to match."

"So you're getting a divorce?"

"Oh, yeah."

"I'm sorry."

"Don't be. I'm going to make the bastard pay through the nose. Little Miss Bimbo is going to be the most expensive fuck he ever had."

"What about the *Blade?*"

"He says he wants it."

"What do you say?"

"Over my dead body."

I smiled.

She glanced up at the front pages on the wall.

"Loverboy has pushed the sales of this paper to a new high. I'm the editor. I get credit for that. Any settlement is going to have to take that into consideration." She laughed. "Loverboy has been very good for both of us, hasn't he, Lucy?"

I suddenly remembered that at one point I'd even speculated that Vicki might be behind the murders— so she could use it to boost *Blade* circulation.

I'd thought it was crazy at the time.

Now it didn't seem quite so far-fetched.

Nothing seemed far-fetched anymore.

But, of course, it didn't matter now. Loverboy was dead.

"How about you?" Vicki asked. "What's going on in your love life?"

"I'm seeing somebody," I said.

"That homicide cop?"

"Yeah. Mitch Caruso."

"Have you slept with him yet?"

"No."

"When?"

"I'm working on it."

Fifty-five

Mitch Caruso was coming over to my house again.

And this time I was ready.

I was making him dinner. A real gourmet dinner. Chicken Kiev. I bought some boneless chicken breasts, cut and pounded them into rolls, then stuffed them with a mixture of butter, chives and tarragon. Then I added a touch of flour, beaten eggs and dry bread crumbs on the outside before I started cooking. For dessert, I made a crème brûlée—a rich French custard with lots of whipping cream and sugar. It took quite a while, but I didn't care. Mitch was going to see a whole new me tonight. She solves murders, and she cooks too. Lucy Shannon, the total package.

Afterward, I hoped this was the night Mitch and I would finally consummate our relationship.

I wanted Mitch to kiss me, to hold me and to whisper sweet words into my ear all night. It had been a long time since I'd felt like that about someone. But I'd opened myself up to him in a way I'd never done before with any other man. I'd broken free of all the fears and anxieties that had always stopped me from doing that in the past. Now it was time for me to finally be happy.

That was my plan, anyway.

But sometimes even the best-laid plans go awry.

Mitch showed up at my door a little after seven.

"Smell that home cooking?" I asked him.

"Very good."

"Just like Mom used to make."

"My mom wasn't actually that great a cook."

"So if it really sucks, we'll order takeout," I said.

He handed me a container of French roast coffee.

"I picked this up at a coffeehouse downstairs on Third Avenue," he said. "I wasn't sure what to bring. I mean, I figured a bottle of wine wasn't a good idea."

"Wine wouldn't have been a problem."

"But you . . ."

"I'm a big girl, Mitch. If you want, you can drink when you're with me."

He shrugged. "I don't like to drink alone. It's not much fun, is it?"

"Really? I used to love it."

I took the coffee into the kitchen and made some. When it was ready, I brought it out on a big tray with some cheese-and-cracker snacks.

Caruso was looking through some of the books on my bookshelf.

"You don't have a search warrant with you this time, do you?" I asked.

"I'm sorry. I was just curious about what you like to read. They say it tells a lot about a person."

My books were almost all true-life crime stuff and murder mysteries. I wondered what that said about me.

"No problem. You can search my bedroom again, too, after dinner if you want."

He didn't say anything.

"That's a joke." I smiled.

We sat down on the couch. As we sipped on the coffee and ate some of the cheese and crackers, I told him about the great meal we were going to have. I also told him about my conversation with Victoria

Crawford. And I even told him about the TV and book offers I was getting.

At some point, I realized I was doing most of the talking.

"Is there something wrong, Mitch?" I asked.

"I'm just a little preoccupied."

"Yeah, I've noticed."

"Sorry."

"What's the problem?"

"You, actually."

"Me?"

"Yeah. You and my uncle."

He put the coffee down on an end table next to the couch. The expression on his face was very serious.

"I talked to him today about you."

"The commissioner?"

"Yes. He told me about his part in Joey Russo. How he knew about it all along and did nothing. I never heard that until today."

I was surprised.

"Your uncle and I, we were supposed to have a deal," I said slowly. "I wasn't going to tell anything about him, and he was going to do the same for me."

"That's what he said."

"So why did he decide to tell you about it?"

"He didn't."

"But . . ."

"I already knew about you," Caruso said. "You told me. Remember?"

"Okay."

"And I figured out the rest myself."

"How?"

"Like I told you before, my uncle is as much of a by-the-book cop as you'll ever find. Once you confessed something like Joey Russo to him, he should have acted on it through the normal channels. But he didn't tell anybody. And he was the one who made sure all the charges against you got dropped.

He just wanted it all buried. There had to be a reason. He was trying to protect himself too."

"Very clever."

He shrugged. "It wasn't that hard. I'm a trained investigator, remember?"

"So what happens next? Do you arrest me as an accomplice for murder? Maybe your uncle, too, for withholding evidence. Is that your plan, Mitch?"

"That's not what I want."

"What do you want?"

"Some answers."

I stood up. I realized I was shaking now. I wasn't sure if it was because I was angry or afraid. Maybe a bit of both.

"Let it be, Mitch," I said. "It's finished. That's the way your uncle wants it. That's the way I want it too. It's not going to do anybody any good to start digging this stuff up again."

"A man was murdered, Lucy. And you've been carrying the guilt of that night around with you for twelve years. I thought you said you wanted to finally break free of that."

"Joey Russo killed thirteen people. If Russo didn't die when he did, there would probably have been a lot more innocent victims. Everything worked out for the best in the end."

"Is that you talking—or Jack Reagan?"

"Maybe Reagan was right."

"Reagan was a lunatic."

"He got rid of the real Loverboy, didn't he?"

Caruso shook his head sadly.

"So that's it, huh? Everything's tied up in a nice, neat package. We just forget about what happened to Russo that night and move on. My uncle gets elected mayor. You become a famous reporter again. Everybody's a winner—except Joey Russo. He's not famous. He's just dead."

"I can live with that," I said.

"Well, I can't."

He took out a file of papers from his pocket and laid them on the table.

"What's that?" I asked.

"The ballistics report," he said. "I got the results today."

"You mean on the gun Fowler used to kill himself?"

"That's part of it."

"Is it the same gun that was used on all four of the new victims—Tischler, Vinas, Blaumstein and Kaffee?"

"Yes."

"So what's the problem?"

"There's also a report on Russo's gun."

"The one you took out of my apartment?"

"Yeah. Everyone forgot about that in all the excitement. I mean, you and my uncle both had this secret little deal going, so he never pushed it. And those ballistics tests took a lot longer anyway, because some of the original case files were so old. But I finally got them. I guess I was simply curious. Policemen are that way sometimes. Just like reporters."

I still didn't get what it was he was telling me.

"Okay, so they matched too. The gun you found in my apartment was the same gun used to kill the first thirteen victims. I told you why it was there. Reagan took it from Russo, then gave it to me. I've just held onto it all these years. You knew that before. So what's the big deal?"

"They don't match."

"What?"

"The ballistics tests say it's not Loverboy's gun."

I guess I always knew deep down that I wasn't going to be able to walk away from it like that.

I'd spent twelve years of my life carrying around the guilt of what I'd done that night in the car with Jack Reagan and Joey Russo. Nothing was ever the same for me after that. It had consumed me. It had nearly destroyed me.

Now I was finally going to have to face it.

Oh, I knew there were all sorts of other possible explanations why the gun didn't match: Russo had two .44s; the ballistics report was wrong; the original-murder case files were old and confused.

But that wasn't it.

I knew what had really happened even before Mitch Caruso uttered the words:

"Joey Russo wasn't Loverboy," he said. "You killed the wrong guy, Lucy."

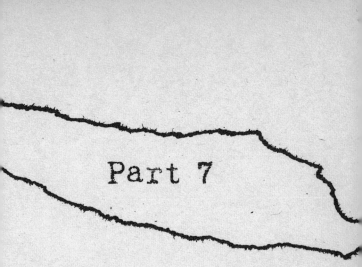

Part 7

I LOVE YOU TO DEATH

Fifty-six

I thought it was over, but it wasn't.

I'd been concentrating all along on the present, figuring that once I found the copycat Loverboy who killed Barry Tischler, Theresa Anne Vinas, Julie Blaumstein and Deborah Kaffee that would exorcise all my own demons from the past.

But I was wrong.

I still had to find the real Loverboy, the one who had murdered thirteen people more than a decade ago and changed my life in the process.

I didn't know how I was going to do that.

So I did the only thing I could think of—I went back to the beginning.

I talked to them all. The surviving victims like Danny Girabaldi and Kathleen DiLeonardo. The still grieving family members like Jack Corrigan. Some of them were nice. Most were polite. A few got impatient because of all my questions.

I didn't care.

I just kept going over everything with them, hoping to pull out a sliver of information that somehow might lead me to Loverboy.

By the time I was finished, I'd filled up several notebooks with information from the interviews. I spent hours poring over the stuff.

The most tantalizing of them all was Kathleen Di-

Leonardo, the Long Island woman shot in the shoulder. She'd been wounded the least seriously by Loverboy. She remembered the most about what had happened. And she'd even managed to catch a glimpse of him before he struck.

That last fact jumped out at me now from my notes as I talked to her again at her house on Long Island.

"You actually saw Loverboy?" I asked.

"Only for a second or two."

"What do you remember?"

"Nothing really."

She seemed uncomfortable talking about it.

"You know he was a man, right?"

"Yes."

"Big? Small? Medium?"

"Pretty big."

"Did he have light hair? Dark?"

"Kind of blond, I guess."

This was the first time I'd heard about any of this.

"Did you tell that to the police?"

"Of course."

"What did they say?"

"They were excited, just like you are now."

"Did they try to get you to identify a suspect?"

"Yes."

"What happened?"

"I never did."

Okay, but somewhere inside her head she had a description of Loverboy. Maybe she could even identify him. I wondered why the police had never put this in any of the reports on the case.

It seemed too good to be true.

And, as it turned out, it was.

I showed her a picture of Joey Russo first.

"Do you recognize the face?" I asked.

"Yes."

My heart skipped a beat.

"The police showed me the same picture a long time ago."

"But he wasn't Loverboy?"

"No."

Next I took out pictures of the two other prime suspects in the case back in the early eighties. David Gruber and Albert Slocum. Neither of them had blond hair or were very big. But you never know.

"Same thing," she said.

"The police showed their pictures to you twelve years ago, and you said neither one was the guy?"

"That's right."

I put the pictures away. I wasn't ready to give up yet, though.

"The police have got some pretty sophisticated methods of identification these days," I told her. "If you feed that to some of the crime-lab people, they could do a computer enhancement. Maybe we could come pretty close to the face you saw."

Kathleen DiLeonardo shook her head.

"Look, there's some stuff you probably ought to know about me. I didn't really get over the shooting as easily as I tell people. The truth is, it messed me up very badly."

She shivered slightly. Not because it was cold. The sun was shining brightly, and it was eighty degrees outside.

We were sitting on the porch of her house, which overlooked Long Island Sound. On the horizon you could see lots of beautiful homes and green rolling lawns and sailboats bobbing on the water.

It was a nice life.

But Kathleen DiLeonardo was a long way away right now. She was back at Queens College on the night Loverboy had tried to kill her.

"I went to therapy for a long time," she said. "I was afraid. I was so afraid.

"Every time I went out, I was convinced Loverboy

was going to come back and finish the job. I couldn't go to school. I couldn't go out at night. I couldn't even go to the store without practically having a goddamned nervous breakdown.

"I didn't trust anybody. I thought my teacher at school wanted to kill me. My landlord. Even my therapists.

"One time—right after the shooting—I became convinced that one of the cops talking to me was really Loverboy. I got so hysterical I tried to jump out a window of the station house. That's why the police never took my description seriously. Christ, I thought *everybody* was Loverboy."

She started to cry softly now.

"I still have nightmares about that night. Not as often. They're down to every few months or so now. I'm still scared. But I'm mad too. Mad at what he's taken from me.

"When I read your story about Robert Fowler . . . well, I understand how Fowler felt. I don't condone what he did. But, God help me, I understand. He tried to do something about his pain. He tried to make somebody pay for it.

"I wish I could make somebody pay for my pain too. I sometimes feel that I'd even kill somebody to do that. Just like Bobby Fowler. Do you understand what I'm saying, Miss Shannon?"

I understood, all right.

More than she realized.

Loverboy had changed all our lives—everyone he came in contact with along his bloody path. None of us had ever been able to go back to being the people we used to be before we met him.

Not Robert Fowler.

Not Kathleen DiLeonardo.

Not me either.

"Do you really think you can find out what happened to him?" she asked.

"Yes."
"The police never did."
"I will."
"Why?"
"I have to."

Fifty-seven

That night I went to see Mitch Caruso again.

He'd been busy too investigating the case. And he seemed to have made much more progress than I did.

"I've got good news and bad news," he said when I asked him about it in the squad room.

"That's the oldest joke in the world, Mitch."

"Which do you want first?"

"The bad."

"Okay, but you're gonna love the good stuff."

He told me first how he'd gone back and checked out every one of the early murders, then cross-indexed them against whatever he could find out about Joey Russo's movements during the same time period.

We could have done that ourselves twelve years ago, Jack Reagan and I. But we didn't. Jack decided to be Dirty Harry instead. So we stopped being cop and reporter that night and became a lynch mob.

Now it was too late for the answers about Joey Russo to do much good.

But I still wanted to know.

"Russo definitely didn't do three of the murders, and probably couldn't have committed at least two of the others," Mitch said. "The three definite noes have witnesses or documented proof that puts him somewhere else at the time of the crime.

"On the first one, the night Bobby Fowler and his girlfriend got it in upper Manhattan, Russo had just started a job as a busboy in a restaurant on West Fifty-seventh Street. He didn't last very long—he got fired a few days later. But he was there when the shooting happened, according to the manager's old records.

"The second one he's got an alibi for is a beaut. Russo picked up a street hooker near the Lincoln Tunnel, only it turned out to be a he instead of a she. Russo tried to get his money back, they got into a big fight and both got hauled in by a passing patrol car as part of a prostitution sweep. He spent the night in jail. It's all in our own records.

"The third one is good too. Russo was in the Army. He enlisted at one point and got sent to Fort Knox, Kentucky, for basic training. That didn't last much longer than any of his jobs. In fact, he got a dishonorable discharge a short time later. But he was at Fort Knox for morning roll call a few hours after one of the murders went down here. Fort Knox is six hundred and forty-two miles from New York City. I looked it up.

"On two of the others, we're pretty sure Russo had an alibi. But the evidence is a little more vague. Witnesses' memories fade over the years, records get lost, people die—that sort of thing.

"The bottom line is your guy Russo is innocent of at least three of the killings—and probably two more also."

I nodded. "Which means he probably didn't do any of them," I said.

"We always figured that it was the same person who did all thirteen."

"Me too."

Okay, so I'd helped kill an innocent man. I'd been

pretty sure of that ever since Caruso told me about the gun. But now there was no doubt.

What happened now?

Was I going to go to jail as an accomplice to murder?

And what about Commissioner Ferraro? He was guilty of withholding evidence in an outright murder case now, wasn't he?

Jesus, what a mess.

"What's the good news?" I asked finally.

"You didn't kill Joey Russo."

My head jerked up in surprise.

"What are you talking about?"

"You had nothing to do with it, Lucy."

"Hey, I know I didn't shoot him. But I was there. I could maybe have stopped Jack before he did it. Taken away his gun or—"

"Russo was already dead."

I stared at Mitch. I still didn't get it.

"I went to see Russo's mother again," he said. "I went through everything one more time with her. The man who came to the door to get her son. What he looked like. But I also asked something else—what time he came."

"I already know what time it was," I said impatiently. "Late. Between twelve and one."

"Do you know what Mrs. Russo said?"

"I really don't see the point of all this."

"She said it was seven-thirty."

"Well, she's wrong. She's an old lady."

"She's sure it was seven-thirty because *Wheel of Fortune* was starting. She always watches *Wheel of Fortune*. And it was just starting when Reagan knocked on the door."

"Is she sure it was Reagan?"

"She described him to me the same way you did."

He told me what Mrs. Russo had said about the way Reagan looked.

"Yeah, that was Jack," I said.

"Don't you see what this means, Lucy?"

"There's a missing five hours between when Reagan met me and said we were going to pick up Russo—and when he really did it."

"What does that tell you?"

"I—I'm not sure. . . ."

"Joey Russo was already dead."

I suddenly realized what he was saying.

"Reagan picked him up at seven-thirty. I figure he tried to make him talk, then shot him out of frustration. When he called you from the bar, he was trying to figure out what to do with the body. You said yourself Russo seemed in pretty bad shape when Reagan threw him into the car. The truth was, he was already dead. That's the only logical explanation. Your ex-lover—the fuckin' great Jack Reagan—set you up."

"Russo—Russo was dead?"

"There was nothing you could have done to save him."

"All these years . . ."

I started to cry.

"I've been living with this for so long. I thought I killed a man, Mitch. I thought I took another man's life. Do you have any idea what it feels like to carry around a guilty secret like that?"

"I—I can only imagine."

Mitch put his arms around me.

"You're free and clear now, Lucy. For the first time, you can just walk away from all this."

"Free and clear," I whispered.

"That's right. You can start over again. You've got the whole world in front of you. *We've* got the whole world in front of us."

I still couldn't quite believe what he was telling me.

"But I've wasted so much time," I said. "My whole

life these past twelve years. The failed marriages. My problems at the *Blade*. The way I've managed to self-destruct everything good that's ever happened to me by the age of thirty-six. All because of Loverboy. And now you're telling me I never killed anybody after all."

"I thought you'd be relieved to find that out."

"I am."

"But you're mad too."

"Yeah, I'm mad. I'm mad at Reagan, Russo—all of them. But mostly I'm mad at myself. How could I have been so stupid?"

"Your biggest mistake was keeping this bottled up inside you for so long," he said. "Pitting yourself against the world. Sometimes there are people in this world who are on your side. You need to remember that."

He hugged me tightly.

"Let it go," he whispered in my ear. "Just walk away."

Then he kissed me.

I kissed him back.

"It's time to get on with your life, Lucy."

Fifty-eight

I've always been a lot better at the professional stuff in my life than the personal.

I mean, even when I was drinking I could jump out of bed at five in the morning, run to the scene of a plane crash and file twenty-five inches of copy before any other reporter in town.

I was never intimidated by big stories, big names, big assignments or big interviews; they were what I lived for.

My trouble came whenever I tried to do the little things that everyone else in the world seemed to do so effortlessly.

Like find the right guy.

Or get married.

Or stay married to the same person for more than twelve seconds.

I didn't want to mess it up this time.

"I haven't done this in a long time," I told Mitch as we lay in bed, exploring each other's bodies in that awkward but exciting way two people do when they're together for the first time.

"Me either."

"Really? I figured you for a real ladies' man."

"I'm very picky."

He leaned over and kissed me.

"Are we going to make love now?" I asked.

"I certainly hope so."

And then we did.

Afterward, we lay in bed for a long time, talking about our lives. He wanted to know about my three ex-husbands.

"Were any of them like me?" he asked.

"No."

"How were they different?"

"Wow, this is like a police interrogation."

"Just the facts, ma'am."

"Okay, none of them did Jack Webb imitations." I smiled, snuggling closer to him.

"Did you love them?"

I shrugged. "Sort of."

"Sort of? That doesn't seem like the recipe for a happy marriage."

"I was lonely. I needed someone. They were there."

"You should have waited for the right guy."

"I did," I said, kissing him. "I just got married a few times along the way."

"How did they handle your drinking?" he asked.

"Badly. Most of the time they'd start out acting as if it didn't bother them. But after a while they'd try to use tough love on me. You know: 'Either you deal with your problem or I'm outta here'—that sort of stuff. It didn't matter."

"Is that what's going to happen with us?" Mitch asked.

"No," I said.

"Why not?"

"This is different."

"You mean I'm different from all those other guys?"

"*I'm* different," I told him.

I smiled.

"Don't you see?" I said. "I'm finally free of Joey Russo and Jack Reagan and everything bad that happened back then. I proved to myself I can be a real reporter again—the kind I used to be. And now I know that I can fall in love too." I kissed him gently on the lips. "I've got my life back, Mitch."

Later, while he slept, I thought about how different Mitch Caruso was from Jack Reagan and all the other men I'd ever been with.

For the first time, I could see being content and happy with someone—whether or not I kept working at the *Blade* or stayed on the police beat or ever touched another drop of alcohol.

I was ready to say good-bye to the old Lucy.

Lying there in the dark, listening to Mitch breathing softly next to me, I suddenly realized I didn't even care anymore about finding Loverboy.

Whatever had happened to the real Loverboy was a long time ago.

Like Mitch said, it was time to get on with my life.

I was thirty-six years old. Plenty of time yet to have a successful marriage, have kids, buy a house in the country and live happily ever after.

I reached over and hugged Mitch, burying my head in his chest as I thought again about how incredibly different it was being with him instead of with someone like Jack Reagan.

There was just no comparison.

Mitch was gentle, Reagan was violent.

Mitch was funny, Reagan was angry.

They didn't even look alike—Mitch had a medium-sized build with shaggy brown hair and a mustache, while Reagan was big with blond hair.

Yep, Mitch and Jack were as different as two people could be. Thank God for that.

I was just drifting off to sleep when the thought hit me. At first, I believed I was dreaming. That when I woke up, I'd realize how silly it seemed. But I didn't. I couldn't get it out of my mind.

I kept thinking about something Kathleen DiLeonardo had said to me earlier that day.

"One time—right after the shooting—I became convinced that one of the cops talking to me was really Loverboy," she had told me. "I got so hysterical I tried to jump out a window of the station house. That's why the police never took my description seriously. Christ, I thought *everybody* was Loverboy."

Jack Reagan was big.

And he had blond hair.

Just like Loverboy.

Fifty-nine

Okay, it was a crazy idea.

In fact, it was so crazy I didn't tell anybody what I was doing at first. Not Barlow. Not Janet. Not even Mitch.

Maybe I'd been covering the Loverboy case for so long that I'd totally lost my mind.

Maybe.

But the more I dug into Jack Reagan's past, the more I began to think that I really might be onto something big.

The fact is Jack fit the pattern of a certain kind of serial killer perfectly. I remembered something Mitch had said about it earlier in one of the stories I did: "Loverboy doesn't have to be a bogeyman—he could be a very charming fellow."

It was true too.

We all think of serial killers as lonely misfits who look crazy or live at home with their mother, like Joey Russo. But some of them turn out to be upstanding citizens with regular jobs who give no indication to the people around them of anything wrong. They say Jack the Ripper was probably a prominent London doctor or even a member of the royal family. Ted Bundy was a smooth-talking Romeo. Even Son of Sam had a regular job—he worked for the post office.

Another characteristic of serial killers is that they're like arsonists—they like to see the results of their work. People who set fires are frequently found in the crowd outside watching a building burn. Serial killers show up at crime scenes and funerals, and sometimes even make friends with cops because it increases the thrill. What better way to do that than being a cop yourself and assigned to the task force investigating the case? Jack Reagan would have been in on every break, every lead, every detail about what the cops were thinking and doing. If he was the killer, he must have loved it.

Lots of other stuff about him fit the pattern too. He was volatile, violent, angry and dangerous—especially when he was drinking.

I also realized I didn't know much about Jack's past. He had never talked about it.

In fact, the remark he'd let slip one day about having a wife was the only indication I ever had that he'd had any life at all before he met me.

According to the police records, he joined the police force in 1969, after being discharged from the Army. He'd served two tours in Vietnam, winning the Bronze Star for bravery. Before that, he'd graduated with honors from high school in Clayton, Missouri, a suburb of St. Louis.

There were a number of Reagans in the St. Louis phone book, but I kept calling, asking everyone if he was related to the Jack Reagan who graduated from high school back then and went on to serve in Vietnam. I finally hit one of the right ones. His name was James Reagan and he was a certified public accountant. He said he was Jack's brother.

I asked him a whole bunch of questions about Jack, his childhood and his family in Clayton. I wasn't really sure what I was looking for. I was just curious.

"Jack could have gone to college and avoided the draft," James Reagan said. "He had good grades and a couple of schools offered him scholarships. But he wanted to do the right thing. He thought he should do his part for his country first. That's the kind of person Jack was. A real stand-up guy. You know what I mean?"

That didn't sound much like the Jack Reagan I knew, but I guess people change over the years.

"How did you know Jack, Miss Shannon?" he asked.

"I was a friend of his."

"A friend?"

"Well, more than a friend. I went out with him for a while."

"You mean in high school?"

"No." I laughed. "We were both a long way past high school when we met."

He seemed confused.

There was something very wrong here, but I couldn't put my finger on exactly what it was.

"Are you from Missouri?"

"No. I live in New York City."

"So how did you meet Jack?"

"Here in New York."

"Jack never was in New York."

I didn't understand what he was talking about.

"Of course he was."

"No, he talked about visiting there someday, but that was before—"

"Mr. Reagan, your brother was a police officer in New York City for fifteen years. I worked with him. I dated him. I talked to him just before he killed himself here twelve years ago."

There was a long pause at the other end.

"Miss Shannon, my brother died more than twenty-five years ago in Missouri."

"Twenty-five years?"

"Yes. He was killed in a mugging in 1969."

Nineteen sixty-nine. The same year my Jack Reagan joined the police force in New York City.

"Did they ever catch the person who did it?" I heard myself ask.

"No. It's still unsolved."

James Reagan had a fax machine for his accounting business. I told him I was going to send him a picture of someone. I asked him to tell me if it was his brother. He asked me what was going on. I told him what I could. He said he'd call me back.

Twenty minutes later, the phone rang.

"His name is Martin Chambers," he told me.

"Who's that?"

"He knew my brother."

"They were friends?"

"I wouldn't call them friends. Chambers was kind of a troublemaker, as I recall—a big drinker who got in some scrapes with the law. He was in the same high school as me but a year or two younger. He and Jack might have been in the same class. It's been a long time and he looks much older in that picture— I had to check an old yearbook to make sure. But that's him, all right."

"Have you seen Martin Chambers since high school?"

"No."

"What happened to him?"

"He left town, I guess."

And moved to New York City, where he started calling himself Jack Reagan.

The Clayton Police Department's records from twenty-five-plus years ago were filed in a basement, and it took quite a while to find them. A young cop named Morelli finally came up with what I wanted. Jack Reagan's file. It was pretty much like James Reagan had told me. An unsolved murder case.

A thought suddenly popped into my head.

"Did you have any other unsolved murders back then?" I asked.

"What do you mean?"

"Oh, a series of killings that might have been related to each other—say against young women or something like that."

Morelli sighed. "You know, I should charge you for my time. You're really busting my balls."

"It could be important," I said.

Morelli said he'd check. He came back on the line a short time later. He'd obviously talked to someone who remembered what had been happening in Clayton in the late '60s. He was much more interested in me now.

"There were five unsolved killings of young women, aged eighteen to twenty-four, which began in the summer of 1968 and continued through 1969," he said. "The homicide detectives suspected at the time that they could be related. But they didn't have any real proof. And they were afraid of starting a panic."

"What happened after that?"

"The killings stopped."

"In 1969?"

"Yes."

"And no one was ever caught?"

"That's right."

The local records on file at the Clayton City Hall showed that Martin Chambers had married a woman named Rita Vlosek in 1968. There was only one Vlosek in the phone book. It turned out to be her mother.

"I'm calling about your daughter," I said.

"Rita?"

"Yes. I need to find her. Can you tell me where she lives now?"

I guess I knew what the answer was going to be even before Mrs. Vlosek said it.

"Rita's dead. She's been dead for a long time."

"How did she die?" I asked.

"She was murdered."

I asked her for the details.

"It happened on Halloween. There was a lot of violence and property damage that night, with gangs running around the city causing trouble. Rita . . . Rita's clothes were ripped half off." Her voice broke. This wasn't easy for her, reliving her daughter's death again. I felt bad about that, but there was no other way. "The police think Rita maybe encountered one of the gangs. She fought back when they tried to attack her and . . . and they killed her."

"Did the police ever catch anybody, Mrs. Vlosek?"

"No."

"How long ago was this?"

"Nineteen eighty-five."

Jesus, the same year that Jack Reagan died.

What the hell was going on here?

A few hours later, I was sitting with Kathleen DiLeonardo again on Long Island. I showed her a picture of Jack Reagan. Her eyes opened wide with astonishment—and a bit of fear too—when she saw it.

"That's him," she said.

"The man who shot you?"

"Well, at the time I thought he was, but . . ."

"You decided you were wrong."

"He was one of the police officers handling the case. I must have gotten confused. I was going through so much turmoil then."

"You were right."

"You mean he . . ."

"I think he was Loverboy."

She looked at the picture of Martin Chambers/Jack Reagan again.

"Where is he now?"

"He's dead."

Kathleen DiLeonardo shook her head in confusion.

"They told me I was crazy."

"Maybe we all were," I said.

Sixty

"Jack Reagan—or to be more accurate, Martin Chambers—was Loverboy," I told Police Commissioner Thomas Ferraro.

"Do you realize what you're saying?" he asked.

"Yeah, I think so. This despicable mass killer was actually one of the lead homicide detectives in charge of the case. Your partner. My lover. Which makes us both look like real horses' asses."

We were sitting in Ferraro's office. The pictures of his family were still in front of him on the desk. His awards and plaques were still hanging on the wall. But all the trappings of power had a hollow ring to them now. Sure, he had a big office, a loving family, a good life—a lot of stuff I didn't.

But he still had to face the demons of his past just like I did.

"You don't have definite proof, do you?" Ferraro asked.

"No."

"Everything you've told me is pretty much circumstantial."

"Circumstantial," I agreed.

"And since Reagan's dead, we'll probably never know for sure."

"That's right."

"But you're sure, aren't you?"

"Yes. Mitch is sure now too."

Ferraro looked at his nephew, who was sitting next to me.

"I went back and checked Jack Reagan's personnel file," Mitch said. "I wondered how a cop with a record like his—he'd been cited a lot of times for drinking on duty and other infractions—wound up with such a prestigious job on the Loverboy task force. Do you know why?"

"He was assigned to me," Ferraro said. "I figured it was the luck of the draw."

Mitch shook his head.

"It was more than luck. Reagan showed up at the scene of one of the early murders. He said he was drinking at a bar nearby, heard about it on a police radio and came over to see if he could help. Same thing happened on the next murder.

"No one thought much about it. They were just routine murder cases. And he was a cop. Everyone was glad to get his help.

"Later on, it was Reagan who put it all together and came up with the idea that a serial killer might be doing the murders. The brass thought it was great police work. They even put a letter of commendation in his file.

"Then he volunteered to be on the task force that was being assembled to catch the madman. Why not? He was already investigating the murders. He knew more about the case than anyone. So they assigned him as your partner.

"Think about it. He'd murder someone, then show up afterward with the cops at the scene. He knew everything the department was doing. Every lead we were following. Even what we were thinking. Then he starts dating the reporter covering the case. He helps her come up with the name Loverboy. He starts sending her notes from the killer. Christ, he must have been laughing at us the whole time.

"It was the perfect cover. The entire police force was looking everywhere in the city for Loverboy. And he was right there beside us.

"Even when something went wrong—like the time he missed killing the DiLeonardo woman and she caught a glimpse of him—it didn't matter. Everyone thought she was confused. Who was going to believe that the shooter just hung around the police station afterward to question the victim? Hell, Kathleen DiLeonardo herself thought she was crazy."

Ferraro sat there in shock.

"Why would he do it?" he asked. "Why kill all those innocent people?"

"Who knows?"

"There has to be a reason."

Mitch shrugged. "Martin Chambers's father was a drunk who disappeared when he was about six. His mother was an alcoholic too. People who knew them back in Missouri say she alternated between smothering the kid with love and physically abusing him because he reminded her of her husband. There may have been some sexual abuse too. We can speculate on that being the reason for Chambers/Reagan turning out the way he did. But I don't think it's that easy. There are plenty of other child-abuse victims and children of alcoholics who don't become serial killers."

"But how could someone like that ever get on the police force?" Ferraro asked.

"It was the late sixties," Mitch said. "The Vietnam War was still on, and there was a big push for recruits. I suppose the standards weren't as high as they are now. And don't forget—it wasn't Martin Chambers's record they were looking at. It was Jack Reagan's. A straight-A student. Model citizen. Nothing for anybody to question there."

"Martin Chambers knew his résumé would never work," I added. "So he decided to become Jack

Reagan. Only he had to make sure Reagan wasn't alive to mess anything up."

"And you think he was connected to the real Jack Reagan's death?" Ferraro asked.

"I think he murdered him to assume his identity," I said.

"That's unbelievable."

I told Ferraro about the string of other unsolved murders in Missouri that ended when Martin Chambers left town.

"The man we knew as Jack Reagan probably killed a lot more people than we even know," I said.

Ferraro shook his head. He gazed across the desk at me.

Then he asked the big one.

The $64,000 question.

"What are you going to do now?"

"I'm not sure."

"If you print this story, it could destroy my political career," he said.

I nodded. "That's a possibility."

"I'll become a laughingstock. A nationwide joke. The bumbling policeman who didn't even know that the worst serial killer of all time was right there beside him."

"It's not going to do much for my reputation either," I said. "I can see the headlines now: 'Bimbo Reporter Slept with Modern-day Jack the Ripper.' This is going to set women in journalism back about a million years."

"They'll probably make a TV-movie about you guys," Mitch said.

"Yeah," I told him. "They can call it *Dumb and Dumber*."

"Who else knows about this?" Ferraro asked me.

"No one."

"So we could bury it here right now, then, couldn't we?"

"That thought did occur to me."

"And no one would ever find out."

It was a nice dream.

I'd thought about it all night before I came to see him, tossing and turning as I wondered if I could live out the rest of my life carrying this deep, dark secret around inside me.

I knew my answer.

So did Ferraro.

We'd both held onto too many secrets for too long.

"I think it's time we finally told the truth," I said.

Sixty-one

LOVERBOY WAS A COP!

**Authorities Probe Dead
Detective's Mysterious Past**

Exclusive
by Lucy Shannon

New evidence has revealed that the infamous Loverboy may really have been a homicide detective investigating the murders.

The shocking new twist to the most sensational crime case in New York City history came just days after copycat Loverboy killer Robert Fowler shot himself to death in the New York *Blade* offices.

Now the original Loverboy—who killed 13 people and wounded 8 others between 1978 and 1984—is believed to have been Police Detective Jack Reagan, a 15-year veteran and a key member of the Loverboy task force.

Reagan committed suicide in 1985.

A joint investigation by the commissioner's office and the *Blade* has also discovered:

- Reagan's real name was Martin Chambers.
- He is believed to have carried out a series

of other unsolved murders in his hometown of Clayton, Mo.

• One of his victims was named Jack Reagan, the man whose identity he assumed.

"It appears that this individual we knew as Jack Reagan did indeed commit the so-called Loverboy murders," Police Commissioner Ferraro said in an interview with the *Blade*.

"He also was my partner on the Loverboy task force and even coined the name Loverboy.

"These facts are as astonishing to me as they must be to everyone else out there. As to why no one ever suspected anything before, I have no answer to that.

"The only good thing I can tell you is that these revelations mean the Loverboy case—after nearly two decades of questions and uncertainty—appears finally to be over."

The article told everything—I didn't hold any of it back. It went on for nearly one hundred inches of copy. There were sidebars on my personal involvement with Reagan, on the impact of these disclosures on Ferraro's political future, and on an in-depth look at Reagan's mysterious past as Martin Chambers.

And so I was front-page news once again.

But if I was worried about being ostracized by my media counterparts for what I'd done, I needn't have been.

They didn't seem to care if I'd broken the rules. I'd covered a mass killer, I'd slept with a mass killer and now I'd broken the true story about the mass killer. They loved me. I was like Michael Jackson or Madonna or Amy Fisher.

Everyone wanted to talk to me about it. *Inside Edition* and *Hard Copy. Geraldo. Larry King Live*. Michael Anson was back on the phone, pleading with me to be part of her movie. Book publishers said my story would be a best-seller.

I didn't accept any of the offers, though.

I told the story only once, in the pages of the *New York Blade,* where it belonged. It was all I had the energy for right now. I wasn't looking to cash in on this or become famous or win a Pulitzer. I just wanted to get on with my life.

That night I went to Headlines.

There was a huge cheer when I walked in. Everyone was there, sitting at one of the big tables. Janet. Barlow. Brian Tully. Karen Wolfe. Norm Malloy. Even Victoria Crawford this time. They were celebrating the *Blade*'s big scoop on the story.

"Here she is—Lucy Shannon, reporter extraordinaire," Janet said, holding her glass up to toast my entrance.

"Speech, speech," Tully shouted.

"Drinks, drinks," someone else yelled.

"I don't drink anymore, remember?" I told them.

"No, we just want you to buy drinks for us," Karen said.

"That I can still do."

I smiled, ordered a round for everyone and a bottled water for myself, then sat down at the table with them.

"I haven't seen you here in a long time, Vicki," I said to her.

"Yeah, I think the last time was the Christmas party."

"Right."

I'd rather she hadn't brought that up.

"That was when you compared me to the Mayflower Madam and Heidi Fleiss, as I recall."

A waiter brought our drinks. I took a sip of the water.

"I'm sorry about that," I told her. "I was . . . I was drunk."

She shrugged. "No big deal."

"I did a lot of dumb things when I was drunk, Vicki."

"Hell, you were probably right," she said.

Damn.

I hated it when I was wrong about people I loved to hate, like Ferraro and Vicki Crawford. Maybe people *can* change for the better. Or maybe I never really gave them a chance in the first place.

"Have you seen the Wall of Fame?" Malloy asked.

"Only about a million times."

"No, I mean tonight."

I looked up at the pictures on the wall. They were all there. Fullerton. Slotnick. Morrison. The legends of the history of the *New York Blade*. But this time there was another picture. Mine.

"Jesus Christ," I said.

"We voted to include you earlier today, after the edition came out," Malloy told me.

"Who did?" I asked.

"It was unanimous."

Everyone around the table nodded.

"Why me?"

"For actions above and beyond the call of duty." Janet smiled at me.

"You mean Loverboy?"

"It was an extraordinary story," Vicki said.

We stayed there into the early-morning hours, laughing and telling newspaper stories. It was a great night. I didn't even miss drinking. I was on too much of a natural high.

At some point I asked Vicki about her impending divorce from Ronald Mackell.

"I think I'll be able to keep control of the *Blade*," she said. "I'll have to give up a lot of other things in the settlement, but that's okay. Circulation and profits are really up from the Loverboy stuff—that helps my case. Shows that I'm not just a rich man's bimbo."

"That's really important to you, isn't it?"

"Yeah, it is. So is the *Blade*. I really care about this newspaper. I like being the editor."

"And if . . ."

"If I don't keep control of the paper? Then Ron takes over again, and I'm out on my ass."

"What would you do then?"

"Probably get a job as a reporter somewhere."

She saw the look on my face.

"Don't look so surprised. I used to be a pretty good reporter."

"I remember."

"Hell, there are worse things a person can do with their life."

"But not too many better," I said.

She finished off her drink and called for a check. It was getting time for her to leave. Me too.

"I've got no regrets about any of it, Lucy," she said. "Ron was a real son of a bitch. But he gave me a nice life and bought me expensive things and handed me this opportunity of a lifetime at the *Blade*. Okay, he cheated on me. But a lot of husbands do."

"Did you love him?"

"I thought I did. At first. But once I got to know him . . . well, let's just say he was a very cruel man."

I stared at her. "You mean he hit you?"

Vicki shook her head. "He was cruel in other ways."

I suddenly thought about Jack Reagan. I remembered the time he had thrown me against the wall of my apartment.

What about his wife? Had he been cruel to her when they were married? Had he ever hit her? Had he gone back to his hometown of Clayton, Missouri—years after he'd changed himself from Martin

Chambers to Jack Reagan—and murdered her in one
final fit of anger?

Why?

Why, after all that time?

And what kind of torment and pain had Rita Vlosek endured at his hands before she died a horrible
death that Halloween night in 1985?

That was when it suddenly hit me.

The answer.

The answer to what I'd been missing all along in
the Loverboy story.

And it scared the hell out of me.

Sixty-two

Mitch Caruso wanted to make love.

We were in bed at my place. He was kissing me very tenderly, but I was having trouble concentrating on the moment. I kept thinking about something else. Something even more important than sex.

"Rita Vlosek died on Halloween night in 1985," I told him.

"Okay."

"We figure Reagan went back to Missouri fifteen years later or whatever and for some reason murdered his ex-wife."

"That's right."

He nuzzled his lips gently against my neck.

"Why?" I asked.

"Why what?"

"Why kill her after all that time?"

"Do we really have to talk about this now?"

"Yes."

Mitch sighed and sat up straight in bed.

"Okay, maybe the Vlosek woman had something on him. She knew the secret of his past as Martin Chambers. Maybe she somehow stumbled onto his new identity and threatened to expose him, and he decided to shut her up for good."

"That makes sense."

"Good." Mitch smiled. "Let's have sex."

"Except for one thing."

"What?"

"Rita Vlosek died on Halloween night, 1985."

"Yeah, you just said that."

"Jack Reagan committed suicide in early October of 1985."

Mitch suddenly realized what I was telling him.

"Then Reagan didn't murder her. He couldn't have—he was already dead. Someone else did it. We were wrong."

"That's one possibility."

I sat up in bed and pulled the sheet around me. It was still summer and it was hot outside, but I was shivering. Maybe it was the air-conditioning in my apartment. Or maybe I wasn't cold at all. Maybe I was just scared.

"Why did you get a search warrant to go through my apartment?" I asked him.

"Jeez, you're not going to bring *that* up again!"

"There must have been a reason."

"Lucy, I told you I was sorry."

"I want to know why."

Mitch shrugged. "We got a tip," he said.

"A phone call?"

"Yes."

"Anonymous?"

"Uh-huh."

"What did it say?"

"That you had crucial evidence connected to the case hidden in your apartment."

"And you didn't think this was just a little bit suspicious?"

"Well, it panned out. It was true. I mean, we did find Russo's gun."

"I never told anyone about the gun," I said. "Not my shrink, nobody at the paper, not even any of my ex-husbands knew I had it. There was only one other person who knew."

"Who?"

"Jack Reagan."

He stared at me in disbelief.

"I think Jack Reagan's still alive," I said.

Sixty-three

No one had ever questioned Jack Reagan's suicide.

No reason to.

Depressed, alcoholic cop leaves the police force, broods about his life, loses his girlfriend, drinks a lot—and then finally kills himself.

It happened all the time.

But was that really what had happened here?

The records showed that police had arrived at Jack Reagan's apartment on the Lower East Side at 8:16 P.M. They'd gotten the call from me at 8:02, but it took them fourteen minutes because there was a robbery in the area at the same time which occupied the closest patrol cars. I got there at 8:22.

The first cops on the scene found Reagan lying on the living room floor. The phone was still off the hook. The gun was next to him. They called for an ambulance, but it wasn't really necessary. The blast had blown off most of his head and face. There was blood all over. The place was a mess.

His death was quickly ruled a suicide—based in large part on my account of the telephone call from him—and he was buried a few days later at a big policeman's funeral filled with teary-eyed cops and flowery speeches about his years of service to the city.

Beautiful, I thought.

A nice touch, Jack.

"There was never any medical confirmation of the victim's identity," Mitch said as he went through the file. "No fingerprints. No hair samples. No dental charts checked."

"Is that unusual?"

"Not really. I mean, they see a suicide in a guy's apartment, they assume it's the guy who lived in the apartment. Anyway, they got a visual ID that it was Reagan from someone on the scene."

"Who?"

"It just says, 'Identification of victim confirmed by individual who viewed body.'"

Mitch paged through the file again. "Maybe the person's name is somewhere else."

I suddenly realized something.

"Don't bother looking," I said.

"Why not?"

"I know who identified Reagan to the cops."

"Who?"

"Me."

Mitch put down the file.

"When I got there, I told them about his phone call to me and the gun blast going off. Then they asked me who he was. And, of course, I told them and said he was an ex-cop. I was obviously very distraught. They asked me a few questions about our relationship, and that was that."

"It was all cut-and-dried," Mitch said.

"Exactly."

"Lucky for Reagan—if he was trying to fake his own death—that you showed up."

"It wasn't luck at all," I said. "He phoned me and did the whole suicide scene over the line, remember? He knew I'd come running over. And he knew I'd be the perfect person to make people think it was Jack Reagan lying on that floor."

"Which brings up a big question. Who died that night?"

"Probably another Joey Russo."

"A patsy?"

"Yeah, some guy Reagan picked up off the street. He'd have to be the same age, build and complexion, of course. He takes him to the apartment, blows his face off with a powerful enough weapon so nobody will recognize the switch, and then calls me to set the whole thing in motion. I'll bet some derelict dropped out of sight on the Bowery or wherever and was never heard from again."

Mitch shook his head. "I'm still not sure I buy all this."

"Isn't there some way to find out?"

"You mean, dig up the body out of Reagan's grave?"

"Yes."

"Jesus, it's been more than ten years."

"Does that mean it can't be done?"

He thought about it. "They could do DNA tests on the remains, I guess."

"And that'll tell us whether or not it was Reagan who's in there?"

"Maybe. But I'd have to get a court order. I'd have to go through miles of bureaucratic red tape. I'd have to answer a lot of questions. It would be a huge amount of work. And the DNA testing itself is a lengthy process. After all this time, it might take weeks or months to get an answer."

"We need to know," I said.

He nodded.

"If you're right, and this guy is still out there, he might come after you, Lucy."

"That thought had crossed my mind."

"Of course, he's probably a million miles away from New York City by now."

"Probably."

Mitch said he'd come over after his shift ended and spend the night at my apartment.

"To protect me?" I asked.

"Sure."

"Or to ravish me."

"Both."

"That's nice."

"Well, I didn't get to do a whole lot of ravishing last night."

"Tonight will be different."

"Promise?"

"I'm running a special at my place tonight—all the ravishing you can handle—as part of my bodyguard recruitment plan."

He leaned over and kissed me.

We were right in the middle of a police station. There were cops all around us, watching. Everyone whooped and hollered at our public display of affection. Some cheered. A few of them even shouted obscene remarks.

I didn't care.

There was nothing wrong with sleeping with a cop.

You just had to pick the right cop to sleep with.

I thought about that all the way home that night. How had I ever let myself get mixed up with Jack Reagan? Sure, he'd been good-looking and charming and I'd been very young. But long before I ever suspected he was a murderer, I knew he was no good. So why had I slept with him? That said something about my character too.

Maybe there was something about him I had needed back then.

The same way I had needed to continually find some sort of high to get through life, whether it be from the adrenaline of a big story or from drinking.

I liked danger, I liked taking chances—I liked living on the edge.

But now I was different. I wasn't the wild, reckless person I used to be, I didn't need a continual high to get through the day—or the night—anymore. I was older, more cautious, willing to take things more slowly. I looked before I leaped a lot more these days. The way I used to be, I was easy prey for someone like a Jack Reagan. But not anymore.

The only high I wanted now was love.

I'd never quite experienced that one.

Now I'd finally found the real thing with Mitch Caruso. I was in love with him. And he was in love with me. Maybe this time I could live happily ever after.

I was still preoccupied with all this when I opened the door of my apartment. That was why I didn't see him right away. I was halfway into the living room before I spotted the figure sitting on the couch and staring at me.

I let out a gasp.

It was Jack Reagan.

He had a gun—a Bulldog .44 revolver—pointed at me.

"Hi, honey," he said. "I'm home."

Sixty-four

He looked different. Much different.

Some of it was from the passing of time. The blond hair was thinner and darker now. He'd put on about twenty-five pounds. And his skin looked weather-beaten, like he'd been out in the sun a lot.

But he'd deliberately changed his appearance too. His hair was cut short. He had a beard. And he wore glasses.

"You're looking real good, babe," the man I knew a million years ago as Jack Reagan said to me.

"You too, Jack." I tried to keep my voice calm and under control. "Death must agree with you."

He laughed. "Sorry about that. But I had to leave in a big hurry. Things were getting pretty hot. I hope I didn't cause you too many problems."

"Nothing that twelve years of psychiatry couldn't help," I said.

He shook his head. "You don't seem very surprised to see me, Lucy."

"I already figured out you were still alive."

"I thought you would."

"Really?"

"You always were a smart girl."

"Funny, I was just thinking about how dumb I was twelve years ago."

He motioned for me to sit down in a chair across from him. The gun was still pointing at me.

"Why'd you do it, Jack?"

"Hell, it was fun."

"Murdering all those people?"

"You don't know what it's like, Lucy. Holding the power of life and death in your hands.

"I used to pick out pretty girls on the street. Then I'd follow them. Watch everything they did—for hours, sometimes for days. I'd savor every little move they made—combing their hair, fixing their lipstick, eating a final meal—without knowing their life was coming to an end. But I knew. I felt like God.

"And then when I did it . . . well, it was like great mind-blowing sex, only better. It's the mother of all orgasms, believe me."

"That's sick," I said.

"No, it's human nature. That's why people like to hunt. That jungle instinct is inside all of us. Only I was hunting humans. Beautiful female humans. It was like combining the two most exciting things in the world—sex and violence.

"Did you know I was assigned to the Son of Sam case? I was there when they caught him in 1977. I watched him being questioned. And I could see the excitement in his eyes when he talked about the killings.

"So I began to wonder what it must be like. I couldn't get it out of my mind. I started to fantasize about it. I used to stand in front of a mirror and act out his murders. Only this time it was me doing them. It was all I could think about.

"And then one night I just did it. The Fowler kid and his girlfriend. I followed them the whole evening. First to dinner, then to a disco and finally to the spot in the lovers' lane where they parked.

"Goddamn, it exceeded all my expectations. Afterward, I was on such a high. I knew I was going to do it again. I was hooked."

I remembered talking with Robert Fowler about the same thing.

Fowler had started out as a victim, and wound up enjoying the killing too.

Maybe it was true.

Maybe there was a bit of Jack Reagan in all of us.

"There's only one problem with that," I said. "You didn't really get the idea from Son of Sam. You were killing people back in Missouri when you were Martin Chambers and barely out of your teens. At least five that I know of. Of course, that doesn't even include your wife."

"Well, well, you've been a busy girl, haven't you?"

"I'm a reporter, remember?"

"I'm impressed."

"I'd also be willing to bet that in the city you're living in now—under whatever name you're using these days—there's a whole string of unsolved killings of young women. Is that true or false?"

He smiled. "That would be true."

We sat there staring at each other.

There was one more thing I wanted from him.

No matter what happened, I had to know.

"Why did you pick me up that first night in Gramercy Park?"

"I wanted to do you."

"You mean sleep with me?"

He shook his head. "I was going to kill you. I watched you covering the story. The way you moved, talked to people, wrote stuff down in your notebook. You were going to be my next victim. I'd never done two shootings in one night like that. But that's what I was going to do."

"What happened?"

"I decided I could use you instead. You were young, you were ambitious, you wanted a big story

really bad—so I decided to give one to you. I decided
it was time that everyone knew what I was doing. I
thought it would make it more exciting. I was right."

"And that's it?"

"Well, I liked you too."

"You fell in love with me?"

"More or less."

"I guess I should be flattered, huh?"

"You were the only one."

The telephone rang. It jolted me like an alarm
clock, suddenly reminding me I was not dreaming.
This was really happening.

"Don't answer it," Reagan said.

The phone rang four times. Then my answering
machine clicked on. After the beeps, I heard Mitch
Caruso's voice. "Hey, Lucy, are you there? Pick up,
hon."

"Who's that?" Reagan asked.

"A friend."

"Your lover, right?"

"I got tired of waiting for you, Jack."

Mitch was still talking, assuming I was in another
part of the apartment and would pick up at any
second.

"He's coming over," I said.

"He'll think you're not home."

"No, he'll be here anyway to wait for me. He's got
a key. He's only a few minutes away. I better talk
to him."

Reagan looked at the answering machine. He made
an instant decision.

"Okay, talk to him. But don't try anything. Just tell
him you can't see him tonight."

"Why?"

"Make up some reason."

I picked up the receiver. Reagan stood behind me
and held it so he could hear both sides of the conversation. He had the gun pointed at my head.

"I'm on my way over," Mitch said.

"Not tonight," I told him.

"What do you mean?"

"I'm really tired."

"Me too. So we'll be tired together."

I tried to think of something I could tell him.

Some clue to alert Mitch that things had gone terribly wrong for me.

But a clue that wouldn't seem strange or suspicious to Jack Reagan.

Something that one man knew about me—and the other didn't.

"Listen, I've just had two glasses of vodka," I told him, "and I'm pouring myself another right now."

There was a silence on the other end of the line.

"What are you talking about?" Mitch asked finally.

"I'm talking about getting myself quietly blitzed, and I prefer to do that alone."

"But . . ."

"Got that?"

I slammed the phone down.

Reagan was eyeing me carefully. But he bought it.

I guess I was acting very normally—for the old Lucy.

"Very good," he said.

But I knew it wasn't good.

Not when Jack Reagan thought I was the only person in the world who knew he was still alive.

Not good at all.

"What happens now?" I asked.

"We're going for a ride."

"Where?"

"Back where it all started."

Sixty-five

That secluded scenic overlook was still there.

Just like it had been on that night a long time ago when Bobby Fowler and Linda Malandro parked their Chevy Nova on the ridge overlooking the waters of the Hudson River.

We went in my car. I drove. Reagan sat in the passenger seat with his gun pointed at me the whole way.

I took the FDR Drive uptown, then got off just before the George Washington Bridge and made my way through upper Manhattan to the spot by the water. I kept looking in the rearview mirror, praying for help. I hoped Mitch had figured it out in time. But there was no Mitch. No police cars. No cavalry riding to the rescue in the nick of time. I was on my own.

"Why here?" I asked as we pulled into the place where the first Loverboy shooting had occurred.

"It seems appropriate."

"A beginning and ending to everything, huh?"

"Something like that."

"An end to Loverboy?"

"An end to everything."

I shut off the motor. There were no other cars in sight. It was a clear, quiet summer night, and the car windows were open. Across the river, you could see

New Jersey. To the south were the bright lights of Manhattan. The *Blade* was back there somewhere. My apartment too. And Mitch Caruso. My whole life, or what was left of it.

"It is very romantic here, isn't it?" Reagan said.

"You want to fool around?" I asked.

He gave me a look of surprise.

"Just like old times," I told him.

"Are you serious?"

"Sure, you and me. Shannon and Reagan. Together again one last time."

"An interesting idea," he said. "The circumstances certainly would add a sense of excitement and . . . well, urgency . . . to the lovemaking."

"You're getting me all hot, Jack."

He shook his head.

"I'm not stupid, Lucy. You'd be thinking the whole time about some way to escape. And it would be difficult to hold this gun on you. A pity, really. So I'm afraid I have to pass on your kind offer."

"Maybe some other time," I said.

"Doubtful."

He took a brown paper bag out of his pocket.

"I will have a drink with you, though."

There was a bottle of vodka inside. Stolichnaya. "Stoli," my favorite brand.

"I don't drink," I said.

"Sure you do."

"Not anymore."

"You quit?"

"Last Christmas."

"But you told that guy on the phone . . ."

He suddenly realized what had happened back at the apartment.

"You were trying to give him a message that you were in trouble," he said.

"My, my, what a bright boy you are."

"But here we are all alone."

"That's right."

"So your little ruse didn't work."

"Evidently not."

He unscrewed the top of the vodka bottle with his free hand and held it out to me.

"No way," I said.

"I'm afraid I must insist."

"Look, you're going to kill me anyway. We both know that. So it doesn't really make any difference what I do, does it? And if I'm going to die, I'd rather die sober. It's important to me. It would be one thing I was able to do right in this life."

"Drink the vodka, Lucy. There are different ways to die. It can be painless or it can be very painful. In your case, I'd like to make the outcome as painless as possible."

"For old times' sake?" I asked.

"For old times' sake."

I looked at the clear liquid in the bottle. Hello, old friend. It's been a while. All that willpower, just to end up like this.

"Here's what's going to happen, Lucy. You're obsessed by the Loverboy story—it's driven you over the brink. So you drive up here to the place where it all started. You're drunk, you're distraught, you're suicidal. You kill yourself at the scene of your greatest triumph. They'll find a note in which you admit you made up all that stuff in your story about poor, long-dead Jack Reagan. And the gun will be in your hand. The real gun this time. Loverboy's gun. The one you kept all these years."

"It won't work, Jack."

"Why not?"

"Too many people know what I know. The cops. My editors. Even your old friend Police Commissioner Ferraro. They realize I'm not crazy. And that this is not all just figment of my imagination."

"Maybe."

"And they're gonna figure out the real Loverboy did this."

"That's all right too."

"You want Loverboy to go out in a final blaze of publicity, huh?"

"It does provide a certain kind of closure," he replied and smiled.

"But it's not over for you, is it? You're going to keep on killing people, aren't you? Maybe not as Loverboy. But you won't stop. You can't stop."

"Like I said before, it is the ultimate thrill."

"You are one sick motherfucker."

He gestured to me with the gun to start drinking.

I raised the bottle to my lips and started to take a sip.

"More," he ordered. "A lot more. Keep drinking until I tell you to stop. I want your alcohol content nice and high when they find you."

I took some more in my mouth. It tasted wonderful. Just like it always had. I closed my eyes and savored the taste and felt the familiar anticipation beginning to spread through my body.

It was now or never.

Suddenly I gasped for breath.

I lurched forward like I was going to be sick.

"What are you doing?" Reagan yelled in surprise.

Before he could react, I spit the vodka in his face. He reacted instinctively, jerking back to get out of the way of the liquid coming out of my mouth. I dove for the gun he was holding.

The .44 went off, bucking violently in his hand.

I felt a burning pain in my side as the bullet creased me and then smashed through the windshield of the car. Reagan tried to fire another shot, but he couldn't wrestle control of the gun from me for long enough.

We battled for it in the front seat. The fight probably lasted only for seconds, but it seemed like hours.

Finally, with every ounce of strength I could muster, I grabbed hold of his wrist, smashed it against the passenger door and forced him to let go. The gun flew out the open window.

Reagan broke away from my grasp and desperately looked around for it on the floor of the car. He didn't know where it was.

I grabbed at the door handle on my side and jumped out, landing on the ground.

Then I picked myself up and started to run.

The pain in my side was getting worse. I looked down and saw a pool of blood growing bigger on my blouse.

Suddenly, behind me, I heard Reagan gun the engine of my car. I realized in a panic that I couldn't outrun him. In front of me was the edge of a cliff, dropping off steeply to the waters below.

I was trapped.

There was no way out.

That was when I saw the gun.

It was lying on the ground where it had fallen after flying out of Reagan's hand during the struggle.

If I could only get to it in time.

Reagan started to speed toward me in the car.

I dove for the gun. Then I came up firing, emptying all six shots at him.

I hit him. He slumped forward on the steering wheel, his foot still pressed down on the gas pedal. The car continued speeding right at me. I jumped out of its path just in time. It missed me by only a few inches.

The car roared on by, crashing through a low fence on the edge of the cliff and dropping off into the water far below.

I watched it sink below the current.

Then, from somewhere in the distance, I heard police sirens.

That was the last thing I remembered until I looked up and saw Mitch Caruso's face above me.

"Am I going to die?" I asked.

"You're going to be fine."

Then Mitch leaned down and kissed me.

"Promise me something," I said.

"Anything."

"I want us to be forever."

He kissed me again.

"I love you, Lucy Shannon."

"I've been waiting for you my whole life, Mitch Caruso."

And then we began living happily ever after.

One day at a time.

Epilogue

Things have finally begun to settle down.

I'm back working at the *Blade* again. I spent a couple of days in the hospital, then a few weeks resting up at home. Finally, when I was about to go stir crazy, Victoria Crawford offered me a new job as a kind of criminal-justice columnist for the paper. I do in-depth investigations, write opinion pieces and sometimes still go out on the street with cops to cover a breaking murder case.

Michael Anson did make her movie about Loverboy. She loved the new ending with the confrontation between me and Reagan at the lovers' lane, even though it wound up a bit differently in the movie. In her version, Mitch Caruso gets there in time to shoot it out with Reagan. I explained to Anson what Mitch had told me afterward: He'd known something was wrong on the phone, so he sent a cop over who watched my house and followed me up to the lovers' lane. But the cop wasn't sure what was going on, and it was a few minutes too late when Mitch got there and they finally moved in. Anson said her way played better at the box office. That's Hollywood.

Thomas Ferraro is still the police commissioner and probably will be the next mayor. All the polls say he's more popular than ever after the Loverboy business. He's become real star material. He's even writing a book about the case. I guess that's the way it works today—if you do something bad, you write a book about it or make a TV-movie deal and become rich and famous. There's no such thing as bad publicity.

Things at the *Blade* are pretty much back to normal too. Barlow keeps talking about going on a diet, Janet is still looking for Mr. Right, and Victoria Crawford got her divorce from Ronald Mackell. The case was handled by a woman judge, who gave Victoria the paper, their Fifth Avenue apartment and a whopping $80 million in alimony—even more than she'd asked for. Meanwhile, Mackell's new girlfriend sued him for palimony. Beautiful. Sometimes what goes around does truly come around.

As for Mitch and me, we're still very much together. We're not married yet; we don't even officially live together. But that's my choice. I've been married before, and I know a ring on my finger is not the most important thing in a relationship. I want to take it slow and easy. I want to do it right this time.

So, all in all, I guess I'm as happy as I've ever been.

I still wonder about some stuff, though.

Like why Jack Reagan did what he did. I mean, what drove him to kill all those people? Outwardly, Jack seemed just like everyone else. He had a good job, he liked to drink, he made love to women. Okay, he was a bit crazy sometimes, but he didn't seem like some sort of sadistic monster. Joey Russo as Loverboy made sense. Jack Reagan didn't. I had a lot of trouble making sense out of all that.

And why did Jack make that anonymous call to the police and tell them about the gun and other stuff in my apartment? Did he really want to set me up for murder? If so, he must have known that he hadn't given me the real gun. He'd kept that all along. Or was he just trying to stir things up, to have some

fun, to put Loverboy on the front page? Just like he
had that night at Pete's Tavern when it all began.

I wonder about myself too. I mean, how could I
have spent all that time with Jack Reagan and never
suspected the truth? What does that say about me?
I like to think I'm bright and perceptive and have
good instincts about people. But I was wrong about
Jack. Horribly wrong. So how can I ever completely
trust my instincts again about anyone else in my life?
Even someone like Mitch Caruso.

I'll never know the answers to those questions.

But that's okay, I guess.

I can live with that.

And the truth is, most of the time my life is pretty
good these days.

Most of the time.

They never found Jack Reagan's body.

The scuba boys searched several days for it, but
came up empty. My car was down there, all right.
But no one was inside. Probably his body was
thrown clear of the wreckage and landed somewhere
else in the water, they say. Then the current got hold
of it and pushed it downriver to a totally different
area, maybe even out into the ocean.

It's almost impossible to find a man's body when
that happens, I'm told. It could wash up on shore
months later. Or maybe it'll never be found.

Nothing to worry about, of course.

I mean, I know he's dead. They found blood all
over the car where he'd been wounded. And they say
no one could survive an injury and a fall like that.

But I still have the nightmares.

There are several of them, but the one I remember
the most—the worst one—has me back at the spot of
the shooting, just before I looked up into Mitch Caruso's face and he told me he loved me. I'm standing
there watching the car with Reagan in it go off the

cliff. It crashes through the fence, tumbles over several times and then pitches straight down to the water below. Just like it did that night. Only this time I see something I didn't see before. As the car goes through the fence, something comes out of the door and lands on the grassy edge of the cliff. It's Reagan. He's managed to jump free before the car went over. He's standing there grinning at me.

Then he starts coming toward me.

That's the point where I wake up—screaming, covered with sweat, gasping for breath.

Crazy, huh?

That's what Dr. Collett says. Mitch too. And everyone else I've told about the dreams.

I knew they were right too.

Until what happened a few days ago.

It was a bright, sunny April morning—with the promise of another summer in the air—when I crossed Eighteenth Street, in front of my apartment house, to try to hail a taxicab. At that moment I saw the car. It was a black Lincoln—just like Jack Reagan used to drive—going about sixty miles an hour and headed straight at me. I screamed and leaped backward onto the hood of a parked car to get out of the way. The Lincoln roared past, missing me by inches. Then it disappeared around the corner of Third Avenue.

The incident made me think again about Reagan. And that empty car they'd found at the bottom of the Hudson.

A few nights later, while Mitch was still working the late shift and I was home alone, I thought I heard a car gunning its engine in front of my apartment building. When I looked out the window, I caught a glimpse of it driving away. It looked like it might be a black Lincoln. But I couldn't be sure.

That night, before I went to sleep, I loaded an extra

police revolver Mitch had left there and put it in the drawer of the end table next to my side of the bed.

Even though I knew it was probably nothing.

Just my imagination running wild.

Acknowledgments

They say writing a novel is lonely work, but it helps when you have good people on your side.

I'd especially like to thank the following:

Philip Spitzer, my agent, whose enthusiasm and encouragement from the very beginning never gave me a chance to doubt.

Kristin Cortright at Avon Books, who got inside Lucy's head so well she told me things about her even I didn't know.

All the terrific women I've worked with at the *New York Post* and *Star Magazine*, who were the inspiration for so much of the material, one-liners, and New York attitude in this book. Like Lucy Shannon, they're great reporters—even if they don't bend the rules quite as much. I can't name you all, but you know who you are.

And, most of all, thanks to Laura Morgan—who has a lot of Lucy Shannon in her, and vice versa.

—R.G. Belsky

For six horrific years, a psychopath held the city in his fist—a media-hungry maniac who committed thirteen brutal murders before vanishing without a trace.

It was the high point of Lucy Shannon's life.

A one-time star reporter, Lucy Shannon built her reputation on the baffling "Loverboy" case. But the ten years since the killer's mysterious disappearance have not been kind to the tormented newspaperwoman—cursing her with three failed marriages, numerous alcoholic interludes and a decade-worth of dark, disturbing memories. But this summer, as a movie crew takes to the sweltering New York City streets to film the Loverboy story, Lucy has the chance to restart her life and revive her fading career.

Because now the nightmare is back.

Once again, a faceless madman has chosen Lucy to be his voice and his go-between, offering her the opportunity to ride his terror to new glory and to put her demons, at long last, to rest . . .

. . . but only *if* she can survive his lethal love.

"Belsky perfectly nails the tone and the atmosphere . . . [of] the newsroom of a New York tabloid . . . Lucy Shannon is a gem with her mordant humor, cynicism and love of a good story . . . LOVERBOY is one of those sparkling, quick tales that one encounters far too seldom."
Erie Times-News

"Lucy will keep you reading. Isn't that what good reporters do?"
Chicago Tribune